D1595433

BAND OF BROTHERS

Early autumn 1943, and the German former banana-boat *Heilbronne*, newly fitted out as a U-boat supply ship, is sailing heavily escorted from Le Havre to the Atlantic. A mixed force of motor gunboats and torpedo boats from the Coastal Forces base at Newhaven in Sussex is ordered to intercept and sink her. For Ben Quarry, Australian navigator of MGB 875, the safety of his girlfriend, Rosie, who is now set on returning to occupied France as an SOE agent, is a matter of greater concern than the hazards he faces at sea. Also, his former mistress, now the wife of his own CO—Bob Stack, has embarked on an affair with one of their brother officers. Ben's got to tell him, though wishes to God he didn't. But in the aftermath of battle, as dawn breaks across the Sussex Downs and the survivors of the flotillas limp home to Newhaven, such issues remain to be resolved.

BAND OF BROTHERS

Alexander Fullerton

CHIVERS PRESS
BATH

First published 1996
by
Little, Brown and Company
This Large Print edition published by
Chivers Press
by arrangement with
Little, Brown and Company (UK) Ltd
1997

ISBN 0 7451 5425 5

Copyright © 1996 Alexander Fullerton

The moral right of the author has been asserted.

All characters in this publication are fictitious and any resemblance to real persons, living or dead, is purely coincidental

British Library Cataloguing in Publication Data available

Photoset, printed and bound in Great Britain by
REDWOOD BOOKS, Trowbridge, Wiltshire

FOREWORD

Into the Fire, the novel preceding this one, tells the story of Rosie Ewing, an agent of Special Operations Executive, on a hazardous mission to set up a new SOE network in Rouen, where the Gestapo have infiltrated the old *réseau* and arrested all its members. Nine-tenths of the story is about Rosie, while in the background is Ben Quarry, Australian navigator of the motor gunboat in which she travels from Dartmouth to the coast of Brittany.

Band of Brothers follows *Into the Fire*, but this time Ben Quarry has the lead. He's in a gunboat flotilla based at Newhaven in Sussex; has managed to wangle this transfer so as to be closer to Rosie. She's working for SOE in London—and threatening, to Ben's dismay, to return to 'the field', i.e. German-occupied France. So this time it's Rosie who's in the background—although she's more often than not in the forefront of Ben's mind.

The action occupies about eight hours of a Sunday night/Monday morning in October 1943. The former banana-boat *Heilbronne*, newly fitted-out as a U-boat support ship, is sailing heavily escorted from Le Havre *en route* to the Atlantic, and a mixed force of motor torpedo boats and motor gunboats from Newhaven is ordered to intercept and sink her.

The background is not far removed from reality. There were flotillas of MTBs and MGBs at Newhaven, and the battle which takes place off the Cherbourg peninsula is based loosely on an amalgam of several Coastal Force actions of which the official 'Reports of Proceedings' were very kindly supplied to me by Mr Len Reynolds, DSC, himself a former gunboat CO, author of his own highly readable memoir *Gunboat 658* (Kimber, 1955), and now historical researcher in the Coastal Forces Veterans' Association. First and foremost, though, I have had the tremendous benefit of months of help and advice from Commander Christopher Dreyer, DSO, DSC☆, RN (Rtd). Now President of that Veterans' Association, in his own distinguished career at sea he commanded several MTB flotillas, including—in 1943—the 24th Flotilla which for a time was based in Newhaven.

A.F.

CHAPTER ONE

He woke rather slowly—on his bunk, more or less fully dressed, emerging reluctantly from a dream in which Rosie had been telling him she'd changed her mind, she'd marry him right away. Rosie, with whom he'd spent last night ... *That* had been no dream—except in a figurative sense, a dream of heaven on earth. There was something wrong too, though—bad, spoiling, surfacing in his memory like garbage floating up. The voice that had woken him grinding on, meanwhile— '—Intelligence Room, Ben, right away—briefing. Wake up, damn it! D'you hear me, Ben?'

Barclay's voice. Alan Barclay was this gunboat's first lieutenant. There were other sounds and reverberations, voices out there and sailors clomping around and overhead. Judging by the dimness of the light in the scuttle just above this bunk it had to be getting towards sunset; in which case he'd been out for the count for bloody hours. Making up for kip he'd missed last night. Barclay still nattering at him and pulling at his shoulder: Ben grunted, lifting that arm to focus slit-eyed on his watch. Five-thirty.

They'd been due to come to immediate notice for sea at 1800—sunset, officially—as a matter of routine. He cleared his throat, muttered in an exaggeratedly Pommy accent, 'Briefing for what, one asks oneself...' Projecting himself off the bunk. Shoes and reefer jacket were all he needed that he didn't have on already. Barclay was telling him he didn't know, for Christ's sake—and Ben remembering that that particular problem—private

1

and personal, which would be why it had sprung to mind before anything else—well, right on the heels of the glory that was Rosie—was by no means the only bad news, here in Newhaven on this October sabbath in 1943. *Very* bad news: the MTB sweep last night— off Etaples—545 badly shot up, Roddy King the motor torpedo boats' SO killed outright and her coxswain and several of the crew wounded. At a time when he himself had been luxuriating in an oak four-poster at the Beauport Place Hotel with Rosie in his arms, the incredibly exciting, longed-for feel and scent of her, and—all right, the hitherto forbidden word—*love*—a year of dreams come true and he— Ben Quarry, Australian, twenty-nine years old— hardly daring to believe in it.

Problems there too, however. She worked for Special Operations Executive, who were currently employing her here in England—helping to train other agents, he'd gathered—but having been back from her last hair-raising sortie only about six weeks—less than eight, anyway—she was under some kind of inner compulsion to go back into what she called 'the field'—meaning German-occupied France.

The thought of it gave him the shivers, and he'd spent part of the night trying to dissuade her.

'I know a cat has nine lives, Rosie, but you're *not*—'

'What d'you mean I'm not? I'm a *super*cat!'

Claws in the darkness to prove it: and her impression of a purr...

That jumble of thoughts had rushed through his mind in the time it had taken him to lace his shoes. He was on his feet now—a head taller than Barclay— who was on the skinny side, as well. Ben muttered,

2

'Right. I'm off.' Reaching for his cap. 'Going over, I suppose.'

Meaning by that, over to the other side, the French coast. And the engines started at that moment—not exactly confirming the supposition, but tending that way, 'warming-through', a procedure which took about fifteen minutes, after which they *would* be at immediate notice, ready to shove off. He was out of the wardroom—out into the galley flat then up the ladder into the plot, or wheelhouse—his own closet-sized domain, since he was the navigating officer of this 'D' class motor gunboat. Pausing to snatch up a notebook and a couple of half-used soft pencils. Up a shorter ladder then into the bridge, where an AB named Bennet was bawling 'We'll Meet Again' while greasing the starboard twin Vickers GO machine-guns, and the telegraphist—sharp-eyed, blue-jawed, name of Ordway—asked him, glancing round from tracing a lead to one of the aerials, 'No idea what the flap's about, I suppose, sir?'

'Not a bloody clue, Sparks!'

None whatsoever. Preparations were being made—the warming-through, for one thing, with other boats of the duty units starting up as well—but departure was not likely to be imminent. You sailed after dark, almost invariably, not in daylight thus advertising the fact to any *Luftwaffe* reconnaissance, for instance. Same applied to the opposition, of course, if some unit was about to emerge from one of the French ports it would surely wait for sundown. Cats lying doggo, eyeing the mouseholes . . . He was out of the bridge, crossing the upper deck abaft it, and a seaman gunner who had the twin Oerlikon in pieces was shouting a reminder to the telegraphist about the Worry-Worry bird, which allegedly flew

3

backwards because it didn't give a toss where it was going but was always desperate to know where it had been. Amazing that one had slept through even the first minute of this racket. He'd had *very* little sleep last night; then had had to see Rosie off to London on a train from Haywards Heath and get back to the base here by noon. He'd had some lunch, listening to the talk about last night's action on 'the other side'— which had involved achievement as well as loss, a tank landing craft had been sunk and an armed trawler left burning—and after the meal he'd been quick to get his head down.

Just as well, too. Tonight, by the look of it, there'd be no sleep. Passing over MGB 866—whose engines chose that moment to start coughing and shuddering into life—over to her port side, thence a ladder fifteen feet up to the stone quayside: turning left, jamming his cap on tighter and beginning to run. 'Baldy' Worbury, 874's first lieutenant, howling at him from that boat's stern as he passed her—'Wages of sin, Ben, wages of sin!'

Whatever the hell *that* meant. Rum bloke, Worbury—bald as a coot at twenty-two. 874 had her engines running too. By this time he was passing the next moored trot—MGB 870 lying outside 863, which was Grant McKellar's. McKellar, half-leader of the gunboat flotilla, had been acting SO during the recent absence of Ben's own captain, a fellow Australian by name of Bob Stack.

Whose wife was cheating on him. Of which fact he, Ben Quarry, was supposed to be apprising him. At least, he'd agreed that it was his duty to do so, last night. In the cold light of day, however, it was about as embarrassing a prospect as could be imagined. In fact bloody impossible.

4

But not easy to know about it and stay mum, either, when it was a mate involved. Even *without* the pigeon coming home to roost.

He'd worked up to full power by this time, sprinting northward along the quayside. Dodging slower-moving personnel and attracting looks of surprise, even humorous comment here and there. Workshops—integral to this Coastal Forces base, HMS *Aggressive*—lined the quay on his right, opposite trots of motor torpedo boats—MTBs, as distinct from MGBs—smaller as well as faster, 70 feet long as compared to the gunboats' 120, roughly. Several of them were warming-through; another started up as he passed her. Billy Chisholm's, that was, 562; with young Raikes, her spare officer, gawping at him from the foredeck. Beyond him, Ben saw repair work in progress on 545, in which Roddy King had been killed last night. A single round of 88-mm from one of the Gerry trawlers had done all the damage, shattering that corner of the bridge and blowing King's head off. The other two boats which had been on the sweep, 559 and 561, were lying next ahead of 545, in the right-angle where the quay jutted outward into the harbour. All the boats pointing seaward—as always, having berthed port-side-to.

MLs—motor launches—occupied the next fifty yards or so, and more workshops filled the space between the quay and the railway line. Over on the other side of the narrow harbour, launches with RAF roundels on their hulls were clustered alongside the Air-Sea Rescue station.

Low cloud, unbroken, darkened the barely moving, oil-streaked surface. You could smell the oil. A breeze from the west slanted the wires of the barrage balloons, silver-grey against the darker

5

overhead.

Slowing, now—down to a fast walk and getting his breathing back into control—trying to—as he approached the London and Paris Hotel. Formerly the railway hotel, it had been requisitioned to become HMS *Aggressive*'s offices and wardroom. From the wardroom anteroom you stepped out on to platform number 1; what had been the railway buffet was the wardroom bar. No loss to the travelling public, for the simple reason that there weren't any; the whole of this coast from the Thames to Selsey Bill was an exclusion zone. Ben entered the old pub by its back door and made his way through and upstairs to the inter-connecting suite of Intelligence Room, Ops Room and SO's office. The SO—senior officer of the MGB flotilla—being his own skipper, Lieutenant-Commander Bob Stack DSO, DSC and bar, RANVR. The one with the wife. But also an old friend, and a fellow Australian. It had been thanks to him that Ben had managed to have himself appointed here, moving from the 15th MGB Flotilla which was based at Dartmouth.

Motivation for the move had been to get closer to Rosie. From down there in the West Country, with her in London and neither of them getting much time off—and any such breaks hardly ever coinciding— you might as well have been in China.

Or Brisbane. Home, was Brisbane.

'Ben.' Female voice, as he let a door swing shut behind him. 'Been taking exercise?'

'Might say that, Judy. Hi, Doc.'

Wren Second Officer Judy Collins—head girl, boss of all the Wrens here—stores assistants, mechanics, cooks and stewards, armourers, torpedo ratings, writers. She'd been talking to the quack—the MO,

6

who'd been a medical student when the war had started, had by this time learnt a lot the hard way. Ben would have paused to ask after the wounded from last night's action, but was aware that his absence might already be holding up the briefing session. Although it had only taken him a couple of minutes to get here. He pushed into the Ops Room— where 'state' boards showed the availability of boats, which were on patrol or at short notice or stand-off for repair or maintenance—and through it to the Intelligence Room, the door to which was normally kept locked but was now ajar with a green-stripe sub-lieutenant framed in it, turning to yell into the room behind him, 'Lieutenant Quarry's here, sir!' From inside came Bob Stack's rasping Australian, 'At bloody *last* . . .'

The green-striper—one of the base staff, handled cyphers, acted as duty officer and so forth—shut the door behind him. Ben joining about a dozen—fifteen, sixteen—of his colleagues, all the duty unit's COs and their navigators—which in the case of the seventy-foot MTBs meant their first lieutenants. He was facing Bob Stack's unsmiling glare, and a friendlier, welcoming nod from the SO(O)—Staff Officer (Operations), an RNVR lieutenant who was himself a Coastal Forces man, 'resting' from sea duty. Ben told Stack—in his early thirties, broad-shouldered with wiry jet-black hair and brilliantly blue eyes— wide mouth, strong jaw, a nose that looked as if it had been broken at least once—a tough cookie, in fact, but there was a lot of humour in that face even if it wasn't showing much at this moment—'Sorry, sir. Came as soon as I got word, but—'

'Let's not waste *more* time.' Stack and the SO(O) were out front, as it were on stage, backed by an array

7

of charts and a blackboard. One blown-up chart of the whole Channel was studded with coloured pins showing units known to be in the various French ports, and the positions of convoys and own forces— patrols out of Dover, Ramsgate, Portsmouth, Portland—wherever—and minefields—every known or at any rate relevant fact or feature. Ben, still puffed, subsided on to a vacant chair next to Johnny Crowther—MGB 866's navigator—and Stack nodded to the SO(O). 'Kick off, Harry, will you?'

* * *

This was a preliminary briefing, the SO(O) explained, based on Intelligence reports and logical deductions. Preliminary in the sense that sailing orders had yet to be received. Units had been ordered to immediate notice for sea, however, in anticipation of a further signal from C-in-C Portsmouth which would follow a sunset reconnaissance flight over Le Havre and/or its approaches.

Situation as follows. Newly fitted-out U-boat supply ship, the 4500-ton *Heilbronne*, former banana boat, was expected to sail tonight from Le Havre westbound, destination possibly Cherbourg but more likely either Brest or straight out into the Atlantic. Ten days ago she'd left the Jade, slipped into Ostend before she could be intercepted, and sneaked into Le Havre after a second coastal hop during the recent spell of foul weather which had severely restricted Coastal Forces' operations. Intelligence had thought she'd taken temporary refuge in Dieppe, now they'd woken up to find her in Le Havre.

Stack cut in: 'Hence this bloody panic. Known it

8

earlier we could've shifted down to *Hornet*, made the interception a lot easier than looks like it may be.' *Hornet* being the Coastal Force base in Portsmouth. He gestured towards the SO(O): 'Sorry, Harry.'

'Fair comment, sir.' Glancing down at his notes. 'Would've made it a whole *lot* easier. However...'

Strategic factors—since time allowed for this ... Intelligence assessments were that U-boat operations in the North Atlantic, which had virtually ceased after their heavy defeat on the convoy routes in May, were about to be resumed. New types of submarine, new radar, at least thirty boats equipped with *Schnorkel*, and a new acoustic torpedo. So—very urgently and vitally, since any effective disruption on the convoy routes could impede the build-up of invasion forces and material—and the *Heilbronne* was obviously intended to play a part in that effort—

Bob Stack again: 'Let's just say the bastard's German and he's afloat, so he's our meat, right?'

There was universal and emphatic agreement. Ben murmured to Crowther, 'Bugger hasn't changed one bit.' He meant Stack hadn't. The SO(O) added, winding up his strategic appreciation, that obviously Admiral Doenitz would want this support ship out on station—or at least at Brest, available to him—sooner rather than later, and since conditions for a breakout tonight were favourable—cloud-cover total, therefore no moon—the odds were that (a) she *would* be making a run for it, (b) she would not be intending to put into Cherbourg.

This brought him down to detail: as much as there was of it at this stage. The *Heilbronne* was reported to be well armed. Obviously would be, for her intended role. Her speed between Hamburg and Ostend and Ostend and Le Havre had averaged seventeen knots:

9

the same might reasonably be expected tonight. As for escorts—from Hamburg to Ostend she'd been accompanied by R-boats and M-class minesweepers, then on the stage to Le Havre in that very heavy weather she'd had the sweepers again—two of them—and two T-class torpedo-boats. According to air reconnaissance there were at least half a dozen of such craft now in Le Havre.

'RAF call 'em "small destroyers" but that's what they are. And that's the kind of opposition you can expect. With luck the PRU recce'll tell us more.' The SO(O) added that before the 'off' he'd also have had the Night Movements signal, up-dated gen on any scheduled convoy and/or 'own forces' movements to be expected during the coming hours of darkness.

He turned to Bob Stack. 'All yours, sir.'

Stack moved to the chart, brandishing a pointer that looked like the end of a billiard cue. Touching Le Havre with it, then the north-eastern tip of the Cherbourg peninsula.

'Le Havre to Pointe de Barfleur by their inshore convoy route—that's to say hugging the coast as near as damnit two-point-three miles offshore, then from here up to the *pointe*—at seventeen knots, four hours. So if they clear Le Havre by say 1900, they'll be rounding Barfleur about 2300. Could be on their way earlier than 1900—that's what we're waiting to hear. Darkness won't be slow coming with the cloud we have. And from here, cruising at twenty-three knots, say—for your lot, Mike—eighty miles, three hours and a half. For us Dogs—' he meant, for the 'D' class gunboats—'at twenty knots, nearer four hours. On the face of it I don't like those margins, *especially* don't relish a headlong bloody rush inshore. May be able to warm the bell a bit—but low cloud could

10

make the air reconnaissance tricky, too ...
However—Mike—'

'Sir.'

Mike Furneaux drew himself up slightly on his chair. Long-legged, dark and smoothly handsome. Well-heeled, too—Eton and Oxford, father an MFH and Deputy Lieutenant of his county. A minute ago, while they'd all been listening to the SO(O), Furneaux's and Ben's eyes had met—Furneaux glancing round not ostensibly *at* him, more seemingly including him in a general survey of the room, but in those few seconds the MTB man's stare might well have been asking, 'Going to spill the beans, are you?'

Might have been a touch of contempt in it, at that. As if he'd have been interested to know, but either way didn't really care all that much.

Which would suggest a high degree of recklessness: lack of concern for the potentially disrupting effect on the flotillas' spirit and cohesion as—in the Nelsonian concept—a 'band of brothers'. The essence of it being team-work, mutual trust, interdependence. It was how it *was*: brothers all in tune, making the same music. You didn't get that—or keep it—by chasing each others' wives.

Furneaux had to be reckoning on Ben turning the blind eye. Could be some special reasoning behind the guess too—depending on whether or not Joan— whose lover he, Ben, had been a couple of years ago—whether she'd kept *her* lovely mouth shut.

He guessed she would have. Unless marriage had changed her more than he'd have thought possible. There was one way in which it evidently and regrettably had *not*. But it was an even more crucial issue now than it had seemed last night—because

11

with Roddy King dead, Furneaux had become the senior MTB officer.

He'd be well up to the job professionally. Bags of experience, a considerable reputation, two well-earned DSCs. Well-liked, too. Despite being—in Ben's own opinion, but not having known him more than a few weeks—a somewhat supercilious sod, at times . . . But as things were now, as the MTBs' SO, he was going to have to work very closely with Stack; there'd be times when they'd need virtually to read each others' minds.

Stack was saying, 'Lieutenant Furneaux, MTB 560, will have 562, 563 and 564 with him. All things being equal, he'll put himself ahead and inshore of the enemy—' the pointer's tip touched Barfleur again—'off the point here—and I'll open the attack from seaward with MGBs 875, 866 and 874, do our best to hog the bowling and give you blokes a clear run in.'

'Using starshell, sir?'

'We'll see, Mike. Maybe. With just a *little* luck—'

'Enemy may do it for us.'

'Exactly.'

Not a bad start: they *were* more or less reading each others' minds. The timing—distances and speeds—*was* a worry. MTB and MGB engines were notoriously unreliable, and running them at more than half power for any length of time was inviting trouble. And you needed to cover the last few miles—ten miles, say—at low revs, silenced. But—assuming a solution was found to that problem—the broad intention was for the MGBs to make a diversionary attack from seaward, on the target's starboard bow; the MTBs, attacking with torpedoes from inshore with the blackness of the land behind them, were to

12

disengage to starboard after firing, MGBs staying clear of them by also disengaging to starboard—the opposite direction, roughly. There was to be a post-action rendezvous position—position XX—at Pointe de Barfleur 045 degrees 15 miles; and several other reference points were established. Navigators making notes of all this. Stack checked the time, and raised an eyebrow at the SO(O). 'Communications, wavelengths, and recognition signals, Harry— you've got all that. One thing I'll say first—I don't want jabbering on R/T. Radio silence includes voice radio, in my book. Until we see the whites of the buggers' eyes, OK?' He saw their nods . . . 'Radar too. Where we're going tonight they'll be expecting us, won't they. It's a prime target and that's the only place we have a chance to hit it.' He'd touched the top of the Cherbourg peninsula with his pointer. 'They know it, and we should not make it any easier for the bastards by advertising our presence. Especially on the way over, with a chance of warning 'em we're coming.' Looking at Furneaux: 'All right, Mike?'

A nod. 'On the way over—yes, sir. But when I'm inshore with my unit—effectively detached—'

'Up to you, then.' A glance at the SO(O). 'Harry . . .'

*   *   *

'Before you saw fit to join us in there, Ben—' Stack told him, ten minutes later in the SO's office—'We were talking about old Rod.'

He nodded. 'Bloody shame, sir.'

'Well—on our own like this, forget the "sir". On duty, in public, sure, we toe the line, but—old mates, right?'

13

'Aye aye, sir.'

A nod. 'Up yours too, cobber.'

At the Felixstowe base two years ago Stack had had command of an MGB—under an SO by name of Hichens, probably the finest ever, who'd been killed in action six months ago—while Ben had been first lieutenant of an MTB, and the Canadian 'Monkey' Moncrieff, who was now skipper of MGB 866, had been Stack's first lieutenant. Being the only Australians in the flotilla, Ben and Stack had naturally become good friends. In fact the three of them had. Then Ben's boat had come to grief in a fracas with German destroyers off the Dutch coast, Ben had been brought back unconscious and woken up some time later in hospital, and he and Stack hadn't seen each other since.

Hadn't seen Joan since then, either.

'Sorry I couldn't attend your wedding, Bob.'

'Through being wrapped in bandages head to foot and semi-conscious, you mean?'

'Oh, I think they had me up and using crutches, by that time.'

'Well ... But you'd met Joan, hadn't you ... Hell, of *course*—'

'Before you did. Might even have introduced you—uh?'

'No.' A jerk of the coal-black head. 'You were around, course you were—knew her before I did, sure. But it was that smarmy pongo—Billy something, Welsh Guards—who introduced us. Regretted it soon after, poor sod ... Remember Billy?'

'Sort of. Vaguely.'

Quite clearly, would have been a more truthful answer. Billy Bartholomew, a friend and brother

14

officer of Joan's brother's, had come up to Ipswich now and again to see her. She'd been stationed in Ipswich then. But old Billy had been wasting his time, she'd only used him as a stalking horse, sort of. Ben was pretty sure he'd never got to lay a finger on her.

Stack asked him, half smiling, 'Didn't cause *you* too much heartache, I hope—when I carried her off?'

'Hell, no.' And *that* was the truth. Joan had had a lot going for her—she really had—but he'd have married her like he'd have married a redback spider. He shrugged. 'The best man won—eh?'

'Well—' a shrug—'Why'd I argue with *that*? Ben, what I was going to say a minute ago—about Rod King—it's an ill-wind blowing good for young Newbolt. He gets 563—he'll be confirmed as CO. King recommended him for command some while back, now he gets it. Ironic, huh?'

Roddy King had gone out in MTB 545 last night because his own boat, 563, had not been part of the duty unit. Mark Newbolt, who'd been 563's first lieutenant but was taking over now as her skipper, had only recently celebrated his twenty-first birthday.

Ben saw no irony in it. Men did get killed, and from his short acquaintance with King he thought he'd have been as prepared for it as anyone.

He agreed about young Newbolt, though. There were several 22-year-old COs in the flotilla, and others not much older, but twenty-one was good going.

'No sour grapes, Ben?'

'Certainly not. I'm lucky to be at sea at all.'

Because after getting crocked-up that time and then as it were cobbled together, he'd been left with only one eardrum that worked. They'd given him a

15

shore job to start with; then it had been a stroke of luck, a sympathetic senior officer agreeing that an MGB navigator didn't need sharp ears—although a skipper or first lieutenant certainly did—that had got him back to sea. And that of course was as far as he'd go, he'd remain a navigator until Kingdom Come.

Or thereabouts.

Which was perfectly all right, he told himself. Not fooling himself entirely, but—well, it was a fact he was a damn *good* navigator, and he took pride in that.

'Incidentally, thanks again for asking for me.'

'Mutual advantage. I get a pilot I know I can rely on, you get to see your sheila once in a blue moon. Saw her last night, huh?'

Ben nodded. 'Did indeed.' He added, 'You and Joan have a cottage near here, Alan Barclay said.'

'Four miles away. Sounds a better deal than it is, mind you, I've—we've never got to enjoy it all that often. Last night, for instance—my first night back, and she's away on one of her long-haul trips. Other times, she's there and I'm not.'

There was a pause, while Ben hoisted that in. Having seen her last night foxtrotting and quick-stepping around with Furneaux. And now, by seeming to accept the lie at its face value—Joan's lie to his old mate, her husband—putting himself clearly offside. He asked him—stuck with it now—'Be back soon, will she?'

'*Is* back. I was out there today, briefly.'

Checking the time. Somewhat distracted: which was hardly surprising, in the circumstances. Talking about the cottage and its surroundings, then: it was at a village called Rodmell—Barclay had told him this, and that it belonged to some relation of Joan's. They

16

were mostly titled, Joan being the daughter of an earl—she was *Lady* Joan Stack—as well as—now—a driver in the MTC.

Stack was saying, 'You must come out there some time, Ben. Did you visit the pub at Alfriston yet, by the way?'

He nodded. 'With Monkey. Got everything there, huh? God knows how.'

'Black market connections, is what I heard. Don't quote me.' Nodding ... 'Anyway—it's good to have you around. Sorry we didn't get a chance to say more than hello yesterday.'

'You had to make your formal calls, you said.'

'Well, I did. NOIC Newhaven here—' NOIC standing for Naval Officer in Charge—a retired admiral masquerading as a captain, with his offices in what had been the Guinness Rest and Relaxation Home—'then Fort Southwick. Daily routine, I can use the blower—scrambler—but having been away so long—well, you know, personal contact...'

He'd been up on the east coast for the past five weeks, relieving an SO who'd gone sick and for whom there'd been no other suitable replacement available. When Ben had arrived at Newhaven, MGB 875 had had a temporary CO and Grant McKellar of 863 had been acting SO of the flotilla.

All back to normal now. Or to what passed for normal. On the surface, and as far as Stack knew, normal.

It felt like being an accessory, an accomplice. Not at all a good way to feel. In Stack's situation, he asked himself, wouldn't you count on any mate worth his salt tipping you off?

It would be a damn sight easier to break this kind of news to someone you *didn't* like, though.

17

Especially Joan being an 'old mate' too. If you could put it that way. Well—you *could* ... Another aspect—less personal, therefore more easily arguable—was that blowing the gaff at this juncture could be extremely damaging; and the other side of that coin was that if all concerned kept their mouths shut the whole thing might blow over, the affair come quietly to an end with effectively no harm done.

Could happen. Furneaux with new responsibilities *might* come to his senses.

If Joan let him.

In the long run, Furneaux wasn't Stack's problem. Joan was. When Ben had been corresponding with Bob about getting himself transferred to this flotilla, the marriage had lasted nearly two years, Bob had been reported as still considering himself the happiest man on earth, and it had seemed reasonable to assume the leopard had changed her spots and it might be safe to fraternize again.

Stack asked him, 'Tell me about your girl?'

'Well. Name's Rosie. Rosie Ewing. Widow.' He shook his head, smiling, at Stack's quick glance. 'She's twenty-five now, wasn't married long. Her husband flew Spitfires, got himself shot down just before I met her. Now she's in SOE.'

'*That* show ...'

'You'd think she was hundred per cent Pom, but Dad was a Frog so she's bilingual. I met her first in London when I had the desk job. Outfit called NID(C). We had a fair amount to do with SOE. Shipping their agents over, and munitions to the French resistance, bringing shot-down flyers out— all that malarky.'

'Which is what you've been doing since, in the Dartmouth flotilla?'

'Exactly. How I got to it. My chief in London—name of Slocum, RN captain—astutely agreed a navigator can get by on one ear. And I ran into Rosie again—we'd lost touch, sort of—'

'Going to marry her?'

'When *she*'ll consent to—when or if.'

'Good on you, Ben.'

Checking the time again, though. 'About bloody time we heard . . .' Jerking round, then, at a thump on the door as it opened.

'Yeah?'

Mike Furneaux: his eyes on Stack—who'd already begun to move—and a jerk of the dark head back towards the Ops Room. 'It's coming in now on the scrambler, sir.'

CHAPTER TWO

Leaning over his chart-table in the gunboat, hearing the familiar sequence of reports and orders from the bridge only a few feet away, up there behind him: Barclay's 'All gone aft, sir', and the clink of the telegraph as Stack gave her a kick ahead on the starboard outer, telling Charlie Sewell, 'Port wheel, Cox'n' and adding to Barclay, 'Let go headrope', and then—with the engines stopped and put astern—'Take off the back spring.' Ben meanwhile scribbling a few quick and simple calculations on a signal-pad. True course—which he'd laid-off on the chart—216 degrees. Westerly variation was a plus, easterly deviation a minus. And—feeling the tremble in the boat's timber as her outer screws backed her away from MGB 866, alongside whom she'd been

19

secured—*and*, since it was now four hours short of high water at Dover, you'd have an easterly set of roughly one and a half knots. Which in four hours' time off Barfleur would have become a westerly of about a knot and a quarter. Another movement of the telegraphs bringing further changes in the vibration: outers stopped, then slow ahead, Stack's rasp of 'All right, Cox'n, take her out', and Petty Officer Sewell's quiet acknowledgement. He'd be putting on starboard wheel to ease her over that way, steering her out through the narrow bottleneck of the harbour entrance. Stack telling Barclay, 'Fall the hands out, Number One.' Sailors would have been lined up for'ard and aft, since taking in all the breast-ropes and springs, and were now being fallen out to secure the deck gear for sea. The boat meanwhile still propelled only by her two outer screws. Ben transferred the result of those calculations to his notebook—course by magnetic, south 40 west—slung binoculars round his neck and went up into the bridge.

The light was going fast. Effectively, it had gone; and it was still a few minutes short of 1830. The darkening effect of low cloud, of course. Over on the other side—the French side—the *Heilbronne* would be clearing Le Havre in similar conditions. The recce flight had reported her as being still inside but that there'd been some movement in progress, four or five escort vessels filing out into the swept and buoyed channel. Being a daylight reconnaissance, the aircraft would have been a Spitfire, one of the very fast, unarmed PRU probes that covered not only the French but also the Dutch and Belgian ports. Whether the enemy would know they'd been spied on was a toss-up. Might not, if the Spit had taken its

20

quick look—using the last of the daylight, ducking under the cloud-ceiling as it were *en passant*—a slant-view from a mile or so offshore, over the Baie de la Seine.

MGB 875 was beginning to pitch a little as she met the incoming tide and the beginnings of the swell; with a faintly pinkish glow still emanating from the horizon in the west, the direction of Selsey, and the wash from her powerful, rumbling progress startlingly white in the surrounding gloom, washing along the dark line of the east pier. It was going to be a little bit bouncy outside, but nothing much; wind only about force 2 at present with no more than a slight chop on the sea, but this long swell out of the Atlantic, a legacy of last week's storms.

The rest of the unit would be clear of their berths by this time, following her out. Ben focused his binoculars on 866, Moncrieff's boat. Hearing Stack growl, 'Didn't know we'd lost Binns, Alan.'

'No, sir.' Barclay ... 'Looked for you to tell you, but—'

'When I was ashore, dare say. Not that it'd have made any odds...'

Binns, a green-stripe—'special'—sub-lieutenant who spoke German, was carried as an extra officer to man the QD gear. Also known as 'Headache', it was a contrivance for eavesdropping on the enemy's voice-radio. Binns had been rushed off to hospital with acute appendicitis and it hadn't been possible to replace him at such short notice.

Stack had had his glasses trained astern. Without lowering them or looking round, telling whoever was nearest the telegraphs—it happened to be Harper, a leading seaman, also second coxswain, who'd come up to report that the gear on the upper deck had been

21

secured for sea—'All engines slow ahead.'

Harper—six-four and about sixteen stone, known to his friends as 'Tiny'—repeated the order, pushing the two centre levers over. Starting the inner pair would push her up to ten knots, from about six or seven, at these low revs. The next step would be to go to half-ahead, working up to cruising speed by the time of passing C2A buoy, about two miles offshore. It was the departure point for all Coastal Force operations from this base; the Newhaven turn-off, as it were, from the swept channel that ran from the Nab Tower at Spithead all the way round to Dover—thence through the Downs to the Thames and on to join the East Coast Convoy Route.

866—Moncrieff—was matching the slight increase in speed, maintaining his distance astern. Stack had taken a glance back to check this. Ordering now, 'All engines half ahead, 1500 revs. Course to the buoy, Ben?'

'South twelve east'll do it, sir.'

'Steer that, Cox'n.'

Power building, noise building, whitened sea broadening where it slid away into the dark. Motion increasing slightly as she met the swells ... Ben watching 866 again—and remembering Moncrieff asking him when they'd been dispersing from the briefing, 'So did you tell him yet?'

Meaning, had he told Stack about Furneaux and Stack's wife. Ben had glanced round to check that they were on their own, then shaken his head. 'No, Monkey, I haven't. Hardly the right time, is it.'

'But you're going to—huh?'

'It's not—*easy*, Monkey.'

'Bloody hell, what's *that* to do with anything? It's a fact, and you and I owe it to Bob to damn well tell

22

him. Christ's sake, Ben, last night you *swore*—'

'I know I did.'

'Changed your mind, since?'

'Not exactly ... Talk about it when we get back, can we?'

Moncrieff had been with him and Rosie at this hotel called Beauport Place last night. He'd recommended it, in fact, soon after Ben had arrived in Newhaven and asked him for advice as to where he might put her up for a night or two whenever she could get down. Its advantages as he'd cited them being that it was accessible from Newhaven but not so close as to be patronized by any others from this base, and that the woman who ran it was—'you know, easy-going?'

Meaning she didn't ask to see marriage certificates.

'How'd I get there?'

'Well—couple of guys on the base have cars. Buy 'em a drink or two—and if they're duty, or somethin', aren't using 'em themselves?'

'You go on your bike, I suppose.'

'Sure.' He had a 350cc Royal Enfield which he'd picked up in Seaford for a song. Ben asked him, 'Your girl rides pillion?'

'Has to. Less she wants to walk.'

Last night Monkey had been out there for the Saturday night dinner-dance, bringing the girl in question, a Canadian Army nurse, from some nearby military hospital. The south of England was teeming with Canadians, there were a lot just round this area and naturally enough Moncrieff tended to consort with them. He was a smallish, compactly-built man, with a reputation for using his fists when provoked. Dark, with a bullet head and eyes like brown stones—and an intense loyalty to Bob Stack, whom

23

he credited with having taught him all he knew and helped him up the ladder to command.

He'd shrugged. 'I'm not letting it ride, Ben. You don't tell him, I will. Damn it, we agreed, last night—'

'I know. I know...'

Glasses levelled astern, focused on the flair of bow-wave under 866's stem, the gunboat itself almost invisible behind it, in the gathering darkness. Remembering Monkey last night half-rising from his chair in that instant reaction of hard-eyed shock, his growl of 'Christ—see what *I'm* seeing?'

Joan, with Furneaux steering her into the room where the dancing was. Ben's first thought had been that Bob Stack must be there too, in the same party—in the bar, maybe ... Whereas Monkey had been certain that he wasn't, and within minutes this had turned out to be the truth.

Ben hadn't even wanted Monkey to be there. He'd very much sooner have been on his own with Rosie. But when the Canadian had announced that he was coming to the dance, bringing this girl whom he'd wanted Ben to meet, why not let's make it a foursome—well, particularly as he'd introduced Ben to the Beauport, it would have been downright rude to have said no. Even knowing that Rosie'd be far from ecstatic when she heard about it.

Making about twenty-one knots now; normal cruising speed, for the 'D's. Stack's final decision had been that the whole force should stay together up to about two-thirds of the way over, at which point he'd detach the MTBs to push on ahead. It wouldn't be a prolonged usage of high revs—which wasn't ever to be recommended, or safe—and it would leave an adequate margin of time in which to cover the last ten miles inshore at low revs on silenced engines.

24

Engine noise was a giveaway. Even 'silenced' you were audible at a mile or even more.

'Course from the buoy, Ben?'

'South forty west, sir.'

They were looking for it now—for the C2A buoy. Three pairs of glasses sweeping to and fro across the bow. Stack in the starboard corner, Barclay in the other, and the signalman, 'Dusty' Miller, between Barclay and the coxswain. A fourth then, as Ben joined them ... The pitching and rolling was regular, not all that uncomfortable. Speed helped, carrying her across the swell, and her length did too. The MTBs—'short' boats—naturally enough hammered around much more than these, in any kind of sea.

'C2A fine to starboard, sir!'

Barclay had spotted it. Stack checked it for himself, then grunted, 'So let's get ourselves to action stations.' He had to be just about the most relaxed, easy-going skipper in the whole of Coastal Forces. Which was saying something. He got results, for all that—terrific results, as witness the ribbons on his chest, as well as the regard in which his crews held him—this one, and the bunch he'd had up at Felixstowe. His total rejection of all bullshit would at least partially account for that. Barclay's thumb was on the alarm buzzer; not only sound, but lights would be flashing in the messdecks, flats and in the engine room. The second coxswain had gone lurching aft: a gunlayer, his action job was on the after six-pounder. It was routine at this stage to go to action stations and test-fire all the guns: and for Ben to return to his hutch—wheelhouse, so-called, although there was no wheel in it, only had been in some much earlier boats—log the moment of passing the buoy, noting the time and log-reading at this point of departure.

He went down the few steps and through the blackout screens, set himself to checking the chronometer time, and the distance run, and the QH coordinates. Briefly switching on the echo-sounder then—to ensure that it did switch on, and made sense. You'd be on the ten-fathom line, near enough, passing that buoy. Check and double-check ... Not that there was any great problem in knowing where you were at any given moment, now you had this 'QH', a navigational aid derived from what the RAF called 'Gee'. At least, all SOs' boats had it, others were being fitted with it as it became available. It was used with gridded charts and was accurate to within about a hundred yards.

Except if your electrics went, of course. Which could happen—from being shot at, for instance.

'Pilot.' Voicepipe: he answered it, and Stack told him, 'C2A's abeam. Altering to south forty west.'

'Aye, sir.' He had the time noted, and the log reading, and the known position served as a check on the QH being in its right mind. Like falling off a log, really. It was just that keeping right on top of it minute by minute made it even simpler, eliminated any uncertainties of the kind that tended otherwise to show up when other peripherals were going wrong. In any case, triple-checking had become a habit. Even though any halfwit could have handled this lot. In the 15th Flotilla, where the job had been to get into pinpoints on a rocky coast under the noses of German coastal defence positions and often in foul weather—well, that *had* called for some degree of skill.

He'd switched off the echo-sounder. It was of no practical use at this speed anyway. Whereas on the Brittany coast, creeping in through those narrow

26

channels, it had been one's primary navigational tool. In fact—on reflection, thinking of what he'd told himself an hour or so earlier when Bob Stack had asked him, 'No sour grapes?'—that line about being a good navigator and wanting nothing more—well, it wasn't entirely true. Had been in those days, the clandestine operations on the Brittany coast, but it wasn't now. Not really.

'Course south forty west, sir.'

The coxswain's voice, audible via the bridge voicepipe. And Stack's, then: 'Test guns, Number One.'

'Aye aye, sir.' Barclay used the sound-powered telephone to pass that order to the gunners—to the power-operated six-pounders forward and aft, the two twin point-five mountings, power-operated turrets just forward of this charthouse, port and starboard, the twin 20-mm Oerlikons on the centreline abaft the bridge, and a pair of Vickers Gas-Operated .303" machine-guns in each of the forward corners of the bridge.

You didn't need two good ears to hear *that* lot. Wouldn't want to be on the receiving end of it, either. Pressing his palm over the one that worked—while the whole boat shook from the percussions . . .

Petering out already, though. Finished. In the ringing, comparative quiet, Stack ordered, 'Secure the guns. Relax to cruising stations.'

Cruising stations, also known as the second degree of readiness, would be the state of things until the unit was well out to sea; then the hands would be sent to action stations again and stay there. Fiddling with the QH again, Ben heard, over the engines' steady thunder and the timber hull's more or less rhythmic slamming across the swells, a distant popping and

27

crackling which would be the other boats testing their guns. For those up top to see it there'd be firework-like displays of coloured tracer, back there astern: a lot of it from the other gunboats, rather less from the MTBs, whose armament consisted only of a twin Vickers GO each side—mounted on the torpedo tubes—a twin point-five powered turret abaft the bridge and a single hand-worked Oerlikon on the foredeck. Torpedoes were the MTBs' main, offensive armament, and they'd have been brought to the ready—depth-settings adjusted to six feet, stop-valves opened, propeller clamps removed, safety-pins extracted from the 'whiskers' on their warheads' pistols; and on the tubes, firing-stops lowered and impulse cartridges inserted.

Ben pushed his dividers into their slot at the back of the table. Wondering whether Stack wasn't cutting things a bit fine, as far as the interception was concerned, whether instead of holding the unit together he shouldn't have been letting Furneaux push on ahead with the MTBs at higher speed right from the start. Present arrangements were fine if the target and her escorts could be counted on to follow the inshore convoy route: but what if some Kraut staff officer had suffered a rush of blood to his square head, elected to depart from standard practice and send the convoy straight across?

At seventeen knots, they'd be rounding Barfleur in nearer three hours' time than four. Three and a half, say—taking into account the fact that the *Heilbronne* hadn't actually cleared the port at the time of the reconnaissance.

All right, so there were the Hunt-class destroyers out of Devonport or Brixham, *en route* to act as long-stops somewhere between Alderney and Cap de la Hague. But that was hardly the point. Wouldn't figure prominently in Bob Stack's thinking either.

Maybe you *could* be certain, about that convoy route. Being a stranger in these waters, Ben admitted to himself, not having seen any action yet with this flotilla, learning the ropes as one went along, more or less...

So *ask* the bugger.

He pulled himself back up into the bridge. Into the whip of the wind, roar of engines, dark figures all in 'goonsuits'—one-piece oilskin overalls lined with kapok for warmth and buoyancy. 'Skipper, sir—'

'Hang on.'

Stack was facing aft with his glasses at his eyes, and the signalman—Miller, identifiable by the fact that he was unusually short and wide—was back there aiming a blue-shaded Night Signalling Lantern into foam-flecked darkness. Flashing some message to 866. Barclay explained into Ben's ear—the good one, picking that one probably just by luck—'Cruising formation. Dogs port, Mikes starboard.'

As had been presaged at the briefing. Dogs meaning the gunboats—Stack's callsign was Topdog, Monkey was Dog Two and Ted Bland in 874 was Dog Three—and the MTBs were respectively Mike One, Two, Three and Four. Mike as in Furneaux.

'Message passed, sir.'

There'd be no acknowledgement. A light flashing forward, the direction in which a unit was travelling, might be seen by an enemy—if there was one lying in wait ahead. You had to assume that Monkey would have got it and read it and that as he shifted 866 out on to Stack's port quarter and Bland brought 874 out on Monkey's, Furneaux would make his own move

29

up to starboard, the other three MTBs angling outward beyond him, increasing revs in order to close up and reducing again as they settled into the new formation—an arrowhead, this boat at its apex, MGBs in quarterline to port and MTBs to starboard.

It was happening now. Monkey was on the move anyway, the white patch of his bow-wave sliding steadily from left to right as one looked astern.

A bit of a fanatic, was old Monkey. Un-Canadian, in that way. Most of them—and they were quite numerous in Coastal Forces, one flotilla in the Mediterranean for instance had only Canadians as COs—mostly, they approached even Aussie standards of informality. Monkey was a hell of a nice guy—bags of guts, and great company ashore—at least, if no-one made him angry—but when he drew the line on some issue or other that was it, the line stayed drawn.

Ben had a feeling that he—Monkey—would end up giving Stack the bad news. Then Stack would want to know why his own compatriot, Ben bloody Quarry, hadn't told him.

Better tell him, therefore. On return to harbour. Get it over with there and then, just bloody *do* it.

'What did you want, Ben?'

It made him jump. Then he'd caught on, got it in context ... 'I was dickering with the chartwork. Struck me—well, may be talking out of the back of my neck, sir, but—'

'If you are, I'll tell you.'

'Thing is, if our Krauts didn't use the convoy route, sir—if they plugged straight over—'

'We'd be fucked.'

Chuckles out of the darkness. Ben agreed: 'What *I* thought.'

30

'Should've mentioned. One—out of Le Havre, bastards *always* use that route. Two—Fleet Air Arm Albacores from Manston'll be doing another recce for us—not inshore, out in the middle, where you say.'

'Ah.'

'I'm not just a pretty face, Ben.' Stack's arm came up, pointing. 'Here he comes.'

Furneaux: a white mound of broken water and white streamers flying like pendants, sharply rising engine-noise as his boat came crashing up on the quarter at maybe thirty or thirty-five knots, size of the mound and volume of noise reducing then as he cut the power, settling into his new station. Identical flurries of foam were falling into place out on *his* quarter: Billy Chisholm's 562, John Heddingly's 564 and Mark Newbolt's 563.

Ben commented, 'Neat enough.'

'Mike's a dab hand.' Stack added, 'Damn shame we've lost Rod King, but his shoes'll fit Mike like they were made for him.'

All the boats were in station. Like pressing a button, and it had all happened. The band of brothers thing, Ben thought. That Nelsonian concept really came to life here, became in some ways the essence of it. He had his glasses up, seeing them like so many flickering white fires in the black surround. Out from Furneaux's—two—three—and four—just visible, Newbolt, at the tail end because he was the most junior, in his first command.

Lucky bugger. Nice guy, too. Tall—an inch or so taller than Ben, maybe—fresh-faced, fairish, with an open, friendly manner. A natural enthusiast. Fine cricketer, apparently, according to Barclay he'd been captain of cricket—and also fives champion—at

31

whatever school he'd been at. But a quick eye and quick thinking were great assets in *this* game too. Ben had been one of several men who when they'd been dispersing to their boats had shaken the youngster's hand and congratulated him, Newbolt mumbling for about the fourth time thanks but he'd sooner have had Rod King still around—and genuinely feeling this, you could see it, hear it and like him for it—even if you *did* still envy him.

Envied the bloody lot of them, was the truth of it. Would have given an arm and a leg, metaphorically speaking, to have a command of his own. *That* was the truth: although he'd take care never to let a damn soul guess it.

Except Rosie. There wasn't anything he'd want to keep from Rosie.

Well—*hardly* anything.

Remembering from way back—*really* way back, as far as his relationship with her was concerned, right at the start, the first evening they'd spent together—the very beginning of that evening too, in the New Yorker, a drinking club in Park Lane, so it must have been over one of about the first two or three drinks they'd ever had together—she'd told him flatly, 'There must have been a girl.'

In his Paris days, immediately before the war, which he'd been telling her about. He'd gone there to learn about painting. To *become* a painter. And his answer to her in the New Yorker, refuting that allegation, had been, 'Painting, is what there was.'

'*And* a girl.'

That tone of certainty. Even then, when she hadn't known him from a kangaroo. It was the evening of the day he'd heard that he was getting back to sea, after about a year stuck behind a desk; and despite

32

the fact it was also the day news came of the surrender of Singapore, he'd been in a mood to celebrate. While Rosie's fighter-pilot husband had been shot down and killed about thirty-six hours earlier and she hadn't much certainty about who she was, or where, or what she was going to do.

What she was doing, even. Like getting drunk with a strange Australian, for instance.

She'd asked him—about the girl in Paris, ignoring his earlier denial—'Where is she now?', and he'd let her have it her way, told her, 'Don't know. Felt she'd done enough slumming, decided to go home.'

Something on those lines. It had been a lie by omission, but not technically a lie at all. What he had not seen fit to mention was that the girl's name had been Heidi, that she'd been German and had a father back in Düsseldorf who was some kind of Nazi bigwig. This hadn't meant anything to him at the time; she was a beauty, Rhinemaiden type, and she'd got a kick out of being painted with her clothes off. That was where it had started, and the reason she'd left Paris was that her family had recalled her. What had shamed him ever since was that he'd been really shattered, having thought that *she* mattered as much as anyone ever could.

He still thanked God he hadn't told Rosie about it. As he might have done, self-deprecatingly, being unaware at that stage that Rosie's hatred of Germans was quite exceptionally intense.

With some reason, too. Knowing what her job was, you could guess at some of it. In her sleep—this last night—she'd moaned, writhed, wept, cried out in French, then *really* screamed, slippery with sweat and fighting him off when he'd tried to interrupt the nightmare then comfort her as she came out of it,

33

still sobbing.

He'd told her later, 'Rosie—listen, you must *not* go back. Not on *any* account, Rosie. Please—promise me, darling—'

'I'm sorry. Crazy dream—'

'What was it about?'

'Oh—nothing.' A long, hard sigh ... '*Nothing. Just*—'

'Just my left foot it was nothing!'

'Nothing I want to remember, Ben. Or talk about. *Ever* ...'

*   *   *

'Char or kye sir?'

He broke out of his thoughts—more or less. In the plot, on the stool that hinged down, forearms on the chart and a shoulder against the bulkhead for stability, inhaling smoke from a duty-free cigarette ... For obvious reasons you couldn't smoke on the bridge or upper deck at night, but you could down here with the ports and companionway blacked out. A mental close-up of Rosie in semi-darkness still blurred his mind—a life-size negative through which he was looking at Carter, Ordinary Seaman William J., acting steward and galley hand and also now under instruction—Ben's—as an embryo 'tanky' or navigator's yeoman. Mainly because he had neat handwriting and could spell, and had volunteered for it.

'Thanks, Carter. Kye'd be fine.'

Cocoa, that meant. The boy glanced at the QH, on his way down to the galley flat. He was pale, with deep-sunk eyes, crewcut yellowish hair and over-large ears, and he came from Liverpool. Ben had

34

never bothered with a tanky—meaning an assistant, who'd correct charts and so forth—but Carter was keen to learn and he'd agreed to try him out.

Checking the QH: through a haze of smoke, transferring the coordinates to the gridded chart.

Slightly off track. Enough, though, to realize you'd be significantly off it if you held this course for another hour, say. In fact you wouldn't—if only in view of the small, gradual changes in the tidal stream's strength and direction as the hours passed; there was also the effect of wind. As things were at present this would be very slight, but it was still a contributing factor.

He called into the voicepipe, 'Bridge!', and Stack's answer was immediate: 'Yes, pilot.'

'Better steer three degrees to starboard, sir. South forty-*three* west.'

'OK.' More distantly, then: 'Hear that, Cox'n?', and Sewell's acknowledgement, 'South forty-three west, sir.'

Carter reappeared, with an enamel mug of Admiralty-issue cocoa. It was supplied in bars which had to be scraped into powder with a knife, and lower-deck gourmets used custard-powder as well as condensed milk to thicken it. A flavouring of rum was not unheard of.

Ben stubbed out his cigarette. 'Thanks.' Nodding then to Wheeler, the radar operator—dressed for the bridge, on his way up to do a stint as lookout. Dark, scrawny, with deep-sunk eyes—the look of a mad priest, Ben had thought when he'd first met him.

'Evenin', sir.'

'Set all right now, is it?'

The 291 radar set; they'd had a lot of trouble with it. Wheeler held up two crossed fingers: 'Never know

35

your luck, sir.' Ben reflecting that Stack wasn't likely to be using the damn thing anyway.

* * *

On his own again, he had the big chart out, to check on whether at the two-thirds stage—2100 say, just over an hour's time—if there was an all-clear from the Albacore reconnaissance, whether times and distances really would work out. For the MTBs particularly, if they went on ahead then at thirty knots.

Should, he thought. He could see it roughly in his head, and had faith in Stack's own prescience. But having thought about it some more—in the back of his mind, almost sub-consciously—and still having that slightly anxious feeling...

No harm in checking, anyway. 'Walking' his dividers along the pencilled track, on course 216 true...

Amazing. The MTBs would be ten miles northeast of Pointe de Barfleur at about 2130. So reducing to ten knots then, they'd be as close inshore as they'd want to be by 2230. While the three Dogs, maintaining the present twenty-one knots, would arrive in that ten miles NE position at 2200. Reducing to slow speed, then, silenced, they'd be half an hour behind the MTBs, which would use that much time getting into their waiting position inshore.

Bloody perfect. Spot-on.

But—he saw this suddenly, as in a double-take—only as long as the reconnaissance report confirmed Stack's expectations, was it spot-on. Otherwise, the end-result might be something like a dead heat. Or even worse ... Pausing again for thought: realizing

36

that Bob's answer would be that if the reconnaissance told him the enemy were dashing straight across—OK, he'd let Furneaux off the leash at once. But—it was a large 'but' too—the recce effort couldn't be infallible, guaranteed. The Albacores mightn't spot what in fact *might* be there. *Easily* might not. Even with their ASV radar.

Solution?

Well—surely to detach Furneaux and his boys not at 2100 but at 2030. More than an hour at thirty knots was certainly not to be risked without good reason—the risk being that of engine breakdowns— but the situation—*viz.*, important target possibly about to slip through one's fingers—would surely justify it.

On the bridge, he expounded this theory to Stack, who cursed but then led the way down to the chart. 'Don't bloody well let go, Ben, do you...'

'Well—'

'Come on. Show me.'

'We're here, sir. At 2100 we'll be—'

'Plot!'

The voicepipe from the W/T office. Ben leant to it. 'Plot.'

'Weather forecast, sir.' Leading Telegraphist Willis added, 'In the bucket.'

'Right.' He fished it up—a small cylinder, pulled through the pipe on a lanyard. Extracting the folded sheet of signal pad, handing it to Stack; he sent the carrier down again. Stack meanwhile reading the forecast out aloud. Wind was predicted to veer from southwest to west by midnight, and to increase to force 5 or 6 by first light.

Not so good. In rough seas, small ships like these were severely handicapped.

37

'By first light—' Stack put a stopper on that kind of thinking—'we'll have sunk the bugger and gone home.'

CHAPTER THREE

As yet there'd been no report from any Fleet Air Arm reconnaissance. The Hunt-class destroyers west of Cap de la Hague would be waiting for it too, Ben guessed. Stack meanwhile had decided that if there was no news by 2030, OK, belt and braces.

'Time now?'

'Twenty twenty-nine, sir.'

'Good enough.' Straightening from the voicepipe. The gunboat with her nose up as she climbed a swell, a rolling mass of black water lifting ahead then creaming aft deck-high, a certain amount of spray lashing over as she levelled and started down again. The swell was no bigger than it had been an hour ago—might even have been down a little—but to a ship of this size it was quite big enough.

The flat-bottomed MTBs would be feeling it a lot more, of course.

'Signalman!'

'Sir!'

'Dusty' Miller ... Ben arriving in the bridge at this moment, joining the skipper, Barclay, the coxswain—PO Charlie Sewell like a permanent fitting at the wheel—a lookout with binoculars at his eyes, and Miller already cradling a blue lamp. Stack was telling him, 'Make to Mike One: Flag 4, K for king.'

'Flag 4, K king, aye aye, sir.'

38

He could have used R/T, voice radio; but the high-frequency type fitted now was long-enough range to be liable to interception. So why risk it? If you could read the Germans' inter-ship chitchat, chances were they'd read yours. It would only need a few words of English to tell them that Royal Navy units were in the offing. Whereas when you were in contact with them anyway you weren't telling them anything—they'd know it. Surprise was a primary objective—virtually an imperative, for small wooden ships going out against much larger and more heavily armed steel-hulled ones. Miller had his blue-shaded Aldis stuttering: a call-up—two or three 'A's to ensure having the addressee's attention—then the message which had been pre-arranged at the briefing. Flag 4 in the Coastal Forces Signal Pamphlet meant 'Attack with torpedoes', and the addition of the letter 'K' as a special code tonight enlarged this, telling Furneaux to push on ahead to Pointe de Barfleur and position his unit for an attack on the *Heilbronne* from inshore. The MTBs were to take advantage of the planned diversionary attack from seaward by the MGBs, but if for any reason this was delayed—late arrival owing to engine breakdown, for instance, or other mishap—they weren't to wait for it.

The choice of the letter 'K' was in memory of Rod King. Stack had told the MTB skippers when they'd been winding-up the briefing, 'Chalk this one up to him, eh?'

'Message passed, sir!'

An advantage of the quarterline formation was that the other three would have read the signal and be ready for Furneaux's move. As *now* ... In 875's bridge several pairs of glasses including Ben's were focused on that leaping patch of white as it seemed

39

visually to explode, the brilliance expanding, bursting outward, and the note of the four boats' engines—twelve in all, three engines each—rising sharply at the same time as it increased in volume. Another pre-arrangement—Furneaux's with his COs—was that at this juncture they'd adopt Order One, line ahead, instead of quarterline. You could see it happening—the three of them angling inward, slanting into his wake—throttles open, the boats flinging themselves at the black undulations of sea ahead.

Furneaux himself already level, and overhauling; had passed, and this was 562 abeam now, thunderous roar beating across the rolling gap of water: then 564, and 563, jumping the swells like game-fish and the four of them well closed up, virtually nose to tail, a single cohesive unit. Stack had his glasses on the last of them—young Newbolt—drawing away ahead now, fine on the bow. 875 beginning to roll and corkscrew across the furrows like a somewhat larger game-fish herself as the MTBs' combined wash hit her. Stack half-turning—'Bastards...'—grabbing at the binnacle for support ... 'All engines 1800 revs, Number One!'

'1800, sir.' Barclay, in the forefront near the telegraphs, cranked the handle of the rev counter. 1800 would give her about twenty-five knots instead of the twenty-one that she'd been getting from 1500. Over the next two hours, therefore, putting her eight miles ahead, arriving off Barfleur roughly twenty minutes earlier than she would have at the lower speed. Touch wood ... 1800 was regarded as the maximum revs permissible on a continuous basis—continuous as distinct from short bursts of up to thirty or thirty-plus knots as was frequently required

40

in action.

Stack had told the signalman to pass 'George 25' by blue light to 866—telling Moncrieff, 'Speed twenty-five knots.' Bland in 874 would read it too. The rolling was savage at this moment, still in the wash from the MTBs—whose departure would make a fine painting, Ben thought—if you could get it right, the real guts of it, not just a picture of boats going fast on each others' tails but somehow put over that sense of purpose, aggression, imminence of action.

How you'd achieve it, he didn't know. Only had a conviction that it *should* be possible. He guessed the answer would come through getting down to it—taking the plunge and then bloody *slaving* at it. Rosie, indirectly, had said something more or less to that effect, just yesterday.

'Eighteen hundred revs on, sir!' Then Miller's report: 'George two five passed, sir!' Yells high-pitched, to beat the racket of sea and engines. Ben lowered his glasses, having to go back down to his plot now, log the increase in speed and the departure of the MTBs, etc. Accepting as he went down that the stuff about painting must have come into his thoughts through having had that conversation with Rosie about it last evening, when she'd asked him whether he'd done any since she'd last seen him, and he'd had to confess he hadn't.

'Except sort of in my head.'

'Ideas for it, you mean?'

'Yeah. I think strewth, I'll paint *that*—'

'Why not do it?'

'Well. One day ...'

He'd made pencil sketches, from time to time, and notes to remind him how it had looked and felt, this or that particular scene, what there'd been about it that had got to him. But why he hadn't taken any of it further than that conceptual stage—well, the obvious let-out was not having the gear handy or the time or a place to do it, but the more basic thing was being scared that if he tried now he'd only be turning visions into dogs' dinners.

She'd warned him, 'Wait too long, you might never do it. Might get *permanent* cold feet.'

'You're so right.'

'But the fact you care and think about it as much as you do—'

'Care about you, Rosie. *Love* you...'

He was in the plot, with her voice in his ears and image in his mind while logging the speed increase—tagged as 2030—and now marked the position on the chart, noting the log reading ... Halfway over, roughly; but the second half should be covered in twenty minutes less. Barring misadventure, of course. Meanwhile—well, it was now *two* hours before high water at Dover, and the tidal stream atlas told him the easterly set would be running at a rate of 1.6 knots. Not enough difference there yet to bother with. And the position by QH—dead right, they were where they ought to be. For the moment, therefore, no problems. Even the continued non-arrival of any follow-up reconnaissance report might be a case of no news being good news. If the Albacores had done their stuff and found nothing, the inference would be that the *Heilbronne* and her escorts were taking the coastal convoy route.

Bloody idiots, if they were.

He went down to the wireless office, which was on the deck below, starboard side of the galley flat, between the officers' heads and the CO's cabin. It was a tiny, cramped compartment mostly filled with radio gear, cramped enough anyway but more so in an SO's boat, like this one, in which you had two telegraphists instead of only one, as well as extra gear. Both with headsets on—they were keeping listening watch, with the switch broken on the transmitting side, for safety's sake—heads turning as he pushed the small door open and looked in: Ordway's expression sharp, terrier-like, Leading Tel. Willis rather donnish, affable, as he shifted the earphone from this side ... 'Social visit, sir?'

'You could call it that. How're we doing?'

The warmth of electrics, cigarette-smoke hanging blue, a pin-up on the bulkhead. Several empty tea or kye mugs, and Saturday's *Daily Mirror*. Nothing much was happening, apparently—nothing on the air other than what Ordway referred to as 'the usual garbage'. But even in the present comparatively quiet sea-state it was thunderously noisy. Something like going over Niagara in a barrel ... He chatted with them for a minute, then went back up to his plot, folded the seat down and lit a cigarette.

A glance at the clock, as he expelled the first plume of smoke. Any minute now, Stack would be sending the hands to action stations.

He wished he'd been able to 'phone Rosie before they'd sailed. To check she'd got back all right—let her know he'd *wanted* to check, had been missing her ever since her train had steamed out of Haywards Heath this morning. He'd told her he'd ring if he could but might not be in a position to, in which case he'd try on Monday evening instead.

'Saying you might go to sea tonight?'

He'd shrugged. 'We do sometimes. Earn our living?'

43

'Don't go getting yourself smashed up again, that's all.'

'I'm not planning on it.'

'You go on like a mother hen about me, Ben, but your job isn't exactly *un*dangerous.'

'Comparatively, it is. And straightforward, damn sight less frightening. Mother hen, huh ... Well, I'll say it again—please, *don't* offer to go back?'

'You look after yourself, I'll look after *my*self. In any case, as things are at this moment—'

'You said in the night they're short of trained agents and sooner or later—'

'I promise you I won't just suddenly disappear. As you said you dreaded most.'

'Dread it all. I want you safe, out of it. Christ, you've done *enough*, Rosie. Why are they short of agents anyway—because so many have been caught, or—'

'Because more are needed. There'll be an invasion before long, and before that—you know what the job is, the Resistance have got to be armed and organized—'

'Change your mind, marry me?'

She'd said earlier, 'I don't want to be widowed a second time, Ben.' And had gone on quickly, cutting short his protest to the effect that there was no reason to think she would be, 'Even if we *did*—get married—we wouldn't see each other any more than we will from now on, please God. Now you're here instead of at the back of beyond. There's no damn *point*—'

'Except I love you.'

'Well, me too. I mean—love *you* ... Ben, let's be together as much as we can, and—'

'When the war's over, then?'

Fingers on the back of his neck: 'Your hair's much too short.'

'Has to be. The admirals insist.'

'Well, the hell with—'

'I agree. But Rosie—after the war?'

She'd sighed. Warm breath in his ear. 'Ask me then, if—'

'No *ifs*—'

'If you still want to. Could be a long time, you know.'

'When do I get to meet your family?'

'Whenever you get some leave.' She'd shrugged. 'Although—I told you, as far as my mother's concerned—'

'You said there's an uncle I'd get along with.'

'Well, yes...'

She wasn't too enthusiastic about her mother, he remembered. Holding her. Smallish, curvy, *lovely* shape, with a lot of soft brown hair, wide-apart hazel eyes and a mouth that made his hair curl just to look at it. He'd seen Monkey Moncrieff looking at it last night too—and the Canadian girl watching Monkey, a certain displeasure creasing her pudgy face and Monkey quite oblivious of it. But that mouth of Rosie's would give *any* man ideas—if he didn't have them already. Rosie Ewing, *née* Rosalie de Bosque—

Action alarm buzzer, harshly insistent—startling him for an instant although in the next he registered that only seconds ago the radar genius, Wheeler, had passed through, getting down there to his set before the rush began. Ben stubbed out his cigarette, reached for the log to record this—time 2045— keeping out of the way then as sailors streamed up from the for'ard messdeck, via wheelhouse and bridge to their action stations. Except in a glassy calm

45

the fore hatch wasn't usable at sea. These were all seamen, and all in goon-suits—guns' crews, mostly, the stokers having their own messdeck aft. Scrambling up now was Harrison, layer of the for'ard six-pounder, singing 'She was poo-ah but she was honest' in a warbling mock-soprano; behind him, Merriman, Foster, 'Percy' Prout, Fenner, Michelson the Oerlikon gunner who'd been a Barnardo boy, orphaned in the '14–'18 war when his mother had been killed by a bomb from a Zeppelin. She'd been pushing him in his pram at the time; his comment to Ben when he'd told him the story had been, 'Should be gun-shy, shouldn't I?' Ben half grinning, watching them and thinking what a bloody marvellous lot they were. Young Carter now—his action job was lookout on the bridge, also to man the starboard Vickers GO—although when it came down to it anyone who was handy used that one. The signalman, or Barclay—even Bob Stack, at a pinch.

Last man through and up to the bridge was 'Tiny' Harper. Shouting to Barclay as he pushed on aft to his six-pounder, 'Messdeck cleared, sir, all hands closed up!'

All hands numbering thirty, plus the three officers—four, if Binns had been on board. In the engineroom, PO Motor Mechanic Bluett, one leading MM and four stokers. Also below—at this end of the ship—were the telegraphists and the radar man—who if Stack was permitting it at this stage would be switching on his set, warming it up and testing it, then shutting down again. While on deck there'd be two seamen at each of the six-pounder mountings, one in each of the point-five turrets, Michelson with his winger Foster at the Oerlikons, and others concerned with ammunition supply,

46

depth-charges and the smoke-making gear. The powered gun mountings were all joystick-controlled, one single control for laying, training and firing; having slid into their seats and donned telephone headsets and tin hats the gunners would have the turrets swiftly training around, barrels elevating and depressing—checking the power—then centred again, loaded, ready.

An hour's wait, at least. Hour and a half, more likely. But it could always happen sooner—*something* could. Checking again, to ascertain speed-made-good since the increase in revs.

Barclay's voice then: 'Going walkabout, sir.'

A tour of the gun positions, he'd mean. As first lieutenant, gunnery-control was one of his jobs. But that had been an Aussie turn of phrase, Ben noted. Reflecting that with a bit of effort from both himself and Bob they might get the bugger educated, by and by.

He was OK, though. Not much of a sense of humour, in fact by Coastal Forces standards a bit formal in his manner, but—he was OK. Might be a little over-conscious of being second in command with a navigator five years his senior. Might account for some of it.

Plunging over the swells like some great porpoise. Rolling rather more noticeably too. With the hands from below all up top now, the centre of gravity would be a foot or so higher than it had been, and this alone would make a difference.

'Plot!'

The W/T office voicepipe. A buzzer had sounded in the bridge, as well. He had only to turn his head to the pipe. 'Plot.'

'Signal in the bucket, sir!'

'Let's hear it, pilot!'

Stack ... This was so to speak a way-station on that voicepipe, which led on up to the bridge, connecting all three positions. But in the light over the chart here you could read a telegraphist's blue-pencil scrawl, and you certainly couldn't up there. He pulled up the copper cylinder, extracted and unfolded the wad of signal-pad, scanned it quickly. Face back to the pipe, then: 'Skipper—to us from C-in-C Portsmouth, repeated Tom, Dick and Harry—ASV search of Baie de la Seine between Cap d'Antifer and Pointe de Barfleur completed without any surface contact. Time of origin—'

'Good-oh. We're in business.'

It looked like it. In recent minutes, though, he'd put this new fix on. 'Skipper—present rate of progress, ETA Barfleur 045 degrees ten miles still looks like 2150. Weather's slowing us by about a knot.'

A moment's silence. If you could call that racket 'silence' ... Then Stack's comment—uncharacteristically philosophical—'Can't do much about it, can we?'

*   *   *

Leaning back, smoking again, thinking how incredible it was that this time last night he'd been with Rosie, at the Beauport Place. Such a short interval of time, such a contrast in space, circumstance, physical contact and this remoteness ... He'd met her at the hotel just after six, having borrowed a battered Hillman Minx from *Aggressive*'s first lieutenant, Jock Hastings, who was a Coastal Force RNVR lieutenant with a DSC but permanently beached now, hobbling around with the aid of a stick after being severely damaged in a motor launch at St Nazaire, eighteen months ago. He'd been duty officer at the base this last weekend, had only asked Ben not to use more gas than he had to, since it had become harder to get of late; this was why Ben had met Rosie at the hotel instead of at Haywards Heath. He'd telephoned her in London the day before, asked her to take a taxi, for which he'd reimburse her.

'Won't be necessary. I mean reimbursement, as you call it.'

'Shortage of petrol's the snag. I'll get you back *to* the station, Sunday morning. But listen, Rosie. In case you're there before me—the room's booked in *my* name.'

'Oh. Is it.'

'You see—I don't know this woman—Mrs Evans-Hart, who runs the joint—'

'Is my name supposed to be Quarry?'

'Well—sooner or later *will* be—'

'Does our room have its own bath, by any chance?'

This was intended as a joke, or dig. A long time ago there'd been a night in London—a railway hotel, only one single room vacant, but the hall porter had told them, 'Does have its own bathroom', and Ben was alleged to have offered to sleep in the bath. He'd done no such thing, had in fact never made any such offer, although she still swore to it as an historic truth.

He'd told her on the 'phone, 'I don't know. I asked for one, she only said she'd see.'

'Depending on whether some VIP turns up, I suppose.'

'Well, probably.'

49

'I'll see you there, then.'

'Right. Can't wait, Rosie—I mean it, really *can't...*'

Actually she hadn't minded about the room, or for having to allow Mrs Evans-Hart—blue hair, too much make-up, eyes like a snake's—to pretend to believe they were married. What really had made her cross had been when after he'd joined her there—in the room, which was fine, quite large with a dark oak four-poster and a view across the park—after they'd made love and come back to earth he'd broken the news that the evening was to be spent in a foursome with Monkey Moncrieff and some girl.

'A bit much, Ben! *Isn't* it?' The glow had faded very suddenly. 'When we finally get to spend a few hours together, for God's sake, we're going to spend our time making conversation, dancing with other people—'

'More than a few hours. Whole night. Rosie, look, I don't like it either, but I couldn't help it—honestly, at least I don't know how I could have got out of it. Anyway, we don't have to dance with them—well, *once*, maybe ... I know it's a bloody bore, but—Rosie darling, we don't have to stay up late, either—'

'No bathroom—' she hadn't seemed to mind this, until he'd told her about Monkey—'and now—well, *honestly*—'

'Four-poster—huh?'

Naked, with an arm up behind her, fingering the carving of that post ... Eyes swivelling to it, then back to him, beginning to laugh.

'What's funny?'

'You. Like offering a child a treat to stop it crying.' She put on a baby-talk voice: '*Look at the nice four-poster...*' Then turned serious again. 'Do these people know we're staying here?'

'Monkey knows *you* are. He put me on to the place, I told you.'

'So they *will* know.'

'Well—does it matter?'

'Not to *you*, perhaps—'

'He's an old mate, Rosie. Wouldn't go telling tales. And she's from heaven knows where, wouldn't know anyone who'd know you or me.'

'It still stinks.'

'I ever mention you're the most beautiful thing in creation?'

'You and your old mates. I suppose I'm lucky you didn't ask the other one along. The Australian.' Her eyes widened: 'Or *is* he coming? Because if he is, you bastard—'

'Uh-huh.' Laughing down at her. 'I swear it. Rosie, darling—'

'I warn you, if he *does* show up—'

'He won't. The base is bloody miles away—one reason for coming here. Promise you, he will *not*. OK?'

Just his wife did...

Their table, where they'd had supper, was in a wide corridor, one of a line of tables against one wall, and the dancing was in what had no doubt been the drawing-room, at one time—double doors farther along, opposite the bar. The staircase came before that, leading up from a wider area that was an extension of the foyer. Inner hall, they'd probably have called it. The hall and front door were round to the right, around that corner. And past the bar and the foot of the stairs was the dining-room proper. Joan might have come out of there, or from the bar: there'd been a lot of people on the move, she was one of them and it was Monkey, facing that way, who saw her.

'Christ.' Interrupting his girlfriend, whatever rubbish she'd been talking ... 'Ben—see what *I'm* seeing?'

He'd craned round, seen them just as they went out of sight into the dance room. His immediate reaction had been one of alarm: Joan was here—as beautiful as ever, there'd been no mistaking her—nor her impact on him, an instant flare-up of memories to which he was not now—as he told himself just as instantly—entitled ... And that had been Mike Furneaux taking her in to dance.

Therefore, (a) Bob Stack must also be here, (b) it wouldn't be possible not to become involved—even for the two parties to amalgamate, if Bob had his way—and (c) Rosie was going to be *really* spitting mad.

The band, he remembered, had been playing 'Don't Get Around Much Anymore.'

He'd glanced rather anxiously at Rosie, then back at Monkey, and begun to say something like, 'Let's stay clear of 'em if we can', and Monkey had snarled, 'Taking it just like *that*?'

Rosie had asked them what was going on. The Canadian girl also wanted an explanation. Ben began, 'My CO's wife—'

'Christ—he *is* here?'

'Damn well is not.' Monkey was looking that way again, but obviously Joan and Mike would have been dancing by then. Shaking his bullet head: 'Ben—Bob is in the base. I *know*. I asked him if he'd join us tonight, bring her ladyship along, and he said she's away, he wasn't even going to bother going home after he got back from Portsmouth.'

52

'So he's had a nice surprise, she's back sooner than he expected. He'll be in the bar, or—'

'If he was here at all he'd have brought her to join *us*.'

'*What* we've missed.' Rosie's wide eyes on Ben. She was wearing a long black skirt and a turquoise blouse, pearl necklace. 'And when you were so certain—'

'News to me, I swear it. Anyway, Monkey here reckons—'

He'd checked: staring at the Canadian, getting the implication. 'You think she's here with Mike?'

'You saw, didn't you?'

'Bob *must* be here—'

'Want to bet? Mike will have picked on this dump for the same reasons we have!'

Ben ignored that. Adding, '—or he'll be coming. That's it—coming on late, so he got Mike—or someone—to bring her along.'

The Canadian girl said through her teeth, '*I'd* like to dance.'

'Sure. Let's.' Monkey got up. A nod to Ben: 'You going to ask them, or shall I?'

'Dance, Rosie?'

'If he does show up, I'm going straight to bed.'

*   *   *

A shout, on the bridge: it cut into his reflection that from the point of view of his own relationship with Rosie you could say it was a mercy the poor bugger had *not* shown up.

Shouts, plural, though. It had sounded like at least two, overlapping. He put his good ear to the pipe, heard Barclay's voice and something about starshell.

53

The skipper, then: 'Near enough due south. Flare, I'd say, more like.' Nearing the voicepipe then: 'Well—could be either ... Pilot—what's due south of us?'

'Baie de la Seine, sir. Coast's about thirty miles, on that bearing.'

'Fading now ... Gone. Alan—all yours, I'll be in the plot.'

He came thumping down. 'Let's have a decko.' Dazzled by the light, blinking ... 'You smoke too bloody much.' Stooping over the chart, simultaneously fumbling a cigarette out of Ben's tin without looking at it. Wet-fingered, too. '*Here*, is us. Right. So on a due south bearing ... No. Hardly. Only thinking—if the Albacores made another sortie—Southwick might have asked for it without telling us—'

'Not likely, sir.'

'No.' Straightening, holding his storm-lighter to the cigarette, blue eyes slitted through the brightness. 'Could've been starshell, too. I'd guess less than—say, ten miles south.' Nicotine-stained finger on the chart. 'Thereabouts.'

'One hour out of Le Havre, on the direct route.' Measuring it with the dividers. 'Could be. If they'd sailed around eight-thirty, say, not six-thirty, and come straight over?'

'Then in another hour, the bastards'll be—'

'Past Barfleur. Off the hump here.'

'And Mike's—'

'Getting close to the end of his sprint.' Ben glanced at the time again. 'Ought to be ten miles off at—well, by 2130 say.'

In about twenty minutes, the MTBs would be reducing speed and continuing inshore with silenced engines.

54

Stack nodded. 'No obvious problems, then.'

'No ... But no certainty the flare's what we're guessing it could be. No certainty at all—uh?'

It could have been dropped by an Albacore, could as well have come from a Dornier. Could have been dropped *on* a fishing-boat, or a surfaced U-boat, or on precisely nothing. Might equally have been starshell fired by the *Heilbronne*'s escort, some nervy Boche with spots before the eyes.

Stack, deep in thought, was gazing at the chart as at a crystal ball, while Ben updated their position by QH.

'Plot!' Barclay again. 'Another one, same bearing, sir.'

'I'm coming up.' Stack crushed his cigarette in the tin's lid. 'Look—we'll be in our run-in position—here—in thirty minutes, say—'

'Thirty-five, more like.'

'All right. Thirty-five.' A glance at the time: nine-fifteen: he nodded. 'I'll reduce to 1500 revs now, and hold on for another—say, another forty-five minutes from now. *Then* cut to silenced outers.'

Ben nodded. Reading it as old Bob's toes curling at the thought of being left out in the deep field, missing all the fun.

CHAPTER FOUR

'Flashing ahead sir!'

Mark Newbolt yelled acknowledgement, having seen it and also read it—a dim blue light calling from his next-ahead, Heddingly, MTB 564, the letter 'R' ordering 'Down 200 revs'. The lamp had repeated it, was doing so again, and Newbolt, goon-suited like all the others and on his seat behind the torpedo-sight in the bridge's starboard for'ard corner, had his hands on the throttle levers, easing them towards closure, feeling and hearing the difference as the power came off her but then realizing—seeing, by naked eye, having had to drop his glasses on their strap—that 564 was already a damn sight too close ahead, must have been slowing even before the flashing had begun. Shutting the throttles all the way, therefore, then shifting to the telegraphs and pushing both levers—two levers controlling the three engines—back to 'slow ahead'. So many levers, he recalled someone remarking, it was like playing a bloody organ. Throttles, telegraphs, torpedo-firing levers, all in this small space in front of him—and right above them, the torpedo sight. No light, of course, you did it all by feel, familiarity. In the next split second, though, he saw that 564 was flashing not 'R's now but 'O's—three long dashes, meaning 'Stop'. The coxswain had seen it too—bawling, 'Stop engines, sir!'

He'd done it. Still too close for comfort, though. 'Starboard wheel, Cox'n.'

In order not to run up Heddingly's arse. Sheering out—into black water, the alternately swelling and subsiding immensity that surrounded them. Into a trough now—a gargantuan belly-flop, jarring impact like hitting rock. She still had way on but was losing it very quickly now with the engines cut, her hull embraced by the heaving near-solidity of sea, passing within a matter of seconds from very little drag to so much of it that it was like applying brakes. Wind and sea taking over meanwhile, the engines' former night-filling roar only a long echo in his skull, more of a mutter than a roar now. The turmoil of white water around 564 was broadening on the beam as his own boat swung on round. Whatever might be the reason for this sudden stop, it would be necessary very shortly to put on enough power to maintain steerage way, hold her at an angle to the swells where they'd be less likely to turn her on her beam ends. Inert you were at the sea's mercy—and the wind's entirely, being flat-bottomed.

Kingsmill had moved up beside him, between him and the coxswain. Tony Kingsmill, a twenty-year-old sub-lieutenant—he'd transferred from 545, in which Rod King had been killed last night, to take over the first lieutenant's job which had been Newbolt's own until this morning.

'Someone broken down, or—'

'Get a position on, Tony.' By QH—which this boat having been an SO's was lucky enough to have. Kingsmill shot below, and the midshipman, Sworder, squeezed up into the space thus vacated between Newbolt and the coxswain's stand. Newbolt calling past him to CPO Gilchrist, 'Lost steerage way yet, have we?'

'Losin' it, sir, aye.'

Gritty tone. Gilchrist, known as 'the Badger' because of the white streak in his beard, was the most senior coxswain in the flotilla. He'd been King's for—well, a long time, in other boats and flotillas before this. Newbolt, conscious of his own status as a brand-new skipper, was aware that he'd be under an eye and critical judgement that might be inappropriately avuncular if he didn't guard against it. He was glad to have him, both as a sterling character and with his comparatively vast experience, but with a pinch of salt as it were— needing to establish himself in as short a time as

57

possible as this boat's CO, as distinct from her jumped-up first lieutenant.

CPO Gilchrist, he guessed—moving the port wing telegraph to slow ahead—was a wise enough man to recognize this himself, even to be impatient to see it happen. Left hand to the port-side throttle then. Choosing that one because it was simpler—the centre engine followed the starboard telegraph. But in any case to circle round, come back into station astern of 564.

'Starboard wheel, Cox'n.'

'Aye aye, sir.' The Badger knew what was wanted, no need to spell it out to him. Winding-on rudder...

'Starshell, red seven-oh!'

A yell from a lookout—one of two—this one by name of Pickering. Newbolt swinging round on his seat, jerking his glasses up and getting it at once, a spark of greenish light hanging out there between sea and clouds—difficult to say how far away—that nucleus and its green-tinted aura drifting downward. Could be either starshell or an aircraft flare. If you'd been in auditory range and stopped like this you'd have known which—shell or flare—hearing either the bark of the gun or the drone of an aircraft.

563 labouring, swinging her bow across the direction of the swells and such wind as there was; rolling like a drunk...

'Steer south fifty west.'

To bring her up astern of Heddingly again, and on the course on which Furneaux had been leading them. Newbolt had his glasses trained over the bow as they completed the turn, looking for 564 but not seeing her yet. 563 standing on her tail and leaning hard to port, driving herself up the black slope ahead: crests and ridges flying—the wind must have come up

58

a bit. As to not seeing the others—he was sweeping across the bow in search of any of them now—it was a fact that with the boats stopped or virtually stopped they could only expect to be in sight of each other when they were reasonably well up.

'Time, Mid?'

'Twenty-one ten, sir.'

Another ten minutes, the unit would have been in position to go to silent running.

'Course south fifty west, sir!'

Toppling down again, spray lashing against the Perspex windshield. Beside him the snotty had his glasses up, for once actually hadn't been sick yet, was muttering something about 'missing the bus'. Might have been talking to himself, certainly hadn't warranted an answer. Mental note—advise him to be less chatty. Although nine-tenths of the time you wouldn't hear him anyway ... Beyond him, on the helmsman's stand, the coxswain's contrastingly solid figure—Pete Sworder was distinctly wand-like—the Badger was knees-bending as he wound-on more rudder—having even his work cut out for him, at these revs. The stand was about six inches high, custom-built for him, immediately behind the wheel. On his left, in the port for'ard corner, was the latched-back door and steps down to the plot, while further aft—about halfway to the back of the bridge—were the lookout stands, one each side and that port side currently occupied by Pickering, whose specialist skill was that of Radar Operator. He was an AB too, though, and up here now because radar wasn't in use and with a crew of only nine men you didn't leave hands idle.

The other lookout, starboard side, glasses up and slowly swivelling, concentrating on the after sector, was Holland, a young OD—Ordinary Seaman—whose mother was in ENSA, allegedly a singer, and currently touring in the Middle East. The drawback to this, in Holland's messmates' view, was that Holland thought he was a singer too.

Might be worth switching on radar, despite the SO's strictures?

He decided against it. Partly for that reason alone—respect for Stack, was what it amounted to—but also because the 286 was primarily an air-warning set limited in its performance even when it was functioning as it was supposed to do, and it was pretty useless on small targets. In any case, by the time it was warmed up and operating this situation would surely have resolved itself.

'Red six-oh, starshell!'

A second one in the same place. Same bearing, anyway, same sort of distance. Nearer five miles than ten, he guessed. Could be something happening around the target—the *Heilbronne*—but on the other hand might be nowhere near it. He left it, swung back, putting his glasses up again to find the others.

'Bloody hell've they got to...'

'Should see him when he starts calling, surely.'

Comment from Kingsmill, who'd come back up from the plot. The operative word in that unsought observation, Newbolt thought, being *should*. Already suspecting what might have happened, although unwilling to believe it: but it was a fact that the blue-shaded lamps were about as dim as they could be, intentionally visible only at close range. An element of panic—instantly suppressed—sprang partly from the prospect of at least *appearing* to be a bloody fool who'd cocked up, first time out ... Whoever had been at fault—Heddingly, for instance, would be a candidate—losing touch with your next-ahead was *your* crime—and perhaps funeral—whatever the circumstances. And the snotty's remark about missing the bus—out of the mouths of babes and sucklings—Sworder being all of three years younger than his skipper—but it could turn out to be not so wide of the mark. With the unit only minutes short of the position where they'd have reduced speed for the run inshore, and the timing not all that sure-fire anyway—well, Christ...

'Are we where we thought we'd be?'

'Pretty well, sir. Looks like the weather's been slowing us half a knot.'

Assume the others *had* gone on?

It wasn't all that unlikely. Passing the order to his next-astern, Heddingly wouldn't have been looking for an acknowledgement, he'd have flashed 'George 30', say—if the order had been to get going at the same speed as before, thirty knots—and crashed off, never doubting he'd have 563 on his tail.

Call Mike One on R/T? With the prospect of being separated from the unit as ample justification?

But in his own briefing of the MTB skippers Furneaux had repeated the SO's warning about total radio silence. He'd been emphatic about it. 'When the time's right, *I'll* break it.'

It would hardly improve matters to fuck up on that as well. Might also smack of the new boy out of his depth and screaming for help.

CPO Gilchrist cleared his throat. 'Skipper, sir.'

'Yes, Cox'n?'

'Reckon we're on our own, sir?'

*   *   *

61

Furneaux swung back from checking on the boats astern of him, and trained his glasses out on the bow again. MTB 560 bucking along at twelve knots on silenced engines, course south thirty-five west magnetic, the Basse du Renier bank seven and a half miles ahead. Before he got that close inshore, depending on what if anything showed up on radar—or even by then in visual range—especially if they were loosing off bloody starshell—he'd turn either east to meet it, or west and allow it to overhaul him. Waiting for Bob Stack to blow the whistle, maybe. Or as the case might be, *not* waiting. He'd discussed these intentions very briefly with Hugh Lyon, his first lieutenant, while they'd been lying almost stopped a short while ago, conferring with him over his—Lyon's—workings on the chart, and finishing with 'God willing', adding after a moment, 'Not that I'd reckon to be the Almighty's blue-eyed boy, just at this moment.'

A typical Furneaux crypticism. Lyon had let it pass, although John Flyte, the boat's spare office had contributed a dutiful chuckle. Lyon suspecting that his CO would have liked to be asked why, what had he been up to? He was a good skipper—a *very* good one, was no doubt going to be a brilliant SO—but was also a bit of a card, with a brand of humour which Lyon didn't always appreciate—in fact he was often aware or half-aware of having his leg pulled. The subject of his own engagement, for instance. Betty was a Wren, based at Stanmore in Middlesex, some secret establishment she didn't talk about—and when he'd mentioned that he hardly ever got to see her, Furneaux's advice had been to call it off, ask her to agree to reconsider the whole thing when the war was over.

62

'Then duck out, smartly. What d'you want to tie yourself down for, for God's sake? Bash it around a bit, old lad. Put it through its paces, while the going's good!'

The sailors adored him, of course.

Anyway, after their discussion over the chart he'd decided to cover these last few miles at twelve knots instead of seven or eight as he'd intended earlier.

Half-turning now, glasses part-lowered: 'Signalman!'

'Sir?'

He was actually a leading signalman, name of Perrot, a newcomer to this crew. Only SOs were allowed signalmen, and Perrot had moved over from 563, in which he'd been Roddy King's. In boats other than SOs' the officers did the signalling. Furneaux told him, 'Blue lamp, quarterline starboard, execute.'

'Quarterline starboard, aye aye, sir...'

If the starshells *had* come from the target or its escort, Lyon thought, there probably wouldn't be long to wait, inshore. They'd appeared on a southeasterly bearing—either starshell or aircraft flares, but the more likely was starshell—during the time the unit had been stopped for 562 to cope with what would have been a breakdown if her Motor Mechanic hadn't been on his toes. The signalman had been keeping a lookout astern, had seen the flashing 'Harry 2'—meaning 'I have two engines out of action'—Furneaux had circled around to come up within loud-hailer range of 562, and Chisholm had told him that his boat's thrust-blocks had been overheating. This meant the two wing engines had had to be stopped instantly and the thrust-blocks given first aid—amounting primarily to lubrication. Overheating wasn't an unusual problem, especially when you'd been running at fairly high revs for some time.

It had taken them about a quarter of an hour, during which time the unit had continued to forge slowly ahead. When Chisholm had signalled 'Ready to proceed', Furneaux had ordered twelve knots and led them round on to this new course.

Perrot reported, 'Message passed, sir.'

'Very good.'

Lyon watched the other boats taking up the quarterline formation—Chisholm's angling out, Heddingly's going out wider astern of him. Looking for Newbolt, then, he couldn't see him.

Blue lamp flashing from Heddingly...

Numerals five, six, three—Perrot called it out: 'MTB 563—' Then, '—is not with us.'

'Not *with* us?'

Lyon confirmed it. 'Can't see him, sir...'

*   *   *

'South forty west, sir.'

CPO Gilchrist's Aberdonian growl... 563 making twenty-five knots, Newbolt aiming to make up lost time and distance, steering a course which cut the corner, as it were, on what had been Mike Furneaux's intended track as stated at his briefing of this unit. Another five minutes at this speed, then he'd reduce to fifteen knots and run in silenced, steering for a point four miles west of Barfleur. He'd be making about twice the speed of the others and steering—touch wood—pretty well up their wakes. Pick 'em up on radar, with luck; he'd decided to take a chance on it, that this situation *did* justify a blind eye to the SO's edict. The 286 was switched on and operating now,

64

sweeping thirty degrees each side of the bow.

Kingsmill shouted in Newbolt's ear, 'Getting a lot of fucking interference, he says.'

That sounded like Pickering, all right. Not unlike Kingsmill, either, who was said to be a good hand at sea but a bit of a tearaway ashore. A parson's son, too. But the fact was, MTBs weren't ideal platforms for radar. Not for the Type 286 anyway—and not when you were cannoning over a swell like this one. Savage impacts every few seconds, jarring all through her fabric—through your own too, for that matter, your spine especially. With such constant pummelling, any and all equipment had to be extremely robust to survive at all.

Let alone anything as delicate and fine-tuned as a radar set.

Sworder—the snotty—was yelling something at him.

'What?'

'Cloud looks like it's thinning, sir!'

He looked up, saw that this was true—to some extent. A slight luminosity there, over the land ... Rising wind, he guessed—tearing holes in it, or trying to. Down here, the smashed crests of the waves sheeting over, white suds lathering the screen.

'Time, Tony?'

'Minute to go, sir.'

Looking around, thinking about a break-up of the cloud—that if it did happen you'd have a moon, and that this would knock the SO's plans for six. Holding the binoculars away from his eyes for a moment, reassuring himself—darkness no less total, *this* far ... In fact not even that patch of lightness over the land was as evident as it had seemed half a minute ago.

Kingsmill had gone back down into the plot, but

65

the snotty and Holland and another hand back there now—Chandler—were concentrating on the looking-out: dark cut-out figures braced against the boat's movement, binoculars slowly pivoting, pausing, moving on, back again ... Newbolt put his own up again. The point about any significant break-up of the cloud was that the moon would be over the land—in the southwest, the way they were heading at this moment and where it had seemed lighter, just now. So an enemy inshore would be up-moon to an attack coming in from seaward; conversely, attacking from inshore wouldn't be a good idea at all.

It looked fairly solid up there now, anyway.

'Bridge!'

He leant to the voicepipe, and Kingsmill told him from the plot, 'Time to come round, sir.'

'Port wheel, Cox'n. Steer south thirty west.'

Throttling down. The Badger's growl on his left: 'South thirty west, sir ...'

'Mid, tell the engineroom—reducing to fifteen knots, engage Dumbflows.'

Dumbflows were the silencers. When engaged, they diverted the exhausts through the engine cooling-water and thence out through the ship's sides. It cut engine-noise significantly, but you could only use it at low revs. Sworder was passing the order to PO Motor Mechanic Talbot over the sound-powered telephone while Kingsmill, returning to the bridge, joined them up front here—wordless, glasses already at his eyes. Newbolt's large frame folded somehow into the bridge seat, his hands still on the throttles, shoulder against the top of the bridge's lightly armour-plated surround, face in the streaming wet above the screen, naked eyes slitted into the heaving dark.

Black as ever. You knew there was a moon up there, but only because the Nautical Almanac told you there was.

Sworder banged the 'phone on to its hook. 'Dumbflows engaged, sir.'

'Very good.'

'Course south thirty west, sir!'

'Radar, bridge!'

The snotty took it. 'Bridge.'

'Three contacts green four-oh, sir!'

Newbolt took over at the pipe. 'What do they look like, Pickering?'

'Small, sir. Could be our unit.'

Highly unlikely—unfortunately. Unless Furneaux was cruising around looking for them—which was hardly probable.

Although he *might*. Come to think of it, he really *might*.

'Range?'

'Three miles, sir. Bearing now—green three-five. Fast-moving, right to left, closing. Range—056, sir.'

5600 yards. It certainly wouldn't be the SO on that bearing. Stack and his MGBs would be on the pod quarter somewhere—a good ten miles away. But if Mike Furneaux had decided he had time to double back and make a quick sweep, get his team back together before the action started: he'd be chancing his arm, certainly, but it wouldn't be the first time he'd done *that*. In fact it'd be right in character.

'Bridge—*four* of 'em, sir, not three—'

'Guns' crews close up.' They'd been at action stations for hours, but in a semi-relaxed mode with gunners and torpedomen in shelter abaft the bridge. 'Port wheel—steer south, Cox'n.'

67

He had a general view of it in his mind—*a* view, how it *seemed* to be. Courses, speeds, distances, a triangle of relative velocities. A few basic facts in the computation, but also guesswork tinged with instinct. The difference between success and failure being to guess *right* ... 563 was rolling harder, with the weather broader on her bow now. 'Mid—radar ranges and bearings. And ask him if he's certain there are *three* of 'em.'

'Course south, sir...'

If it's three—believe it. If not, stay clear...

Down to about eight knots. Believing in it—the probability of this being Mike F.'s unit—because it definitely would be in character. Mike on his first trip as MTB SO, extremely loth to accept having lost one of his boats. It was *his* unit, he'd want to have it together and he'd be cutting a bit of a dash by turning back to rope him in. Furneaux style absolutely—putting his stamp on the unit right from the word 'go' ... Newbolt had swiftly cleaned his binocular lenses, had them up again levelled into the darkness on the bow. Hearing Sworder at the voicepipe—it sounded as if Pickering was having problems—and Kingsmill on the sound-powered telephone to the guns—which included the torpedomen, Lloyd on the starboard side and Burrows, port, who'd be manning the twin Vickers machine-guns mounted on the tubes. Newbolt thinking—suppose this was *not* Furneaux and company. It almost surely was, but—suppose for instance these were patrolling R-boats ... Well, you'd lie doggo, avoid contact with them, concentrate on the primary objective—getting down there and rejoining the unit, not risking a disturbance that would give warning of a Royal Navy presence—and incidentally, taking on more than you could

68

handle. This was an MTB, for God's sake, not a gunboat.

There was still time, anyway—to get the hell out, if necessary.

'Mid, what's radar doing?'

'Getting a lot of interference, sir. Last range was 025, bearings green 25 to 30—gone all jumpy now, he says.'

'What's the challenge and reply, Number One?'

'Challenge is W, reply P Peter, sir!'

'Be ready for it. Mid, tell him to sweep green 25 to red 25.'

Radar seemed to have shot its bolt. The range couldn't be more than about 2,000 yards now. A mile: but they'd pass a damn sight closer. In fact, if they were *not* the other three of the unit—one might *not* have all that much time, or room for manoeuvre. If one had thought of playing safe, when radar had first picked them up—as going by the book maybe one should have—turned away then immediately, instead of slowing and altering to an interception course as he now had ... Alternatives from this point being to crack on the power and beat it, pronto, or—starboard wheel, creep past astern of them ...

If it came to that. Why not—in the next half-minute ... Biting his lip, controlling and regretting that flare of panic. He had his binoculars trained out fine on the bow, sweeping over a sector of no more than twenty or thirty degrees: where they'd show up, he thought, any second now.

Unless *they'd* altered, in the minute since radar lost them?

Like riding a wet and noisy roller-coaster, meanwhile. Sworder shouting that the radar picture was still confused and Pickering thought there might

69

be jamming: interrupting this, a howl from Kingsmill: '*There*—green one-oh, sir!'

He was on them too. *Not* his own unit.

Like a kick in the gut...

Three of them, all right, but either E-boats or R-boats, steering about 030—to pass even closer than he'd thought. He'd reckoned not only on their being MTBs but also on their course being more like 050. They were R-boats—*Raumboote*, motor minesweepers, higher profile than E-boats, and better armed as far as guns went but without torpedoes and nothing like as fast... Speed was one's own advantage now—one's *only* advantage. The decision had been made for him, as it had turned out he had neither of those alternatives. None at all, as a light blazed from the leader—a challenge, the letter 'V' for Victor. Newbolt shouted to Kingsmill, 'Give him a J!' Full ahead meanwhile, jangling the telegraphs to and fro a couple of times and leaving them on 'full ahead'. Throttles wide open. Not a single alternative now, you were *in* it. A burst of 20-mm fire from the one who'd challenged, red tracer arcing up and over the top. Kingsmill was replying to the challenge, clicking-out the letter 'J' at him—by intention it was a delaying tactic, a dodge that had been known to win a few seconds' respite, on occasion—when the enemy was sufficiently irresolute.

'Steer ten degrees to port, Cox'n.'

He'd screamed it over the engines' roar, three supercharged 1500-horsepower Sterling Admirals at full blast. Thudding impacts under her bow as she flung herself ahead, then progressively lighter ones as she lifted, rising towards the plane. Range—by naked eye—about eight hundred yards. At

70

something over thirty knots now—thirty-four, thirty-five—and right up there then—smooth as silk, the speed she was made for, *existed* for. Newbolt clapping a hand on CPO Gilchrist's shoulder, shouting in his ear—'The leader—hard a-starboard at five hundred yards then reciprocal course—OK?'

'Aye aye, sir . . .'

Flat out. Forty knots.

All you *could* do, now. Hit hard, and run like hell.

(Except that one should also be bunging out an enemy report, on W/T. Catch up on that in a minute, though: wording would have to include some explanation of being on one's own.)

Putting the wheel over at a range of 500 yards, with her greatly increased turning-circle at this speed, would mean engaging at about 200. Point-blank, effectively. Which should be—all right. She'd be a high-deflection target herself, while her gunners would be shooting from a comparatively stable platform.

'Tony—open fire on the turn, range'll be two hundred, two-fifty yards.' He'd had his glasses up again for a second: 'They're R-boats. Target the leader first.'

'Oerlikon open fire?'

The first and third—*and* second—were shooting at them now—having decided to ignore the phony answer to the challenge—but it was all going high and wide. He told Kingsmill yes, Oerlikon open fire. *Raumboote* had 37-mm and 20-mm guns: things would get worse before they got better, for sure, but after the turn you'd be passing them like an express train—combined speeds maybe sixty mph—even at close range you wouldn't be an *easy* target. Tracer thickening and coming closer—blinding . . . 563's

71

Oerlikon opening up, a high snarling racket audible over the rest of it, green tracer lobbing away towards that leader. Four hundred—three-fifty yards … Tracer coming the other way was multi-coloured, seeming to lift slowly then pick up speed and scorch by in a flash: except *that* lot, a stream of it slashing explosively down the starboard side, a stink like horses being shod that cleared within seconds on the wind: either the deck there or the tube or the side of the bridge—which had 3/8ths steel plating all around it—bullet-proof, but not 20mm-proof. The Oerlikon in the skilled and determined hands of AB Summerhayes was hitting hard, had just caused what looked like an ammunition explosion—and at least *one* gun silenced—on the leader's forepart.

Close enough now, though. *Too* close. A thump on the coxswain's arm—'Bring her round!' Gilchrist stooping for a grip on the wheel, flinging it over. Kingsmill's thumb on the buzzer signalling 'Open fire', the Oerlikon shifting to the second in line and the Vickers GO on the port side opening up, a double stream of green and red tracer which was a mix of armour-piercing, high explosive and incendiary blasting the leader's bridge then down his length and shifting to join the Oerlikon on target number two; the point-fives were also in it now, shifting similarly after a solid blast into the leader's stern. A lot was coming this way as well, and there'd been hits aft, he thought—certainly *now* there had been, he'd felt several impacts and there'd been a blue flash somewhere close—amidships, somewhere. The leading German was well astern and number two had been hard hit—there'd been a gush of flame from that one's bridge, and the Oerlikon had just shifted to the third and last—which had begun to turn away to

72

starboard, while number two with the point-fives still raking it was going the other way, turning to port across 563's stern. Giving itself very briefly the advantage of an end-on target instead of one flashing by at forty knots—and making full use of it, a storm of gunfire blasting from astern. The starboard Vickers was having a go, then, its tracer arcing back over the quarter into that completely dazzling blaze of tracer from the one who'd crossed astern. Smart effort by Seaman Torpedoman Lloyd—although Kingsmill with his all-round view would have put him on to it. The other Vickers GO and the Oerlikon—Summerhayes still doing good work down there—hose-piping tracer into number three while the point-fives and Seaman Torpedoman Lloyd still blasted at the one astern. Newbolt yelled at Kingsmill—grabbing his arm and pointing—'Shift to *him!*'

The tail-ender, as it turned away. Point-fives already shifting, though—to this one's stern and the back of his bridge as he swung away.

'Port wheel!'

To turn outside him. Much wider turning-circle: the range would be opening fast now. He hadn't heard his own voice, giving that helm order, but Gilchrist had: or he'd only needed the bang on his shoulder, no words. Forcing the wheel over ... A shock right aft, then—and a closer one, the back of the bridge—or it could have been the point-five turret. There'd be a reckoning, before much longer; you prayed not to have casualties—knowing some were inevitable, but still praying. If he'd just turned away and tried to run, he'd probably have been *harder* hit: attack being the best method of defence, as Mike Furneaux had asserted more than once—on

73

the subject of brushes with E-boats, admittedly, but there wasn't all *that* much difference ... 563 with a full third of her length clear of the water, skidding round under a flood of light suddenly from overhead—starshell, which must have come from—well, one of the others, who were in the background now. This last one had reversed its wheel, was turning back to port—at greater and increasing range now but still taking sporadic punishment from the point-fives. Its own guns had ceased fire, he realized—nothing was shooting at them now—and it was on fire, by the look of it its whole afterpart, internally.

'Cease fire, sir?'

'Yes. Midships, Cox'n. Ship's head?'

'South forty west, sir—'

'Steer south ten west.'

She was slowing, though—even before he'd begun to close the throttles. Damage aft ... The engineroom confirmed it: centre engine stopped. Which would also cut out the hydraulic power to the point-five turret, the pump for it being on that engine. She was losing way rapidly. Wind and sea roughly on the beam, beginning to make themselves felt.

Leading Stoker Chivers answered the telephone ...

'It's not *good*, sir. Trying to keep the wings going, but—'

'Report when you can.'

Assuming that one was *not*, please God, about to become totally immobilized—in which case one would be at those bastards' mercy, if they followed up ... But—irrespective, it was time to break wireless silence, legitimately and necessarily to send out an action report on W/T. By-blows of which would be to let Furneaux know where 563 was—and in what condition—and let the SO know there were

74

R-boats around.

R-boats being properly MGBs' meat, not MTBs'. As would no doubt be pointed out more or less forcibly, at some later stage. Not by Mike Furneaux, though, he guessed...

'Starboard wheel, Cox'n.'

To keep her stern-on to them. There were no illuminants in the sky now, but you could see the one that was on fire still, easily enough. He called over his shoulder, 'Number One!'

'First Lieutenant's aft, sir.' Sworder ... Newbolt told him, 'Get on the blower, tell the guns to reload and stand by. And check they're getting the emergency hand-pump going.'

For the point-fives' hydraulic power. You weren't out of it yet; whether or not the R-boats came hunting now, there could be other enemies around—might well be. And the state of things in the engineroom sounded a lot worse than Chivers' 'not good'. There'd be casualties for sure; and this would *not* be a good time or place in which to become immobilized.

Searching the darkness ahead. Annoyed with himself for having given the snotty that order; he had to remember he was no longer a first lieutenant. Kingsmill would *obviously* have seen to the emergency pump being put to work: and would be making his rounds now, for casualties and to assess such damage as was immediately detectable.

The reckoning...

'What are we steering, Cox'n?'

'South forty west, sir.'

'Right...'

Explosion, half a mile back. He'd whipped round in time to see a shoot of flame just as it died down, but

75

then a much bigger, spreading one, followed by a second blast of sound. There was some cheering here and there—assumption of an enemy destroyed—but he was still thinking about the aftermath now, the bill, and the shape of the immediate future, which to a large extent had to depend on whatever was happening in the engineroom at this moment. Whatever the problems were, PO Motor Mechanic Talbot would be getting on with it, and meanwhile was best not badgered for a prognosis.

Had heard nothing from radar, he realized, since the action had started. *Still* hearing nothing. He glanced round: 'Mid—'

The engineroom telephone buzzed. Speak of the devil...

'Bridge.'

'Talbot here, sir. Stopping the port wing.'

'How long for, Chief?'

'Can't say, sir. No longer'n we have to, but—'

'Starboard wing's OK, is it?'

'Not really, sir, no... But—stopping port *now*, sir.'

Hanging up...

'Skipper, sir?'

Kingsmill, at his elbow. Newbolt had been putting his glasses back up, and continued with that movement. 'Yes, Tony. Let's hear the worst.' Resuming a search across the bow: there probably *were* other enemy units about—otherwise why would that fellow have bothered to make a challenge, he'd have known whatever he met was hostile ... Kingsmill told him, 'Several hits aft, sir. Engineroom's in a hell of a state—there was a burst internally, damn lucky they weren't all killed, but the only casualty in there was Stoker Nield, half his left hand blown off. Sort of concussed too though, I

76

think. Fox was killed, I'm sorry to say—not much of him left, looked like a 20-millimetre hit him in the chest—and Lloyd was hit in the thigh. He and Nield'll be brought up in two shakes—I'm getting ready for them now. Quite a bit of damage amidships here too, sir—perforations back there, for instance. Bursts on the plating—from the one that turned across our stern, he did most of the other damage too—anyway, fragments penetrated. And the aerials here, of course—'

'Aerials?'

Hardly taking it in, at that moment: he'd turned for another look astern, at that German still burning, as likely as not sinking—best part of a mile away, by this time—and another silhouetted against the glow, passing this side of it—moving slowly, might be passing a tow or trying to take off survivors. It was surprising that one should be still afloat, after those explosions.

Exactly 2200 now. The whole action had lasted just under four minutes.

Able Seaman Fox, from Preston, had been a valuable as well as popular member of the ship's company. Great fisherman, with a keen eye for the presence of mackerel. He was married, too—only a few months ago, to a girl from Manchester who had a job in a munitions factory and was living with his parents.

If one hadn't deluded oneself into believing the *Raumboote* were MTBs, Fox would be alive, his wife and parents *not* in line for misery.

The W/T aerials—getting back to this now, with some sense of shock—had been brought down, the upper section of the mast and its yard splintered, and the 286 dipole aerial as well as the shaft it turned on was just scrap-iron. Starboard side of the bridge here too—it looked as if something had taken a bite out of the 'egg-box' wind-deflectors—where the R/T aerial had been, for Christ's sake, just a few feet aft of his own seat in this corner. That whip-aerial had gone, completely. Looking back at the mast—he could see its splintered top and tatters of gear hanging from it against the now diffuse and distant glow of the burning R-boat—he was amazed he hadn't seen it before—or been aware of anything like it at the time. Hadn't even seen it in the starshell's light. And this other damage within virtually arm's length of him . . .

There'd be no action report going out for sure. No radar either; Pickering could take over Fox's job— ammo supply back aft, as well as depth-charges and the CSA smoke-making gear, Chloro-Suphonic Acid.

The telegraphist, Shaw, would also be available for other employment. As lookout and for any signalling that might be called for at some later stage, perhaps. Use Chandler elsewhere, then.

The lower, right-angle spur with the QH aerial on it looked all right. Small mercies—*if* it was.

'Tony—see if the QH is working. If it is, get a fix on and give me a course to steer for Basse du Renier. Before you start on the casualties, all right?'

'Aye aye—'

'Wait.' He'd changed his mind. 'Mid—*you* see to that. And get Shaw up to clear away this shambles. Tony—might put Pickering in Fox's place.'

'Done it, sir—he's there.'

'And Lloyd's job?'

'I've moved Burrows over, and Mottram port side, temporarily.'

'Good.'

78

Not bad, anyway—for a cleric's son. Newbolt had a hand on the starboard throttle, easing that surviving engine down to just enough revs to keep steerage-way on her. With things as they were already he wasn't imposing unnecessary strains elsewhere. The telegraphist, Shaw, might conceivably be able to rig some sort of jury aerial for the R/T, he hoped. It was the TCS voice-radio with a whip-aerial, antenna-type, a great improvement on the older sets, but not having had it long one didn't know all that much about it. Shaw would, of course. Another hope was that Lloyd, the torpedoman, wasn't going to be out of action for long, that he might be able to manage down there, at a pinch, if and when the time came. Perhaps with assistance— from Chandler, for instance. Then—glasses up, sweeping from broad on one beam to the other— wondering whether maybe he *should* have stayed clear of the R-boats: turned away earlier, when radar had first picked them up, made himself scarce. Although aggression and engaging the enemy whenever there was an opportunity to do so was supposed to be at the heart of this racket—one had certainly never heard of anyone being encouraged to run away.

He still *should* have.

'Shaw?'

'Yessir.' The telegraphist was groping around in the mess of cables and other junk. 'Proper mess we got here, sir.'

'When you've sorted it, can you do something about getting R/T working? Jury aerial?'

'Well—I'll have a go...'

'Good man. Sooner the better.'

Sworder came back up. Kingsmill too. The snotty

79

reported, 'Course should be south thirty-two west, sir.'

'Steer that, Cox'n.'

'South thirty-two west, sir, aye aye...'

'You handled her damn well, Cox'n.' He had his glasses up, sweeping slowly across the sector from which the R-boats *might* come hunting—if they'd any reason to guess their assailant was languishing here. Hearing Kingsmill at the rear of the bridge calling, 'Let's have you, then!' Gilchrist hadn't acknowledged the compliment: or if he had, it had been inaudible. Meanwhile these were the wounded men whom Kingsmill was summoning: cheerful tone, for a stoker with part of a hand gone and a torpedoman with bullets or fragments in one leg. Kingsmill would have laid out his gear in the wheelhouse, amongst it as well as bandages and iodine and forceps for extracting any easily-accessible bullets etcetera would be ampoules of morphine, also the new sulphur-powder—sulphanilamide?—which was such a major boon to the untrained medical practitioner.

Newbolt called as the group came through the bridge, 'Bad luck, you fellows.'

'Could've been worse, sir.'

'Yeah.' One of them laughed: 'Six inches higher, they'd've 'ad your goolies.'

Fox would have been joking about it too, Newbolt guessed, if he'd been with them ... They'd gone on down—a knot of four men, two of them needing help. This wasn't by any means a *steady* platform now, with so little way on.

Another thought occurred. 'Mid?'

'Sir?'

'Go round the guns, see they have fresh pans and

80

belts on and the ready-use topped up, empties cleared away. Tell 'em I say they did bloody well, but stay on their toes—it's nothing like over yet.'

Buzzer from the engineroom: he snatched the 'phone up. *Hoping* to be told he could go ahead on the port wing now ... 'Bridge!'

PO Motor Mechanic Talbot told him, 'Sorry to say it, sir—'

'Christ—*don't!*'

'Yeah, well. Any other way—but there's not ... Got to stop starboard, sir.'

CHAPTER FIVE

Ben flipped the folding seat down, sat, glanced at the recessed deckwatch and reached across Admiralty chart 2613 for his navigator's notebook. 2154 now. He fiddled a Senior Service out of the tin, lit it, then took a pencil from the rack and noted under earlier entries the course-alteration they'd just made—at 2150—to south fifty west. Position then 045 Pointe de Barfleur seven and a half miles: he also noted *9 knots on silenced outers*.

Pencil back where it belonged, then. Leaning with his shoulder against the bulkhead, idly watching a figure change in the window of the QH—a grey metal box bolted to the wheelhouse side above the chart table. Half an hour to go, roughly—other things being equal. Stack's intention was to hold on until he was about three miles off the point and then turn west-northwest, cutting to about six knots on one engine—or as little as it might take to stem the weather—and expecting by then to have the MTBs a

81

mile or so inshore of him. You didn't need a precise R/V position with them, for the simple reason that the target would act as a magnet drawing the two units together.

Stack's concept. He'd made it work a few times, apparently.

Four and a half miles to go now, anyway—at nine knots, half an hour; but hoping that within that time radar might pick up the van of the *Heilbronne*'s escort—alternatively for a squawk out of Furneaux on R/T when *he* did.

If the buggers hadn't slipped past already.

He sucked in another lungful of sweet Virginia, exhaled it slowly. Thinking first of Rosie tucked up in bed in the flat she shared with another girl in Regent's Park; then of last night, the fact that at just about this time they must have been on the dance floor, with the three-piece band—two geriatrics, a schoolboy and from time to time a heavyweight female vocalist—switching from one slow foxtrot to another, and bloody Furneaux—it *must* have been just about at this time—looking down his nose at Rosie, that supercilious look—and Joan asking her—laughingly, in what was very much her own manner—'You poor thing, how did you get lumbered with *him*?'

Meaning himself, Ben Quarry.

'Tracer, green three-oh, sir!'

A lookout's shout. Young Carter's, he guessed. Then Bob Stack's, and Barclay's in the background saying there was nothing there now, Carter swearing there definitely had been . . .

'Don't doubt you for a minute . . . Close up guns' crews, Number One.'

It was about time for that, anyway. But—green 30

... Ben laid it off lightly on the chart and measured some distances—anticipating the question he'd be getting at any moment. Jotting in the notebook meanwhile *2156, tracer green 30.*

'Pilot!'

'Sir.'

'What might be on green three-oh?'

'Nothing, sir. Closest it'd come to the bulge—towards Cap Levi, that is—is four miles. That'd be eight miles away. MTBs should be closer inshore and a lot nearer Barfleur.'

'Too right.'

No-one else had seen this tracer, and there'd been none since. Ben was asking himself whether if it had been up to him now he'd have altered course to investigate, or held on. It wouldn't have involved much of a diversion. But the answer was, surely, that there was no time to waste on *any* diversion whatsoever: Stack would hold on, leave whoever was doing *what*ever out there to get on with it.

In Stack's place, he thought, he'd have had radar watch set by now and he'd be telling 'Mad Priest' Wheeler to search around that bearing of green 30. After all, if there was some sort of action in progress there, you wouldn't be giving *much* away—if anything.

Not a chance, though. Wheeler had done a one-hour trick as lookout and was back up there now, port side.

Carter again, then: 'More tracer, same bearing, sir!'

A moment's pause...

'Right. Got it. Well done, Carter ... Bearing is—green three-five, say. Hey—'

'Starshell starboard, sir!'

83

That had been a shout from the back of the bridge—the signalman, Miller, getting in first this time. Starshell on or near the same bearing as the tracer, presumably; Ben made a note of it. Time—2158. If Stack *was* going to allow himself to be distracted by whatever might be happening out there, he thought, decision-time would be *now*.

Conceivably, that action could involve—or *have involved*—an advance unit of the *Heilbronne*'s escort, or a covering force of some kind. Supposing the *Heilbronne* had got by already—rounded the point before Furneaux and his boys had got there?

If it had, it *had*. It would be up to the Hunts now—out west there. But God forbid...

Stack arrived in the plot like a ton of coal coming down a chute.

'Quick decko, Ben...'

A cigarette too: if only a few drags...

'We're here, sir—couple of minutes ago. This is the bearing you saw the tracer. *Could* be Mike—circumstances we don't know about?'

'He'd have put out an enemy report. So'd anyone else, once they'd let rip.' Pocketing the lighter, breathing smoke. Eyes on the chart meanwhile—as well as dripping all over it—reinforcing the picture he needed to keep in mind. Ten o'clock shadow darkening the tough, wide-jawed face.

A nod 'OK.'

'You wouldn't use radar even with that action in spitting distance of us?'

'No. Wouldn't tell me anything I really need to know, and it *might* give away our position here.'

'Well—I suppose—'

'So why chance it?'

He nodded. 'OK—sir.'

'What I *do* know is what we're here for, Ben.'

'Right.'

Crushing the cigarette out, leaking smoke as he turned away. 'And I *want* this bastard.'

Savage tone, wolfish look—directed at the *Heilbronne*, obviously, but the latent violence—in a normally mild-mannered man, irrespective of what he *looked* like—making Ben, alone again now, wonder how he'd react if or when Monkey did tell him about his wife.

You wouldn't want to be in Furneaux's halfboots. That was for sure. You really wouldn't. Furneaux might have been making a secondary error, thinking of Bob Stack as he might have of one of his own kind of people. Which he was not. In fact he might break Furneaux's bloody neck.

Stack would just about have got back up there and had time to have picked up his glasses when there was a shout of 'Ship on fire, sir—green five-oh!' Other voices then, including Stack's and Barclay's ... Ben noting, *2200, vessel on fire green 50.* He thought of going up there to take a look, but they'd all lost sight of it literally within seconds. Fire out, or ship sunk— probably the latter, to have vanished so suddenly. He lit another cigarette instead: aware that Stack was right, he *did* smoke too much ... Thoughts back to Furneaux, then—last night on that dance floor, Furneaux's fleeting look of alarm, and then the smile, deliberately assumed composure ... 'Why, Ben! What are *you* doing this far from home?'

Stupid bloody question. He'd ignored it. Furneaux smiling down at Rosie—a rather supercilious look: 'Well, *well!*' But she'd been looking at Joan—or at Ben looking at Joan ... They'd stopped dancing, were in a small, tight but distinctly awkward circle, the crowd of other dancers shuffling round them. 'Hello, Joan.' He'd thought for a moment she was expecting him to kiss her, but Furneaux wasn't giving her that much rope ... 'Hello, *Benjamin!*'

As lovely as ever. Maybe more so. Tall, dark, skin like ivory, huge dark eyes, stunning shape in a green dress that went marvellously with her colouring. She was his own age, but she still looked about twenty. Smiling glance at Rosie, and then that 'You poor thing' line. Ben had told her, 'Actually, she's a very lucky girl, name of Rosie Ewing, and I'm a very lucky man, at least I will be when she consents to marry me. Lady Joan Stack, Rosie. And this is Mike Furneaux. Is Bob here, Joan?'

'*Actually*, he isn't.'

'What I thought. But since you were here—well ... You know he's my CO now?'

'Of course.' The smile had faded. 'He told me you were joining him.' There'd been a renewal of effort then, brightening up: 'I've been looking forward—madly—'

'Look—let's dance.' Furneaux, unsmiling. 'I'm sure Ben didn't come here to stand around and—'

'Ben and I are old friends, Mike, and we haven't seen each other for an *age*. Last saw him in hospital, now I come to think of it—you didn't even know who I was, Ben!'

'I think I remember, vaguely. So I must have done. You and Bob were engaged then—right?'

She'd seemed not to hear that. References to Bob seemed to be dampeners. Instead—belatedly—'How d'you do, Rosie. Actually, you could do worse, you know. *There*, Ben, I've put in a word for you!'

'Speaking from experience, should one take it?'

Rosie: with her claws showing. Joan in two minds

86

for a moment, then shrugging: 'We did know each other quite well—didn't we, Ben. So—yes, the devil one *does* know ... *All* the girls were after him, of course ... Ben, let's have a natter before the evening's over?'

Furneaux said, 'Might allow it. Two minutes, maximum?'

'Bloody cheek. You'd think the swine owned me.' In the swine's arms, though, moving to the music, calling over her shoulder as they drew apart, 'See you, Ben. You too I hope, Rosie ...'

'Well.' Rosie had begun dancing at arms' length, almost. '*Wasn't* that nice. Another old mate—how condescending can you get, incidentally?—*and* an old girlfriend—'

'Someone I knew, that's all.'

'So I gathered. Never guessed I was coming to a sort of general reunion. Any other old flames likely to roll up?'

'Well—let's see, now ...'

She'd taken it all very well, he thought. Despite Monkey grinding on about Bob having to be told and Ben as a fellow Australian being the best man to do it, and the nurse—Monkey's girl—wanting to know about Joan's family and where and when they'd known her before this, and so forth. Ben had suggested, after meeting Rosie's eyes a couple of times, 'You tell her, Monkey. We'll leave you to it. Least, I hope we will.' He'd asked Rosie—although they'd only been sitting down about three minutes— 'Dance? Please?'

She had every reason to have been needled, he thought. To start with, finding they had to be in a foursome instead of on their own. Then Furneaux's condescending manner, and Joan being such a dish, really startlingly so, and Rosie's instincts or intuition doubtless alerting her to the fact he and Joan had been—well, close, at some earlier stage. However long ago, it *would* have grated—just as it would with him, if Rosie had introduced some Adonis who was displaying anything like that semi-proprietorial, teasing attitude towards her that Joan had towards him. In fact it was simply Joan's way—nothing to do with him, not now, not in a long time now, in fact as far as he was concerned *never*, at any depth. Whereas he and Rosie were all-important to each other, despite the obstinacy she had about marriage, they wanted all they could get of each other. He thought that to her he might be primarily a kind of refuge— from the state of nervous tension she was living in at this time, preoccupation with the idea of returning to SOE work in occupied France despite the fact— which he'd come to recognize even more clearly during the ensuing night—*last* night—that the prospect terrified her.

The thought of which tortured *him*.

But it was probably going to happen, at some time. He knew that once she'd made her mind up nothing he said would stop her.

Dancing again, though. Fortunately Joan and Furneaux weren't on the floor. Probably having supper, having arrived so late. The vocalist was giving tongue: *It's not your swee-eet conversation ...* Ben suggested, 'Meet in London next time, shall we?'

'*Now* you're talking. Might even use my flat, sometimes.'

'What about what's her name?'

'Goes home, now and then, at weekends. I'm sure we could arrange it, if you can ever get away properly—I mean for long enough.'

88

'There'll be times. Maintenance periods, so forth ... Darn it, this was supposed to be so far from the base there wasn't a chance we'd run into anyone.'

'It doesn't matter. Never did run smooth—isn't that the theory?'

Oh, no-o-o ...

'But I want it to. As much as anything on earth. It's *got* to.'

Just the nee-ahness of you.

'Rosie—mind if we don't stay up late?'

'Not in the very least.'

'Thank God for huge mercies.'

'*Something's* slightly huge.'

'Your fault, entirely.'

'Oh, *is* it—'

'Also the fact I love you—truly, desperately—'

'Tell me upstairs.'

'Bet on it. But listen—I'm sorry—again—but I *must* have a word with Joan Stack. Having said I would, and—her husband being an old friend—it's *bloody* awkward, actually—'

She'd laughed, mimicking him. '*Actually?*'

'Oh, God ...'

'Better watch that, Ben. I love you as you are.'

'Rather glad you do—old gel—*actually ...*'

*   *   *

'Pilot!'

'Sir?'

'Come up a minute.'

'Aye aye, sir.' Grabbing his binoculars off their hook ...

It was pitch black to start with, after the chart-table light. He paused with his back against the top of the companionway while his eyes became acclimatized, or began to. Making out relatively motionless dark figures in the usual places, the gunboat soaring and plunging on the swell: rolling too, in her slow southward progress in a deep rumble of muffled engines.

Astern, that white smudge in the dark was Monkey's MGB 866, but he'd have had to have put his glasses up to see 874, astern of her. He moved over to Stack's corner instead, putting a hand in greeting on Barclay's shoulder *en passant* ... 'Skipper?'

'Found your way up, then...' Sarcasm... 'Notice a difference, anywhere?'

'Not—as yet—'

'Try the overhead.'

His eyes were more or less attuned to the dark by this time. Putting a hand out to the side of the bridge to steady himself against the roll—she'd be a lot more comfortable at twice the speed—he glanced up, and saw at once what Stack was showing him. The cloud—breaking up. Not all over, but here and there: even a couple of stars visible, in cracks here and there, and an area of radiance—perhaps not radiance exactly, but less-dark cloud, right ahead there.

Absorbing the full message, then: thinning cloud and half a moon behind it—over the land.

'Strewth.'

Eyes down, on Stack—solid black except for the whites of his eyes, against an all-white background as she leaned hard over, driving her shoulder into it. 'That's torn it—*will* do, if—'

'Damn right.' Turning away, as the boat juddered her way up out of the trough. Putting his glasses up. 'Change things, couldn't it.'

'Certainly could ... Alan, here.' He gave Barclay

90

elbow-room where he'd been before, in the forefront, moved himself to the starboard side, behind Stack. Looking astern at the other gunboats—finding he could just make out 874 now, astern of Monkey. But putting his mind to this new, unexpected development-primarily the fact the MTBs might find themselves better off attacking from seaward ... although by this time Furneaux would have them close inshore. Lying cut, probably: or just stemming wind and sea. Might have been there for some while: Stack had put *his* foot down, so to speak, after seeing those starshell at—well, 2112, 2115, when a degree of anxiety had set in—and it wasn't unlikely that Furneaux might have reacted similarly. In any case he'd be in there now, in ambush as it were, he'd have an eye on the thinning cloud over the land and he'd have to decide—if he hadn't already—whether to bank on the target showing up before the moon did—in which case he might risk staying put—or to play safe, take his unit a few miles out to sea while he had the chance.

And let Stack know about it, presumably. Although that would mean breaking R/T silence.

Sweeping over the beam again. No sign of any ship on fire.

'Time now, pilot?'

He lowered his binoculars, checked his watch's luminous dial. Might give old Bob one for Christmas, he thought. 'Twenty-two thirteen, sir.'

'And what time's moonset?'

That was a thought.

'Less than an hour, sir, I'd guess. I'll check.'

He stumbled down. Feeling remiss not to have thought of this himself. In the Dartmouth flotilla he'd invariably had all such data in his notebook—

and in his head—every trip, before putting to sea. He flipped through the Nautical Almanac, found the answer, and came back up. 'Moonset's 2308, sir.'

The gunboats would be in *their* intended waiting position, about six thousand yards offshore, by 2240. With Furneaux and company a mile inshore of them, the two units thus more or less straddling the target's predictable track, the established convoy route. But if by then the moon had broken through, the MTBs' position would be somewhat invidious—to put it mildly. Furneaux would be daft to attack with the moon behind him; he could hardly stalk the convoy from that side either.

Or maybe he could. If he stayed inshore but kept well ahead—several miles ahead, say—until moonset?

But the *Heilbronne* would be making seventeen knots, allegedly. If she turned up off Barfleur now, by moonset she'd be passing Cherbourg—or slipping in there, even. Slipping out again when the weather was such that Coastal Forces couldn't operate.

On the other hand, if she didn't round Barfleur in the next half-hour—

'Alan.' Stack called to Barclay. 'If you were Mike One, how'd you play it?'

'Attack soon as I had the chance, sir.' Barclay must have been thinking it out too. As a second-in-command should. In the next ten minutes his CO might do a Roddy King—or fall overboard, have an epileptic fit—whatever—and the problems would then be *his* to solve. He added, 'From seaward, with or without the moon. I'd switch over now while I had room.'

'Ben?'

'Yes—I reckon … I was thinking about moonset,

but between now and then—seventeen knots, he's into Cherbourg—or, his escorts have played hell with us, driven us off even—'

Barclay interrupted, 'Looking on the bright side?'

'M-class sweepers, Alan, and/or T-class torpedo boats—four or five of 'em, four-inch guns for Christ's sake? All we want's the target, then the hell out—right? But listen—suppose it's half an hour now before they're round the point—it's then another half-hour to moonset, also half an hour at the *Heilbronne*'s seventeen knots to Cap Levi. So if Mike stalked him from ahead—'

Stack cut in—not needing their views, only testing their tactical judgement—'That what you'd do, Ben?'

'No, sir. Because (a) it'd be giving that strong escort half an hour to clobber us, (b) longer an attack's delayed the better chance *Heilbronne*'d have of getting into Cherbourg. I was only seeing that alternative—suppose they showed up suddenly and Mike didn't have room to move out—and with the moon behind him by that time—'

'So you'd shift out by a mile or so. Would you count on me guessing what you're up to?'

'On you allowing for it as what I *might* do—yes.'

'Alan?'

'Yes. As you *are* doing.'

'How it should be. Yeah, spot on.'

'But he might come up on R/T in any case, to make sure of it.'

'I'd think more of him if he bloody didn't. Hell, if I'm guessing what he's at—and we all know how we'd play it from there on—huh?'

Meaning the tactics for an attack by a mixed force of MTBs and MGBs. The combined flotillas would no doubt have exercised such operations, practised

93

them in varying scenarios—maybe used them in action too, on occasion. The only goof who didn't know much at all about it being bloody Quarry—the new boy here ... He had his glasses up, sweeping slowly back down the starboard side, his body balanced against the erratic motion. Six pairs of binoculars in all, all at it—the signalman right aft, lookouts at the sides and himself here, Stack and Barclay in the forefront. Black night, black sea thumping, surging, a small white explosion from each impact streaming over and away to port. Ben with an echo in his mind of Bob Stack's comment *How it should be*—meaning minds in tandem. His and Furneaux's, for Christ's sake. The thought of it triggered a snapshot of Bob's wife as she'd looked last night when finally he'd had a minute alone with her—alone except for dozens of mostly Canadian pongos and their women frolicking around. Joan's wide eyes on a level with his own: fantastic eyes, it amazed him that he'd half forgotten ... He'd asked her whether she and Mike were staying here—knowing the answer, as it happened, because Monkey had been brash enough to check—and she'd told him yes, of course we are—aren't *you*? Typical of her as she'd always been—straight answer to a straight question and if you don't like it, sod off ... Asking him then, 'The pot's not thinking of calling the kettle black, is it?'

'Meaning?'

'You know damn well. Unless the smash-up you had destroyed your memory as well as your poor old ears?'

'But neither of us was married, Joan. Nobody was being cheated on. And this is an old mate of mine you're—'

Rosie had come into sight then, returning from the ladies' room. He'd reminded Joan, 'You used to tell me remember?—when you'd committed yourself to one guy you'd go straight?' She'd shaken her head—expression of wearisome contempt—and he'd added quickly, 'You meant it, too. Dropped *me* like a hot potato, for instance—uh? Why not get back to that—for your sake, Bob's sake—*all* our sakes...' There'd been no time for her to answer, as he'd put out a welcoming hand to Rosie: 'Better?'

* * *

'Message passed, sir.'

'Very good.' Mike Furneaux had his glasses up, looking back at the boats astern of him, Chisholm's 562 and Heddingly's 564. He'd got the unit in line ahead now, instead of quarterline. Unit less one...

'Port wheel, Cox'n.'

'Port wheel, sir.'

Petty Officer Thompson—a big man, Furneaux's height, but heavier. Home town Huddersfield: married, three small children, two girls and a boy. Throwing the wheel over... 560 had been leading the unit on south seventy-five east, was now reversing course to head back westward—from this end of her beat, so to speak. Pointe de Barfleur bearing south twenty east—155 true—distance four thousand yards. The left-hand edge of land—the point, in fact—was discernible on radar, but to the left of it looking southeastward into the Baie de la Seine there was nothing on the screen except for what Taff Davies, the Radar Operator, referred to as 'grass'.

She was coming round slowly—making only a few knots on the silenced centre engine, wings stopped.

95

562 starting her turn now, Chisholm tucking her stem inside the curve of 560's wake.

563—Newbolt—was still absent and unaccounted for. There'd been what had looked like a short and sharp action—culminating in a sizeable explosion—fifteen or twenty minutes ago, a few miles north, and obviously it *could* have involved 563.

But Newbolt would have sent out an enemy report, in that case. The alternative—well, didn't bear thinking about.

Furneaux hadn't said a bloody word about it.

'Steer north seventy-five west.'

'North seventy-five west, sir...'

Lyon, returning to the bridge, moved up between them. He was a head shorter than either his skipper or the coxswain, but stocky, big-boned—a back-row forward. He told his skipper, 'All happy back aft, sir.' Referring to the guns' crews, whom he'd been visiting. Only the point-fives were manned, at this stage, although they were at action stations; the others—the Oerlikon gunner, Markwick, and the torpedo-cum-Vickers men, ABs Wiltshire and Garfold, were in shelter abaft the bridge.

Lyon queried, wondering whether the skipper had noticed—'Cloud's thinning, sir?'

'Yes. I'm afraid it is.'

There was a *lot* of motion on her, at this stage in the turn—struggling round, with the weather on her beam. MTBs were built for speed, not for wallowing. Who was it who'd first referred to them as 'flying bedpans'?

Furneaux lowered his glasses, glanced up again—at the landward sector in particular.

As of now, it was still overcast, stars and moon still covered. Elsewhere—in the north and west—there

96

were some cracks here and there and one sizeable clear patch. But again—with the wind from the west there was no obvious or immediate threat of any clearance here.

'Sub?'

'Sir!'

John Flyte, the boat's 'Spare Officer': smallish, fair, aged twenty. Furneaux told him, 'See what radar's getting, if anything. Ask Davies if he thinks it's land-clutter, if we'll get *anything* this close in.' To Lyon then: 'It *is* thinning, you're right. Plenty of time to move out though, if we have to. Other hand, if it stays as it is now...'

Wordless thinking, then. The kind he did most of. Glasses back up. But he added suddenly—surprisingly—'SO's expecting us to attack from inshore. If we can, we will.'

It made sense, Lyon thought. Especially as the main strength of the escort would normally be on the seaward side, where the gunboats would keep them busy, when the time came. Looking back into the bridge as the boat listed hard to port, bow down, foam swirling across her forepart, washing around the Oerlikon and smashing against the front of the wheelhouse, flying over ... He'd ducked behind the screen: straightening then, looking back into the bridge again, identifying the various dark, goon-suited shapes as Leading Signalman Perrot in the port after corner and on the lookout stands AB Bellamy and OD Woods, respectively port and starboard. Bellamy who captained the flotilla football team, and Woods whose mother and father had been killed a few months ago in a raid on Plymouth.

Didn't know much about Perrot yet. Only that he

97

was single and came from somewhere in the Midlands.

'Course north seventy-five west, sir.'

Lyon turned back, cleaning the front lenses of his glasses with an already damp wad of absorbent paper. The target and its escorts could reasonably be counted on to make their appearance somewhere back on the starboard quarter, as they rounded Barfleur—and even the 286 radar, highly temperamental as it was, should surely be capable of picking up a ship the size of the *Heilbronne* at a range of at least five miles. Even her escorts, some of which would be likely to show up first, T-class torpedo-boats displacing about 1300 tons and/or M-class sweepers of about 700—on a good day you'd expect to get them at, say, three miles. So working on that— three miles—if they were making seventeen knots—or call it eighteen for simplicity, since that was divisible by three—they'd cover those three miles in ten minutes.

The point being—if you got them at that sort of range and the moon was looking dangerous, that was about how long you'd have—ten minutes—to get out to seaward of them, across their bows far enough ahead not to be spotted.

How Furneaux's mind would be running, Lyon guessed. Most of the time you *had* to guess.

Glasses up again now, sweeping across the bow.

'Searchlight—' a yell from Perrot—'port quarter, sir!'

Barfleur: on the point itself, or near it ... A finger of brilliance appearing to shorten as it swung away eastward. Furneaux had his glasses on it, Davidson too. There was the hope it might conveniently illuminate something—like the *Heilbronne* or one or

98

two of her escorts as they came around the point. Have to be damn close in, though: and the coast wasn't anything like steep-to, either near the point or anywhere around the bulge.

But they wouldn't be burning that light for nothing.

Looking for skulking MTBs?

Or using it as a substitute for the Barfleur lighthouse. They did quite often switch on a coastal light when a convoy was due to pass: a courteous gesture, in the view of Coastal Forces ... But in that case they might be reckoning that the Barfleur light itself would be visible too far out—with the implication that MTBs from England might also be some distance offshore, could *not* yet be in here on their convoy's route?

Wishful thinking...

He left it, swung back to search the sector ahead. Expectation of the target coming up astern at any moment didn't mean you could take anything else for granted. Especially with Cherbourg just around the corner.

'Skipper, sir—' John Flyte blundering up, hanging on there in the corner while 560 stood on her ear ... 'There *is* land-clutter, but—'

'Radar, bridge!'

'Wait, sub—'

Lyon answered the radar call. 'Bridge.'

'Two surface echoes—green one-oh range 052 and—green twelve, 055 sir!'

Fine on the starboard bow, at respectively 5200 and 5500 yards. Flyte, who'd only just come up from visiting Davies, muttered 'I'll be damned' and went below again.

'Both closing—drawing right, sir.'

99

Furneaux was in his corner with his glasses up on that bearing. Searchlights astern were one thing, unidentified enemies approaching from ahead quite another. Stooping to the pipe: 'What do they look like, Davies?'

'Medium-small, sir. M-class, or trawlers, like.'

The size of the blip in the tube was all he had to go by.

'Ranges now?'

'Ranges—051, and—053, sir. Bearings green twelve and—one-five, sir.'

He'd taken another quick look at the sky over the land. Lyon in a sort of reflex looking up too: false alarm, though, there'd been no great change.

'Port wheel, Cox'n. Reversing course. Signalman!'

'Port wheel, sir—aye aye, sir.'

Perrot had answered from the port side—the high side, at this moment. Furneaux told him, 'Blue lamp to 562—nuts starboard, then "Do not engage" and "Follow me round".'

Nuts starboard meant enemy in sight starboard: they weren't, but it would hold good for radar contact. There were signal-pamphlet code-letters for the other two phrases too, and Furneaux undoubtedly knew them, but he had a signalman now: having a dog, why do your own barking? Lyon appreciating that by making this about-turn to port he'd also be increasing his distance from the enemy's westward track. They'd be locally-based ships, he guessed, out of Cherbourg. The Germans would have been expecting an attempt at interception, and since it was as important to them to get the *Heilbronne* out to the Atlantic as it was to their enemies to nobble her, they'd be fielding whatever they had available.

100

Such as—here—a pair of M-class sweepers or armed trawlers, say, reinforcing whatever escort the U-boat support ship had brought with her. And—remembering that recent schemozzle—other units already out there.

But *these* might have been in that action. In which case, Newbolt in 563—*something* had blown up...

And the skipper would be as sharply aware of it as anyone. If not more so.

'Radar, bridge!'

'Bridge.' Furneaux ducked quickly to the pipe. Davies told him—the Welsh tones high with frustration—'Lost 'em, sir! It's all grass now and jumpy again, it could be jamming, sir!'

'All right.' A pause. 560 bedpanning round ... Then: 'I'm reversing course, Davies, turning to port, see if you can pick 'em up again on the quarter when we're round.'

'Aye aye, sir.'

'*Fuck* it.' Straightening, looking up at the sky again. 'Steer south seventy-five east, Cox'n. Ship's head now?'

Perrot called, 'Message passed, sir!'

'South ten west, sir.'

'What's the searchlight doing?'

'Still there, sir, sweeping.'

There *was* a slight luminosity over the land, southwestward. It would have been why he'd asked, 'Ship's head now?'—to get his bearings, know which way was which. Crashing around as she was, and under helm, wind and sea seemingly coming from every direction at once...

'Close up the guns, sir?'

'Point-fives'll do for now.'

'Aye, sir.' Lyon was searching over the port

101

quarter for the ships radar had lost and of which bearings and ranges were now entirely notional. Traversing to his left, seeing Chisholm's boat closing in astern, Heddingly's still turning. Back across the quarter then—keeping the glasses moving. In darkness you saw an object best by sweeping over it, not by looking directly at it.

'Radar—'

'Radar, sir?'

'Search between red one-seven-oh and red nine-oh.'

'Red one-seven-oh to red nine-oh . . .'

'Plot!'

Flyte answered.

'What's our distance from Pointe de Barfleur, Sub?'

'Two point two miles, sir.'

'Radar, bridge!'

'Yes, Davies?'

'Nothing in that sector, sir.'

'Keep trying.'

Straightening: and yet another look skyward. He'd be considering the chances of the moon staying hidden long enough for an attack from inshore to remain a practical proposition, Lyon guessed. Especially knowing there was a patrol out there which, if one needed to shift one's ground seaward at short notice, one might run into—almost inevitably then giving the game away, losing the vitally important advantage of surprise.

CHAPTER SIX

Ben had called up to Stack, to tell him, 'In position, sir, near as damnit. Might come round to south five west, though. Stream's setting west now.'

'Steer south five west, Cox'n.'

Charlie Sewell's echo then, distant-sounding through the pipe with the background of sea-noise and engines' rumble. 'South five west, sir . . .'

'Time now, Ben?'

'2232, sir. Half a mile to go—we're five minutes ahead of schedule. Might reduce to 1400 revs?'

'I'll do that.'

Ben noted: *2233, reduced to 1400 revs, silenced outers.*

Down to six or seven knots, now. With some further reduction in noise—which when you were only three miles offshore and liable to run into God knew what at any moment, wasn't a bad thing at all.

The guns were closed up and ready, gunners in tin hats, eyes slitted through balaclavas knitted by the kindly ladies of Women's Institute branches all over England. Woollen garments worn under goonsuits were mostly of the same provenance.

Rosie had asked him—*en route* to the station that morning, when he'd told her he mightn't be able to 'phone tonight—'Isn't it frightening, Ben? Don't *you* get frightened?' He'd thought about it, casting his mind back, then told her, 'You get tense, before it starts. You know—tight gut, sort of thing. But then you're too busy.'

'Can't be much fun, being shot at.'

'None at all. But you're shooting back at them too.
103

I don't remember whose it was, but there's an Old Master painting of two dogs fighting—know the one I mean?' She hadn't known it; he'd explained, 'What gets you is each of 'em's only concerned with what he's dishing out. Seemingly doesn't give a fart what's—you know, like the other's fangs are in him. Action's like that. Afterwards you might get windy, but at the time—see, there *isn't* time. Happens so fast … Nothing like *your* bloody horror of a job, incidentally. I swear to you, *that*'d scare me bloody rigid … Rosie, you've done it—done it *twice* and got out again, thank Christ, so—'

Her hand on his … 'Leave it, Ben?'

Alan Barclay was in the bridge's port forward corner, near the hatchway; he shifted to let Ben out. Emerging from his burrow into darkness, muffled engine-noise, weather-noise and a cutting wind. On this course the gunboat was rolling more than pitching.

'Searchlight still burning?'

'See for yourself.'

Not with the naked eye as yet, he couldn't. He put his glasses up, picked the light up at about thirty on the bow. Distance from here about 8,000 yards. Whatever it was there for … It was a weak-looking beam—and foreshortened at the moment, from this angle. Still heartening, though—an indication, touch wood, that the target and its escorts mightn't be long coming.

It wasn't as dark as it had been. Cloud-cover was still about ninety-five per cent, but its thinning had improved the general visibility, he thought, since he'd last been up here. He could see not only 866, Monkey's boat, quite easily—874 now too, as his vision adjusted itself. Crossing over to starboard to

104

join Stack: passing behind Charlie Sewell—at the wheel as if rooted there—and observing that others present were young Carter, the Liverpudlian trainee tanky, and the out-of-work Radar Operator, AB Wheeler—and the signalman, of course, Miller.

'Up for air, Ben?'

Stack's eyes cat-like in the shifting darkness, binoculars momentarily removed a few inches from them. Ben told him, 'Also to mention we'll be six thousand yards offshore in three minutes' time. You didn't decide—I think—whether to lie cut or patrol on an east-west track then.'

'We'll come round to west, and—tread water ... Three minutes, you say.'

'Two, now. Be 2240, then. Not as black as it was, uh?'

A grunt. Stack with his glasses at work again. 'Other hand, the cloud's still there. No moon, doesn't look like there will be either. I'm betting on Mike sitting tight now. Stay where he is and—as we planned it.'

'Waiting for us to move first?'

'When we have a target, up to us he doesn't *have* to wait.'

'Might best hold on as we are, then. Get in closer.'

'Maybe ...'

Ben had his own glasses up, sweeping slowly from bow to beam on this starboard side. Eyes fairly well-adjusted by this time. He reminded Stack, 'A minute to go, sir.'

'We'll alter to southwest. Gain bearing on 'em *and* close in a bit. Another quarter-mile inshore, maybe. Guessing-game, at this stage ... What's magnetic for southwest?'

'South fifty west, near enough sir.'

105

'Starboard wheel and steer that, Cox'n.'

'Starboard wheel, sir. South fifty west.'

No need for any signalling. Moncrieff would follow round.

'Number One—depth-charges on the top line, are they?'

'Yes, sir. Fifty-foot settings.'

'And starshell?'

'I've warned 'em, sir.'

'Starshell' in fact meant illuminating rockets, which were fired from the side of the forward six-pounder mounting.

'Course south twenty-five west, sir.'

'Very good.'

Ritual reply ... Stack with his glasses trained out to port—close to the beam, now she was on this course—to where that searchlight was still poking around. Erect on his seat, his line-of-sight over the coxswain's head, over Barclay's too, Barclay on the port side also favouring that sector. Good reason therefore for Ben to concentrate his own looking-out effort on this starboard side. He settled down to it: sweeping slowly, carefully, feet straddled, body balanced against the laboured corkscrewing motion she'd adopted on this course. The swell was less noticeable than it had been, he thought, wind and a short, choppy sea gradually replacing it. More white water, and more salt-spray flying; binoculars' front lenses didn't stay dry for long.

Cleaning his own—again—in shelter close under the wind-deflector, using a handful of cotton-waste. Remembering Rosie's question about whether one got frightened when going into action: but that recollection for some reason blurring into one of Joan, long before she'd become Joan Stack, asking

106

him with her bare arms round his neck and her mouth close to his ear—he'd had two ears that worked, in those days—'Don't believe in wasting any time, Ben, do you?'

She'd been right—he never had. Although this had in fact been their second meeting, at a party in a house near Ipswich, and the conversation—fragments of disjointed conversation—had taken place in an upstairs nursery, with the light off. That there was no lock on the door had worried him, a little, particularly as with some help from him she'd removed her smart Beevac uniform with its green tabs and silver ornamentation. He'd never heard of BVAC until he'd met her, but knew by this time that it stood for British Volunteer Ambulance Corps, that it dated from the previous war and that Beevacs weren't paid. Joan had become one because the organization had commandeered a wing of her family home, which was somewhere on the Welsh border; she'd been on the point of joining-up as a 'Free' Fanny—a fairly incredible statement, at any rate to Australian ears, but he'd then learnt that FANY stood for First Aid Nursing Yeomanry, also dated from the '14–'18 war, and that the 'Free' ones, like Beevacs, made a point of doing without pay— but there they'd been, the High Command or somesuch, basing themselves right there in the ancestral pile—so she'd joined them. 'The uniform's really *damn* smart—don't you think, Ben?' She'd told him at an earlier stage, 'I drive bodies around, in a brake converted to an ambulance. It's mostly the airfields up this way that keep us busy. Absolutely *ghastly* sometimes, the poor brave darlings . . . You're free *some* weekends, are you, Ben? Can you fix them in advance?'

107

'No. Never. But there are maintenance periods, for instance. Engines tend to break down quite a lot, and—repairs, sometimes, and so forth ... You're really *beautiful*—well, as you know—'

'I have a beautiful disposition, too. Not that it's much use to you if you're out there on your little boats night in, night out. You are, I know, Polly told me. Killing Germans, before they kill *you*. *Frightfully* good idea ... Except weekends as well, *that's* not so good. Ben, listen—have you ever been to Melton Mowbray?'

She'd sounded a bit potty sometimes, but was actually very bright. An original, for sure. Her father had died not long before this and her brother Gareth had become the Earl. How Ben had met her was that she was working from a BVAC detachment at Ipswich, just up the road from Felixstowe where he, Bob Stack and Monkey Moncrieff had been based at that time, and a fellow MTB officer, Sam Garnish, had a sister Polly who was also a Beevac, and she'd brought Joan with her to a party at Felixstowe. Then at the second encounter—a dance, during which he and Joan had holed-up for a while in the nursery— Ben had brought Polly, and Joan's escort had been this Welsh Guards friend of her brother's. The brother had been expected but had gone down with 'flu, so Billy Bartholomew—'Billy Bigarse', Monkey had called him—who was to have given the Earl a lift down in his Alvis Speed Twenty, in the event came on his own. And proceeded to warn Ben, after complaining that he and Joan had been dancing together all the time, that he and she were unofficially engaged. It was an 'understood thing' between him and her family, he'd alleged.

Ben had asked her about it in the nursery, and

108

she'd snorted.

'Think I could be *that* desperate?'

'Well. Why I asked. Didn't seem too likely.'

'Even less so than he may choose to think. He keeps asking, and he's rich—so Gareth's in favour—'

'Makes no odds?'

She'd shaken her head. 'I'd *love* to be rich, but—crikey, not with *Billy*...'

Melton Mowbray—that question she'd fired at him—had he ever been there, which at that stage he hadn't—was simply a place-name that appealed to her, which she'd therefore had in mind as a *venue* for a weekend. There'd been others too—Market Harborough for one. The criteria had been that the names should have a good ring to them and that they should be well removed from any naval connections or locations where she or her family were known. The risk of bumping into some acquaintance was small enough in Ben's case, since he knew hardly anyone in England and virtually no-one who wasn't in the Navy, but for Joan it was a very different matter. Total strangers recognized her, from having seen photographs of her in such journals as *The Tatler*. He remembered her asking him—it might have been at Ashby-de-la-Zouch—'Wouldn't want me getting a reputation, would you?'

She *had* a reputation. Sam Garnish had told him, having had it whispered to him by Polly, that to Polly's certain knowledge she'd had at least two steamy affairs which all her friends had known about. Also that brother Gareth really *had* been trying to pressurize her into marrying Billy Bigarse, before she became virtually unmarriageable in their own stratum of society. Ben had truly liked her, though. She'd been enormous fun, and forthright, in an odd way completely honest. She'd really got under his skin, for a while—or begun to, the affair hadn't been *only* physical. But he must have had his guard up, even then; when she'd told him that once she did commit herself that would be it, for keeps, no other man would ever get a look in, he'd pretended not to recognize it as an encouragement to *him*. Then again, the line about not getting a reputation—not at Ashby-de-la-Zouch, but at Hucknall-Torkard, this had been—she'd added, 'I'm only a year younger than you are, you know?' He'd been twenty-seven then, and had happened to know that she was actually a year *older* than him; but her point had been that it was perhaps getting on for time she married, before that reputation of hers became just the tiniest bit sullied. And when he'd queried why she couldn't simply snap her lovely fingers at any one of a hundred or so highly eligible young men, she'd asked him, 'D'you think we've got money, Ben? With that awful great mausoleum of a house to keep up? We haven't a *bean*. My dear papa drank most of what we did have—and the rest's debt, all *sham*!'

'Why not transfer to one of the services where you'd get paid, at least? What d'you live on, meanwhile?'

'Oh, one manages...'

'What about old Billy?'

'While you're at it, why not offer me the shady side of Jermyn Street?'

The brother helped her, he thought. Wherever *he* got it from. Selling things from the ancestral home, perhaps—pictures, silver. There'd certainly been some of that going on.

But then old Bob had come on the scene, and dropped at her feet like a clean-shot duck. The first

110

clear indication of it that Ben had was when she'd asked him, in a pub in—in one of those places—'Bob Stack doesn't know about you and me, does he?'

'Of course not. Nobody does.' He remembered it now—a mid-week rendezvous in an improbably-named hamlet not far from Diss in Norfolk, both of them as always with alibis that put them not only elsewhere but also miles apart ... 'Why d'you ask?'

'Sam Garnish, perhaps?'

'Are you saying you've told Polly?'

'I'm not *mad*, Ben!'

Then she'd shrugged, thinking about it. In memory, he could see it, see *her*: and the bar, seedy old yokels eyeing her across the room, a reek of shag tobacco and the rain pelting down outside in a solid, semi-frozen deluge. It wasn't the Ritz, that was for sure. She'd acknowledged, 'Polly might have—put two and two together and made five, I suppose.'

'Better be careful, then.'

'My darling, I *am*, you know I am, but—'

'Why'd you ask about old Bob?'

'Because—' he'd seen her hesitate, then decide to go ahead and tell him—'I think he's going to ask me to marry him. Actually, he did sort of half-propose, I pretended not to understand ... I'm *almost* sure that's what he was getting at.'

'Good grief.'

'What does *that* mean?'

He'd shaken his head, thinking it had to be a joke...

'*Why*, Ben? Bob's all right, isn't he?'

'He's tops. Absolutely. Sound as a bell. But—hell, you wouldn't want to marry an Aussie, would you?'

'Try me and see.'

'Why pick on Bob, though, what's *he* done?'

'*Funny* swine, aren't you. But—like you, in a way, he's—well, *different*.'

'From Billy Bigarse and his mates, you mean. Yeah, that's a fact. I still couldn't see you and old Bob—well, strewth—'

'I *like* him, Ben!'

'So do I, like him a lot, but that's no—'

'He's no pauper, either. His father's got about a million acres out there, he told me.'

'News to *me*. But—OK, if he says so.'

'And two million sheep. Or thereabouts, I wasn't making notes, actually.'

'Actually. No. I suppose you wouldn't. Comes to the same thing, anyway—miles and miles of bugger-all except bloody sheep. That draws you, does it?'

'Not—irresistibly, no. *Bob* does, though.'

Frowning, serious, not wanting to be made fun of ... Ben thinking—still not really believing in it— *Pinch me, I'll wake up...*

Bob had had a blind spot about her too, though. Still did have, presumably. Poor bugger. But how could you have warned him? She'd meant that stuff about committal, going straight and spurning all others: at the time she'd clearly meant every word of it. Warning Bob off her, even if one could have brought oneself to do it—which for obvious reasons one had not—well, no-one in his right mind could have. And if one *had*, Bob would have disregarded it. He'd been seeing it as she did or even more so—the real thing, till death do us part, etcetera. All you'd have done if you'd tried to cast any sort of shadow was write yourself off as an eighteen-carat shit.

*   *   *

112

Rumbling southwestward. 2244 now. He'd memorized, for later entry in his notebook, the time of the last alteration—2239—and had the overall picture in his mind, as well as one knew it—the outline of the coast from Pointe de Barfleur to Cap Levi, roughly where Furneaux's MTBs would be patrolling—or lying cut, as the case might be—a couple of thousand yards inshore—and the line of this unit's slightly oblique approach from seaward. The main imponderables being (a) the timing of the *Heilbronne*'s arrival off the point, (b) the strength and disposition of her escort, and (c) where any other enemy forces or patrols might be. Guessing there had to be such forces: otherwise who'd been letting off all that tracer? Who'd blown up and then lain stopped and burning?

German versus German—just possibly. It *had* been known. Itchy trigger-fingers, faulty recognition, assisted sometimes by bad staff-work. Otherwise—Mike Furneaux off the rails, running his own show?

Less likely. Especially as there'd been no enemy report.

Cleaning his front lenses again. Thinking that whatever was out there, it wouldn't be at any great distance now. Not if the *Heilbronne* still *was* coming. Which please God she had to be ... This was the natural focal point, the meeting of the ways; whatever was about to happen would happen *here*. The gunboats at low revs taking it hard meanwhile, plunging and wallowing ... Bob Stack searching across the bow, Barclay over on the port side still, further aft the lookouts' black shapes outlined against whitened sc astern. Each of them, as it were, isolated, absorbed ... He put his own glasses up again: clean and dry, for the moment. Starting abaft the beam, training slowly left, body swaying to

113

counter whatever angle was on the boat while head and shoulders stayed level, the lenses' intersecting circles shifting slowly around a barely definable horizon.

Stack was probably right about not using radar if you didn't have to. Might well have taken his cue from Peter Dickens—a highly successful and popular SO of MTB flotillas up there on the east coast in recent years, who'd stated at one briefing at which Ben had been present that he'd as soon switch on radar as he'd break W/T silence or light a cigarette. Adding—or this might have been on some other occasion—that in his opinion the radar sets available to Coastal Forces were significantly inferior to the human eye, in all but the most extreme conditions such as a combination of pitch darkness and thick fog.

The Yanks had bloody marvellous radar in their PT boats. If Coastal Forces could have had *that* gear it would have been another thing altogether.

Sweeping back now, left to right. A small up-and-down movement now and then helped to identify as much of an horizon as was visible. Reflecting further on the business of Bob Stack and Joan: that he must have known she'd had a fling or two. Odds on, she'd have told him so, as much from wanting to play it straight as to forestall any gossip he might hear later. And he'd have accepted it as water under the bridge, none of *his* damn business, any more than past affairs of his own were hers.

And she would *not* have named names. Say that for her, she did have her style.

Glasses wet again . . .

'Light flashing—' a yell from Wheeler—'red seven-oh, sir!'

114

Barclay then: 'Letter V—Victor—challenge!'

And repeating, flickering out of the night again broad on the port bow—direction of Barfleur, roughly—'V', three shorts and a long. It wasn't the current *British* challenge.

Wasn't all that close either. It was the flashing one had seen, not the ship or ships. But still—like a long sigh in the depths of your brain—the feeling of *Here we go* ...

'Hard a-starboard, Cox'n.'

Turning her stern to it. Time—2247.

'Signalman—stand by to give 'em a Z.'

'Flashing *astern*, sir!'

Carter: but everyone seeing it then—as she swung, answering her helm, and over the top of 866 as Moncrieff began to follow round—an answering lamp, brighter and closer than the one who'd challenged. The letter 'C'—long short long short.

'Steer west, Cox'n. Miller, belay that order.'

'Steer west, sir.'

Bewildering, for a moment: Ben with his glasses up, searching over the starboard quarter for the ship or ships who'd have been coming south astern of this unit—actually on its port quarter, when they'd answered the challenge from somewhere on *their* port bow. Would be passing astern now—or shortly. If they didn't spot the gunboats—and at that range there was reasonable hope they might not ... MGB 875 steadying on west, 866 curving in astern of her, 874 still halfway through the turn. The challenger, coming from the Barfleur direction, would be the wing ship of the *Heilbronne*'s screen, he guessed: hadn't of course been challenging this unit at all. Hadn't bloody well *seen* it. The ship or ships who *had* been challenged—who'd been so quick with their reply—had obviously been on their toes for it—had to be some unit heading south to rendezvous with this lot. He saw them now. So did Wheeler—their shouts conflicting: 'Ships crossing astern, sir!' and 'Enemy astern, sir!'

'Yeah. I'm on 'em.'

'Course west, sir ...'

Barclay: 'Look like R-boats.'

Stack's voice then—out of a loudspeaker—'Mike One from Topdog. Are you receiving me? Over.'

R/T, for God's sake. Not until we see the whites of their eyes, he'd said. Well—maybe. Figuratively speaking ... He'd clicked off the microphone, was agreeing with Barclay: '*Definitely* R-boats ... Pilot—what's our position relative to YY? Number One, warn the guns—enemy ships around, not repeat *not* to open fire without orders ... Ben—'

'Sir?'

'When you've got that position—enemy report. Send it.'

'Aye aye, sir!'

He landed on his feet in the wheelhouse, grabbed the ruler and dividers. Time, 2249. Position by QH wouldn't have changed by more than a thousand yards, but he updated it as a preliminary. At the voicepipe then, hearing Mike Furneaux's voice through atmospherics: 'Topdog—Mike One receiving you. Over.'

'Skipper, sir?'

'*Yes*, Pilot!'

'Reference position YY one-oh-three degrees two-point-one miles, sir.'

Stack repeated the figures to himself. Then—on the air again—'Mike One and all units. Topdog. My position YY one-oh-three degrees two-point-one

116

miles. Course west. Two R-boats crossing astern of me, steering south to join another unit, probably starboard wing of the screen, halfway between me and Barfleur now. My intention's to follow, stick to 'em until we see the target. Now note this: enemy challenge tonight is V for Victor, reply C for Charlie. Out.'

He'd clicked off. There were R/T loudspeakers in the bridge and here in the wheelhouse and below in the W/T office—where the telegraphists would be logging all messages in and out.

Ben heard, 'Starboard wheel, Cox'n.' Then, 'Where are they now?'

'Port quarter, sir.' Barclay. 'Altered away slightly, I think.'

'Wheeler, you on 'em?'

'Yessir.'

'*Stay* on 'em, as we go round. If you lose 'em, sing out.'

'Aye aye, sir.'

Circling to starboard—the gunboat shouldering her way round, her forepart battering across wind and sea at this moment—Stack would be aiming to keep a safe distance from them and at the conclusion of the turn to finish up almost directly astern of them. They might well serve as cover—as far as being spotted from the *Heilbronne*'s screen was concerned. Touch wood. The Krauts in those small but well-armed escorts had sharp eyes and magnificent Zeiss binoculars. Ben was drafting the enemy report: addressed to C-in-C Portsmouth, it would go out on 2000 kc/s, on which the Hunt-class destroyers of Plymouth Command would also be listening. He checked it, called the W/T office and sent it down to them through the tube.

Radar would be handy now, he thought, returning to the chart. He could start a plot without it, obviously, but lacking ranges other than wild guesses ... He flapped the seat down: the way she was rolling now, beam-on to the sea as she turned, ship's head about north, you needed a firm base. But the guesswork needn't be all that wild, come to think of it. To start with, the R-boats passing astern couldn't have been as much as a mile away—1,500 yards would be more like it. Otherwise you wouldn't have seen them, not that easily. And *their* officers and lookouts should be ashamed of themselves. Concentrating on forward bearings, no doubt, searching for the convoy they'd known would be rounding the point at about this time. Not that that excused them ... Anyway—base the R-boats' track on their having passed 1,500 yards astern, course south, speed say—call it ten knots. And the other, the target's leading escort—with Pointe de Barfleur on his quarter and the target itself plus other escorts all in that gap of navigable water inside him—if he was on the starboard wing of the screen they'd have to be ...

2,500 yards, say?

Allow him sixteen knots. But that was *no* distance—given the fact that all parties were on the move and would be more or less converging. He leant to the voicepipe—reminding himself that although Stack was taking it for granted Furneaux's unit was still inshore of the convoy route, this *was* at present only an assumption.

Barclay answered his call: 'Bridge.'

'Skipper?'

'Hang on.'

She had to be nearly all the way round, by now.

You could feel it. Hear it then too—Stack asking Charlie Sewell, 'Ship's head?'

'South—close to due south, sir.'

'Steer that ... Wheeler—well done, all-round lookout again now.' Into the pipe then: 'Yes, pilot?'

'Enemy report's gone out, sir. Also, plot suggests the starboard wing of the screen's about two thousand yards south, sir.'

'Yeah.' He sounded unsurprised. 'At most...' Ben mentally riposting, *So it's time you bloody well saw the bugger* ... Stack's voice again, then, more distantly: 'What's that, Alan?'

'The R-boats altering to starboard, sir.'

'*Are* they...'

'Ship to the left of them—looks like—'

'Miller—blue lamp astern, tell 'em stopping one engine.'

'Aye, sir.'

'—T-class torpedo-boat I *think*, sir—'

The telegraph clinked. 'Pilot—stopping starboard outer. Starboard wheel, Cox'n, steer south twenty west. What's beyond or astern of that bugger, Alan?'

'Nothing—as yet, sir...'

Ben made a note of the time and reduction of speed, then went back up to the bridge. Doing no good down there: Bob seemingly having a plot in his great Outback brain, what did he need a navigator for anyway? Whereas another pair of eyes up here—plus virtual disbelief in there not being other *Heilbronne* escorts within binocular range by now... He asked Barclay, 'Where are the R-boats now?'

'I'm on 'em.'

Right ahead, then. 'And the *Torpedoboot*?'

'They're sitting on his quarter, and we're on theirs.'

Training left. There *had* to be others of the escort

119

following. Not to mention the *Heilbronne* herself...

'Bugger-all.' Stack's voice from the other corner, sounding angry. 'We're stalking one T-class and two R's. Where the bloody hell...'

'Course south twenty west, sir.'

The searchlight wasn't burning now: wasn't visible anyway. Nothing back there, except a slight glimmer on the sea beyond the spread of the unit's wake, a hint of phosphorescence along the edge of it.

Moonglow, for Christ's sake.

'Time, Ben?'

Two minds with but a single thought—except he'd called the question into the voicepipe. Ben shouted across the wind, '2302, sir.' It was a half-moon, waning, had managed to slip some of its dying light under the trailing edges of the cloud-cap—which was itself disintegrating...

Barclay had muttered, 'Clear-cut view of that T-class *now*.'

You had to hope the German didn't get any kind of view of *you*. Or of Furneaux's MTBs. Who—touch wood—should only have to lie low for a few more minutes. Extremely fortunate near-miss timing, from that point of view. From here the R-boats were barely visible, despite the moon: you wouldn't have seen them if you hadn't known they were there to look for. Making twelve or fifteen knots, Ben guessed.

Keep going, boys. Out of the way, let the dogs see the bloody rabbit...

He'd whispered it aloud, caught himself doing so. This *was* a somewhat nerve-tightening situation. Point being—if there *was* a bloody rabbit. Possibilities—the unpleasant kind—were that it might have got by before the MTBs' arrival—so this

120

would be the rearguard, not the van—or that it was taking a more northerly route, was up there—somewhere—*now*, this little lot serving as a decoy to keep any British Coastal Forces busy and their radar blinded?

If they'd taken the corner wide, as it were, it might in some way or other connect with that otherwise unexplainable flare-up of action an hour ago. Hour and a quarter, roughly ... Wouldn't make all *that* much sense, but—really, you wouldn't want it to, either. The alternative you wanted to believe in was that for some reason best known to themselves they'd sent one front-runner well ahead of the main body.

Put off their stroke by flare-dropping aircraft earlier on, maybe?

But you could take that further: they could have been *turned back* by the flare-dropping. Back into Le Havre to await the promised worsening of the weather.

Bob was using the R/T again. 'Mike One, from Topdog—you hearing me, Mike? Over.'

'Loud and clear, Topdog. Over.'

'No target or escorts in sight yet. Only those R-boats and the T-class aforementioned. They'll be getting by you, about now. I'm reversing course, remaining in this vicinity. Out.'

Delighted to be reversing course, too—without having been spotted by the escorts. Which not only had sharp eyes but were more formidably armed and faster than D-class MGBs: were never therefore to be trifled with ... Ben had his glasses up, sweeping across the port quarter—where the bastards *ought* to be ... R/T again, then: 'Topdog—Mike One. I have those three on radar, bearing 330 range one mile.

121

Moon's just down, so—bring on the dancing girls, huh? Bob—Mike Four lost contact about 2110, not a peep since, whereabouts unknown. My position is YY 136 two miles. Out.'

Stack's growl: '*What* a happy fucking Christmas.'

The seepage of moonlight *had* dried up. That was the only good news. The sombre headline was Mark Newbolt and his crew—missing. Accounting for the outbreak of tracer: even—at the worst—for the lack of an enemy report. If he'd not been in a position to get one out. Those R-boats, maybe: or even the *Heilbronne*'s escort, as in one's thinking only minutes ago—*if* they'd been taking the corner wide.

'Starboard wheel, Cox'n.'

'Starboard wheel, sir.'

Cavorting more erratically as she swung: at low revs on one engine the rudders dragging her round only sluggishly, even though turning to starboard was the easier way, with that outer stopped. Ben making a mental note of the time of this alteration—2312, near enough. Would have expected it to have been over and done with, by this time. Still hope, of course: getting a bit worried now—as Stack was—but still *hope* ... He'd been looking-out mostly on the quarter, towards Barfleur—grasping the binoculars one-handed for a moment, needing the other hand to grab for support at the rail above the companionway as she rolled way over and hung there—longer than she should have before recovering, starting back up again. He'd got himself jammed into the corner, glasses sweeping across the beam—then stopping dead ... Shifting— then back again—needing about a second and a half to be sure it was real—that *they* were—and real *what* ...

122

Finding his voice then: 'Red one hundred and red nine-oh—two more T-class!'

CHAPTER SEVEN

Mark Newbolt had enemies in sight too. He'd sighted them three minutes earlier and for a moment had been frozen in that same natural reaction of disbelief—only worse, because in accepting the reality it was difficult not to admit to oneself that it looked like curtains.

Still did. Worse every minute, in fact. Bastards closing in while you lay bloody helpless. *Effectively* helpless. You'd fight, obviously—once it started and for as long as it lasted—but it wasn't going to get anyone anywhere, except dead.

A preliminary worsening of the situation had been the unexpected appearance of the moon. Low over the peninsula, a brilliance that was entirely unwelcome.

'Skipper, sir—' Sworder, the midshipman, arriving back in the bridge—'PO MM says he hopes to have one wing going before much longer, sir.'

'Very good.'

The hell it was. You needed it *now* ...

They'd come into sight shortly after the moon had broken through. Huge-looking, looming blackly against that coastal glow, crossing rather slowly from right to left, steering to pass close. Antiques, possibly, but still big and powerful-looking. Tall funnels. They'd have 37-mms at least, maybe some 88s. On 563's port beam now, but she was being thrown around so much that the relative bearing was changing all the time.

The only relevance—when the time came—would be which guns would or wouldn't bear. The gunners had been alerted, warned not to open fire without orders.

'Mid.'

'Yessir?'

'Get all SPs and papers together in the wheelhouse, ready for ditching. Get Shaw on the job, most of it's in there.' In the W/T office, he meant. 'He'll have a weighted sack for it.'

'Aye aye, sir.'

'Moonset *how* soon, Tony?'

'Four minutes, sir. No—three, now.'

Three minutes too long. Preparing to ditch secret documents, codes, etcetera wasn't defeatism, only realism.

The second in line was the bigger. Four or five hundred tons, perhaps. The leader was no tiddler, either, but not that big. Couple of hundred, say. Making five or six knots, no more. Another unit out of Cherbourg, almost certainly—in line with the earlier guess that they'd send out whatever they had, to help get the *Heilbronne* out into the Atlantic. These would be categorized as *Vorpostenboote*, meaning patrol craft—trawlers, steam drifters, former fishing craft or pilot vessels on which they stuck a load of weaponry and sent out with their coastal convoys or in defence of minesweeping or minelaying operations.

Any second now ... They'd put a starshell over first, most likely; then use her for target practice.

'Turning towards, aren't they?'

Kingsmill ...

But the light played tricks. That, and your imagination.

563's stern was towards them, at the moment. Range something like a thousand yards. Might take her for a drifting wreck, when eventually they spotted her. *When*, not *if*. Being down-moon had of course been helpful: and having no way on, not even steerage-way—and being small, half-buried in the sea, virtually part of it . . .

'Moon's down . . .'

It was indeed. Making those two—over the port quarter now—suddenly much less distinct. Ditto this boat to *them*—please God . . . They were steering to pass within—he reckoned—about five or six hundred yards, and to the point where they'd be closest— when they'd have this wreck abeam—they had about 500 yards to steam. Quarter of a mile at six knots— two and a half minutes. At which stage, incidentally, they'd be in ideal torpedo-firing range—*and* beam-on. But also infuriatingly and frustratingly safe, for the simple reason that not having a screw that worked you'd have no way of turning the boat to aim the bloody things.

Except by a total fluke. If wind and sea happened to point her the right way—and if you had the deflection set correctly, and fired at the right moment. The odds against such a miracle occurring were so long that it was a waste of time even to think about it: despite which he was setting the torpedo sight, allowing even more hopefully for a ninety-degree shot and estimating the enemy's speed as six knots.

Out of desperation, not expectation.

Buzzer from the engineroom. Kingsmill snatched the 'phone off its hook. 'Bridge!'

The rasp of a voice in the telephone, Kingsmill's explosive *'Right!'*—Newbolt lowering his glasses—

and then his first lieutenant's dumbfounding report of 'Starboard engine's ready, sir!'

Timing so neat, it was almost funny. Right hand moving the Chadburn's telegraph to slow ahead: and a glance to his left, seeing Gilchrist at the wheel and alert—as always, despite the long period of inaction … 'Port wheel, Cox'n.' Easing that throttle open. 'Ready both tubes.' Against the grain, in one way: these torpedoes had been intended for the *Heilbronne*, not to be wasted on some shabby *Vorpostenboot*. Beggars weren't choosers, though; when you'd fucked-up as thoroughly as this, you had to take whatever chances might come your way—and thank God for them.

Still only a very slim hope. Any second, those things' guns were going to open up—he *knew* it, even in the act of removing the latches from the torpedo-firing levers and hearing Kingsmill shouting over the side of the bridge first to Burrows, who was in Lloyd's place, and then to Chandler who'd replaced Burrows on the port tube.

'Tubes ready, sir!'

563 was coming to life. Vibration from the starboard engine, and a thrilling change in the feel of her as she took charge of her own destiny again.

'Midships, Cox'n.'

'Midships, sir!'

Coming round, slowly. The trawlers were grey tall-funnelled shapes expanding very slowly in the lenses of his binoculars which he'd lined-up with the torpedo-sight. Taking the rudder off because having started to swing she'd continue doing so, with only that starboard screw driving her, and he didn't want to overshoot on the swing if he could help it. CPO Gilchrist had reported 'Wheel amidships': Newbolt moved the starboard telegraph to half-ahead and gave her more throttle. Optimum speed when firing torpedoes was twelve knots; 563 would be making less than that, probably more like eight. Or six, even. Please God, remaining unspotted until she'd sent the fish on their way. The lower speed would make her less conspicuous but would affect—to some extent, but in present circumstances unavoidably—the torpedoes' initial dive, the depth they plunged to before their own depth-keeping mechanism brought them back up to the running depth—which had been pre-set at six feet for the *Heilbronne*, would be all right for these big trawlers too. The object being to strike well below the waterline but not to risk missing by 'running under'. The rest of the art was to aim the fish ahead of their target by a precisely calculated angle of deflection so that they and the target would contrive to meet each other, the torpedoes striking the target's side at an angle of as near as possible ninety degrees. Firing from eighty degrees on the target's bow was fine, although the ideal was ninety. Torpedoes' running speed being forty-five knots, angle on the bow and enemy speed as set on the sight ... The tubes were angled seven and a half degrees outward from the MTB's centreline, but the torpedoes' own steering-gear would turn them inward, once they were in the water, by six and a half degrees, leaving an effective spread of two degrees. At a range of 500 yards this would put them sixty feet apart.

'Come three degrees to starboard, Cox'n.'

'Three degrees to starboard, sir ...'

Gilchrist hunched over his wheel, eyes fixed on the magnetic compass. Aiming the boat aimed the torpedoes; to that extent—if the settings on the torpedo-sight were correct and the torpedoes ran correctly, it was *his* aim that decided whether you hit or missed. Newbolt stooping with his hands on the triggers, stooped so as to sight along the firing bar with its backsight and foresight, watching for the target's stem—the flurry of white bow-wave—to cross that line of sight. In the moment of firing he'd shout 'Fire both!', and if this remote-control gear failed—through a failure of hydraulic pressure for instance—the men down there would use their mallets instead to hit the firing-pins; either way, detonating cordite impulse-charges to blast the fish out.

Dispensing with the glasses now. Six hundred yards' range, he guessed.

'Two degrees to port, Cox'n.'

He hoped his voice wasn't as shaky as his hands were.

'Two degrees to port, sir...'

Steering with that degree of accuracy wasn't easy, with a flat-bottomed boat propelled by one wing engine in a moderately jumpy sea.

'Starshell, sir!'

'Yes—all right...'

Didn't want to know. Wasn't from these ships anyway: and—could wait ... These moments called for intense concentration: second by second, with the white flare of bow-wave approaching from the right—which was the direction of that threatening spread of greenish light to be ignored for a few more seconds but on its own a bloody menace ... seconds to go, and now *every* prospect of being spotted.

'*Damn...*'

Turning away!

The leader foreshortening as he turned. His helm

128

had to be hard over: and the other was following him round ... A squawk from Kingsmill ended in a querying '—*seen* us?'

No they bloody well hadn't—thank God...

'Starboard wheel, Cox'n!'

Not with any idea of using torpedoes now, only to stay end-on, a smaller target. If they'd seen her they'd hardly have turned away: not even to comb torpedo-tracks, the short way would have been to turn *towards*. They'd also have opened fire—which he'd been half expecting, only praying to get the fish on their way before it happened... Gilchrist pushing the wheel over, looking up from the compass card now, a greenish pallor on his broad forehead and a glitter of it in his eyes—focusing on the spreading curve of the trawlers' wakes and the diminishing grey shapes beyond it.

The starshell drawing them?

They'd turned that way—towards the action...

But *still* turning—not settling on any southward course. Nothing like.

'Goin' about, sir, ain't they?'

Reversing course, that meant, heading back the way they'd come from. So—patrolling here, on an east-west beat, covering interception routes from the north? That probably was the answer. And too bloody late, chums. Late as well as blind.

Another shell sparked like a cigarette lighter in the sky, expanding to fill that sector with its weird light as the last one faded.

'Midships.'

'Midships, sir...'

These fish would do for the *Heilbronne* after all. Touch wood. If one hadn't exhausted all one's luck now: which one might well have ... He told

Kingsmill, 'Secure the tubes, Tony.' And the coxswain, 'Steer to the right of the starshell.' He still had his glasses on the trawlers—the smudgy vagueness of them that wouldn't have been half as easy to spot if it hadn't been for the green glow distantly beyond them. Most likely *were* patrolling: they'd steadied on about north seventy or seventy-five west, reciprocal of the course they'd been on before. Covering approach routes from anywhere on the south coast—Portsmouth, Portland ... Towards Cap Levi, he guessed: anticipating westward movement by the *Heilbronne* and company.

'Tony—get a position on and give me a course for halfway between Barfleur and Cap Levi.' Picking that as a mark to aim for because one might assume the starshell would be roughly marking the location of the convoy now, and by the time he could get down there it would either be all over or several miles further west. Another factor was that after being shoved around by wind and sea for an hour or more one's idea of present position wasn't all that reliable; tidal stream would have changed too, setting westward instead of east.

'Ship's head now, Cox'n?'

'South five degrees west, sir.'

'Steer that.' For the time being ... Easing the throttle further open. 'Mid?'

'Sir?'

'Ask Petty Officer Talbot whether there's any prospect of getting another engine or two back—eventually. And if so, how long. Where's Shaw?'

'Wheelhouse, sir, fixing the R/T.'

'All right.' All he'd wanted to know—that the telegraphist was still working on it. Time now—2316.

From Stack's gunboat they saw another green starshell break open up there—westward, ahead. There'd also been one or two inshore, on that bow. Radar had no contacts out that way as yet—had nothing that wasn't in sight—and wouldn't have picked up the MTBs at anything but close range anyway. Stack told Charlie Sewell's stolid, mostly silent presence, 'Come five degrees to port, Cox'n.' He put his glasses up again—to port, the hazy, barely detectable smudge of an M-class minesweeper on this seaward side of the convoy. At present they had only this one and the two torpedo-boats in sight— sporadic sight, maximum visibility distance had it not been for the starshell, all of which was being put up by one of the T-class. The inshore one—Ben had seen a couple of the flashes as it had pooped them off. Now he, Stack, Barclay and probably the port-side lookout as well had binoculars probing the darkness around the sweeper, searching primarily for the *Heilbronne* but for other escorts too.

Before they saw *you*.

'Bloody radar...'

Stack, growling to himself ... Wheeler had reported that at any range beyond a couple of miles he was getting nothing but interference, and suspected there might be jamming.

Time—2319. Another enemy report, longer and more detailed had gone out to C-in-C Portsmouth. MGB 875 now running on both outers, with revs on to give her fifteen knots, and with the other two gunboats still in line astern of her. After the sighting of the two *Torpedoboote* he'd immediately hauled away to port, circling northward and right around,

131

switching on radar at the same time and ending up at a distance where they weren't visible all the time but on a course slightly convergent with theirs. Needing to know all he could about their disposition, as well as where the target was: and aware that he had only a few minutes in which to assess all this and then make his move—that he couldn't hang around for ever, leaving Furneaux down there not knowing whether or when to make *his* move.

A click in the bridge loudspeaker, as he switched on the TCS voice-radio. Having made his mind up, Ben guessed.

'Dogs Two and Three. Stand by. Quarterline starboard, execute. Over.'

Monkey's Canadian rasp, then: 'Dog Two, Roger. Out.'

'Dog Three, Roger. Out.' Ted Bland's quiet, flat tone never varied. If he ever did get excited—or anxious—nobody would ever know it. His people were farmers, in Somerset. Ben remembered his own answer to a question of Rosie's last night: 'You get tense before it starts. Tight gut, all that...' Feeling it now too, and remembering the feeling from way back, but recalling also that once the shooting started you *did* forget your gut or dry mouth or whatever else ... Stack beginning again meanwhile, 'Dogs Two and Three. I'll challenge and then go for the nearer T-class. Give me a head-start, Monkey, then you and Ted cross astern of me and hit the sweeper. Then through the middle, do what you can and R/V a quarter-mile astern. Over.'

'Roger, Topdog. Out.'

Ted Bland acknowledged too. Neither of them having to be reminded that they needed to get in there, do their stuff and then vamoose, fast, so as not

132

to get in the way of the MTBs and restrict their ability to (a) manoeuvre, (b) fire torpedoes. Or that Stack's order to 'hit the sweeper' implied any assurance of the enemy's destruction or of one's own survival. 'Sweeper' had a fairly harmless sound to it, but an 'M' had a four-point-one, one or two 37-mms and at least eight 20-mms. Could do a *hell* of a lot of harm ... Ben could see the other gunboats already on their way out on to the quarter. From there, a turn to port and increase to full ahead should with luck take them across this boat's wake and into hitting range before that sweeper knew much about it—especially with a good chance of 875 attracting most of the attention herself as she raced in towards the *Torpedoboot*, challenging at the same time.

There was no reason the deception shouldn't work. Having the correct German challenge, and there being other enemy units at sea to confuse the issue. Those R-boats, for example.

Another starshell cracked open. Green candelabra to replace the short-lived moon. Not so good for Furneaux. The sooner Stack made his move, Ben thought, the better—to distract the escorts and disrupt that starshell activity, and with luck to start some fires to light up the MTBs' target for them.

Moncrieff and Bland were in position. Stack turned from checking on them, lowering his glasses.

'All engines half ahead. Revs for twenty-two knots. Ben—'

'Aye aye, sir.' He was on the spot to do it. 'Telegraphs at half ahead.' Barclay was at the sound-powered telephone talking to the gunners. To Harrison and Prout on the six-pounder for'ard, Tomkins backed up by Merriman on the port point-fives and 'Banjo' Bennet with 'Soapy' Leathers

133

starboard, Michelson with Foster as loader on the Oerlikons and 'Tiny' Harper supported by Fenner on the six-pounder aft. All sweating a bit in their goon-suits, Ben guessed. Freezing cold down there, with spray as well as wind, but that didn't have much to do with it. A T-class torpedo-boat wasn't *easy* meat.

Revs building, all four engines. Dumbflows disconnected, obviously. Screws biting, 875's forepart lifting. If you'd had lances they'd have been levelled, sabres drawn ... Impacts through and over the waves like thumping heartbeats in her double-diagonal mahogany-planked hull. Stack shouted in his good ear, 'Warn Bluett—shortly be ordering full ahead!'

The engineroom telephone, and thumbing the buzzer to draw attention to it: Bluett, PO Motor Mechanic, down there in bright light between the close-packed oil-gleaming masses of machinery, acknowledging the warning by passing it to his minions in a high, noise-piercing scream. While up here in the ice-cold blast of wind Stack bawled at the signalman, 'If he challenges it'll be a V, Victor, and the answer's C, Charlie. If he doesn't, we'll challenge *him* with V Victor—when I say.'

'Aye aye, sir.'

Clear-glass Aldis ready in his hands: eyes in the gap in his balaclava switching between the sweeper—which was abaft the beam now—and the much narrower, stern-on shape of the torpedo-boat.

They'd see this bow-wave and the hump of white water under her counter at any second. *Should* have already. Ben acknowledging to himself that what he'd said to Rosie about one's gut feeling tight for a minute or two had been an understatement. Not a deliberate one—he'd forgotten, that was all. Looking

134

back over the quarter, he saw that Monkey and Ted Bland were still holding their formation and had as yet no great display of white around them. Shifting to the sweeper, then—training right from there, in search of the elusive bloody *Heilbronne*. Still damn-all ... But—at last—these had been much slower off the mark than they usually were—a white light was stuttering 'V' for Victor from the sweeper's bridge.

'Give him C, Charlie!'

They'd have been challenging—instead of the more usual procedure of putting up starshell and then letting rip—because they'd know there were other ships around. R-boats, for instance. Clack of the Aldis lamp ... The challenge was being repeated: Miller following suit again. Stack was at the telegraphs wrenching them once back and forth for the engineroom's attention, then jerking them to full ahead.

'Alan, tell the guns—'

He broke off: the *Torpedoboot* was challenging now too. Miller on it at once: dash-dot, dash-dot. Stack resuming to Barclay, 'Tell 'em we'll engage bow-on, hit the guns on his stern, likely a 37-millimetre right aft and a four-point-one on the superstructure. Knock 'em both out. The other four-point-one'll be on his foc's'l, he may turn to bring it to bear, which case that can be Michelson's and Harper's job. I'll be turning to port, getting out of it damn quick before they get their eye in, so—quick on the draw, OK?'

To Sewell then, 'Ten degrees to port, Cox'n. Let him think we're steering to pass close.'

Astern, the others were making their move. Good timing, by Monkey. 875 up to about thirty knots now, Barclay shouting over the wire to the gunners.

135

Jerries weren't going to sit and watch this missile dashing in at them for long without smelling rats—recognition signal or no recognition signal. Fairly hurtling, wind in your face like flails. Everyone but him wearing tin hats, he realized, and shot down to get his own from the wheelhouse, eyes half-closed in the two seconds he was down there, to preserve night vision. Back up again: less than a minute had passed since the first challenge. Scrambling into the lunging, swaying bridge he heard gunfire, then Stack's 'Let 'em have it!' and immediately the crash and flame of guns. Red and green tracer floating slowly up and then cracking over was what he'd heard for openers. He'd had the idea of taking over the starboard pair of Vickers here in the bridge, but with no more signalling to do Miller had got there first, had the guns unclamped and—this moment—cocked. They wouldn't bear, anyway, until Stack turned her. Tracer was streaming over, quite a lot of it and blinding, although none seemed to be coming close. *Yet.* A theory was that the German gunners were given too much protection and tended to hide behind it. Also of course there was a lot to be said for having caught the bastards with their pants down. 875's forward mountings were hard at it—the six-pounder and the two twin point-five turrets, one each side below the bridge's forefront—at the corners of the wheelhouse, in fact; as he was seeing it from here their tracer seemed to be merging into one common point of impact. Highly effective, at that—if those were flames on the German's stern ... They *were*—he'd been blind for a moment but saw now that the after superstructure was on fire, those turrets continuing to pour their streams of high explosive, armour-piercing and incendiary into the blaze. Where the after four-point-one was and had either been silenced or deserted: blinding if you looked straight at it, and a mass of smoke rolling away down-wind, the guns' individual sounds and rhythms drowned in one solid, continuous roar. Stink of cordite—and/or of that fire, you were down-wind of it—and the enemy was turning, as Stack had more or less predicted, coming round to starboard to bring that other gun to bear—as he plainly would, with the after one knocked out. Hits for'ard here now—37-mm probably, crashes down for'ard and something down there shattered, debris flying: Barclay was on his way down. Stack holding on, despite some evidence that they *had* got their eye in; the range was no more than about 300 yards, Ben reckoned. He'd seen what had looked like an explosion on the *Torpedoboot*'s forepart, starboard side, in these first seconds during which it had been exposed, Michelson was raking the German's bridge with tracer and 20-mm explosive shells from his twin Oerlikons, and the after six-pounder was hard at it too, Harper hammering shell after shell into the midships superstructure from where a fair amount of 37-mm fire was coming. Or *had* been. There was a fire up for'ard where the explosion had occurred: and the German was turning back, starting a swing back to port. That had probably been a six-pounder hit amongst ammunition—on a ready-use locker maybe. Ben with even his bad ear ringing, but hearing Stack's shout of 'Hard a-port!' To disengage—ninety seconds of it having been more than enough—and one didn't know the worst yet. Disengaging mightn't be so bad if Stack could hold her in dead astern—in effectively 'dead ground', with those stern guns knocked out. The gunboat heeling hard as she

137

turned, still under full rudder for as tight a turn as possible. Noise lessening significantly as the for'ard guns found themselves shut out of it; it was slackening aft too, as the range opened— astonishingly, with nothing shooting back at her now.

Bloody lucky. Ben was as much surprised as relieved at how well they'd got away with it—this far. Really, *bloody* lucky ... With the range opening fast—and the *Torpedoboot* skipper doubtless with his hands full, fighting at least one fire, also probably with heavy casualties.

Stack's voice: 'Cease fire!'

Making it official: it *had* ceased, pretty well. Ben pressed the buzzer: Barclay was still down for'ard, where those hits had been a couple of minutes ago. Here, engine-noise ruled the roost again, with no guns to drown it. Distant gunfire, though—ahead— tracer-sparks matching the thin snarl of Oerlikons, and the flashes of shellbursts, on and around the M-class sweeper which Stack had allocated to Monkey and Ted Bland. To the right of it, what looked like an MGB was static and on fire but still fighting back, with something like four hundred yards between them. Stack told Sewell, 'Steer for *that*, Cox'n.' The radar voicepipe was bleating, and Ben answered it. 'Bridge.'

'Skipper, sir.' This was Barclay, in the bridge behind him. 'Point-fives are wrecked, port side, Merriman was wounded and Tomkins is dead. Direct hit from a 37-mm, probably. There were other hits for'ard but no flooding's—detectable, so—' He'd paused for breath. Adding then, 'Merriman was hit in the face and chest. Got him into a bunk for'ard, sir, given him morphine, when there's a chance I'll—'

138

'Christ.' Stack had been silenced. Wordless, for the moment ... Ben too—reminding himself that not everyone stayed lucky. Stack's shout emerging from surrounding noise again: 'Say Tomkins is *dead*?'

'Yes, sir. And Merriman—'

'Christ...' A sigh: a movement in the dark like a dog shaking itself, coming out of water. 'All right. No other damage, you say—'

'Well—'

Explosion ... Head up again, to see the glow of it dying down over whichever of the other two boats that was. Barclay was saying there was no other serious damage as far as he'd been able to see, no other casualties either. Ben thinking again about luck—the awesome truth for instance that one direct hit from a four-inch was all it would take to sink you. Conversely, the partial balancing of such odds-against by virtue of being such a very *small* target ... Stack had reduced the revs; she was down to something like twenty knots again. Astern, the *Torpedoboot* was still on fire aft. Ben ducked to the pipe again, invited the radar man to start again. Poor old Tomkins: he *was* old—or rather, had been—well up in his thirties, one of the older hands—married, with children of whom he carried snapshots to show around. As Stack well knew, of course. Wheeler was telling him, 'Surface contacts, sir—one right ahead—or it could be two in line, I think, range 1700 yards—an' there's a bigger one on green two-five, 3000...'

'Plot it, Ben.' Stack, listening and now cutting in. 'Go down and—'

R/T call: 'Dog Two to Dog Three. Want help, Ted? Over.'

That had been Monkey. So the one stopped and

139

burning was Bland. He hadn't replied to Monkey's transmission yet, but Stack was now on the air, calling Dogs 2 and 3, telling them he was about to put himself between Dog 3 and the sweeper, and what was Dog 3's present state?

Radar again ... In present circumstances you really didn't need it, except that one of those contacts—the bigger one he'd mentioned—was probably the *Heilbronne*. Which one *did* need. Ben shot down to deal with it from the wheelhouse and make some sort of a plot based on a new QH position, plus whatever ranges and bearings one had or could estimate.

Howling wind, and cold ... A hole in the forefront, port for'ard corner, and an elongated one in the port side. This was above the wrecked point-five turret, of course, looked like the entrance and exit of a shell that had passed through without exploding. Probably at the same time: when Tomkins and Merriman had got *theirs*.

'Topdog. Dog 3.' Bland's tones from the speaker had a jerky, breathless quality. 'I have—fire aft but—responding to treatment. Other damage we—can cope with. Taking this sod's fire off me 'd help. I've some casualties. Engines'll be OK, probably, soon as—'

Interference ... Then he was audible again, signing off. Ben meanwhile had cleared some rubbish, moved the chart out of the wet and had Wheeler back on the voicepipe, was jotting down radar bearings and ranges before getting a new position from QH and sorting it all out on a plotting diagram.

Back to the voicepipe ... Wheeler telling him, 'All grass to the right of the big'un, sir, the rest of it comes an' goes, like. Them two astern's close

140

together, sort of.'

'The torpedo-boat we've been engaging.'

'And 'is oppo, sir.'

The other T-class, the starshell expert; he must have moved over to stand by his chum. If he stayed there it would make things easier for the MTBs, presently. But more immediately important was *this* one, Wheeler's 'big 'un'—the *Heilbronne*, sure as eggs. And its position—based on this gunboat's present QH position and the range and bearing by radar, then *that* position as a range and bearing from the reference point YY. For Furneaux immediately, and for an amplifying enemy report to go out on the Portsmouth Operational Wave. He was getting this ready now—scribbling it out on a signal-pad...

'Topdog—Dog 2.' Monkey's voice, loud and clear. 'I'll engage your sweeper on his starboard side, if you like. Lit a small fire on an older-type M-class five hundred yards astern of him, meanwhile. Over.'

Buzzing and crackling...

Stack's voice out of the speaker then: 'Monkey—Topdog. Well done. How about a depth-charge on your way by? Then come on round, form-up astern of me and we'll take it from there. Over.'

'Roger, Topdog. Out.'

Ben had the *Heilbronne*'s position. Should be able to *see* the bastard by now. But he'd still needed it in figures, for the signals. He sent the scrawled one down the tube to Willis, and went back up, emerging into darkness with red tracer whipping over and Stack shouting, 'As she goes, Cox'n, through the middle!'

'As she goes, sir!'

'Stand by.' Barclay, talking to the gunners. He was pretty good, Ben thought, very level and unflurried,

141

you might well have thought this was an exercise. Natural to him, with that quiet and reserved everyday manner of his, maybe. But *damn* good, with Tomkins dead and Merriman the AA3 in God knew what state down there. The most he could have done for Merriman at this time was give him a heavy shot of morphine, poor sod...

'Skipper, sir—the *Heilbronne*'s bearing and range from Barfleur—'

'You do it, Ben.' Stack had his glasses on the sweeper that was belting 37-mm and 20-mm explosive shells at them, one stream of it coming at a much lower trajectory than the rest just at this moment, lashing past at about head-height—tin-hat height—but mercifully wide. Stack adding, 'R/T to Mike One, give him that position and the shape of things here. Tell him we'll clear out soon as we have Ted with us. Open fire, Alan!'

Crash and flame of guns. In the course of the past half-minute the M-class had tired of potting 874 and shifted all it had that would bear to *this* target. While Bland, lying disabled out there to starboard, was still engaging it with—well, only Oerlikons, now. Other guns knocked out, Ben guessed. No Oerlikon now, even: he'd have had to cease fire anyway as 875 moved in, fouling his range. The German on the move again meanwhile—white bow-wave visible, which it hadn't been in recent minutes—and 875 pitching up with all *her* guns very much in action. Giving Bland a chance to make at least temporary repairs: essentially, to put fires out and get an engine going.

Ben had fumbled the microphone of the R/T out of its stowage, crouched down now close against the armoured side of the bridge, starboard side, under

142

the canopied ledge that served as a daylight-hours bridge chart-table.

Switching on...

'Mike One from Topdog, d'you hear me? Over.'

Crackling ... Then: 'Topdog—Mike One, receiving you loud and clear. Over.'

The man himself. Tonight, *not* dancing the night away. Or the other thing, either. Ben told him—this *other* man—'Position of the target five minutes ago was half a mile south of YY, steering west. There are two T-class a thousand yards ahead of her—one of them on fire, and the other seems to be standing by him—one M-class on target's port beam and two more M's between five hundred and a thousand yards on her seaward side. We and Dog 2 are currently engaging the leader of this pair in order to extract Dog 3 who's having problems, but we'll be out of your way directly. The T-class that's on fire and both the seaward-side M's have had some guns knocked out and fires started. Good luck. Out.'

Crouching over the microphone, trying to shield it as far as possible from the continuous racket of the guns. He'd felt some hits while he'd been talking, Stack had reduced the revs, and had also had wheel on, manoeuvring under more or less constant helm, making the boat harder to hit but also keeping all the German's attention while Monkey came up on him on the seaward side. There'd been a hit aft, then ... Then more crackling in the speaker, and Furneaux's voice: 'Topdog—Mike One. I can see your fireworks. Can't delay more than five minutes, though. If the scene's dark when you disengage, illuminations on the seaward side would be nice. Out.'

'Nice'. Funny word ... Checking the time by his watch's luminous dial: 2336. On his feet, then,

143

replacing the microphone, in a blaze of multi-coloured tracer and a sight of the sweeper's lower bridge with flames inside it, also a seaboat in davits abaft the single funnel well ablaze, and six-pounder shells bursting in that area. Stack was shouting into a telephone, 'All right, Chief—best you can.' Focusing his glasses on 874, Ben saw no movement of any kind, but no fire either now. Stack told him—a shout into his good ear although it wasn't all *that* good by this time—'Port outer's been hit, bugger it!'

'866 coming up astern, sir!'

'Hard a-starboard, Cox'n.'

'Message passed to Mike One, sir. Says he'll leave it five minutes max, and if the fires are out when we disengage he'd be glad of illumination on the seaward side.'

'He'll get it. Give me the mike ... Hey, see *that*!'

Monkey's depth-charge—just about under the sweeper's stern. He'd have dropped it close ahead of her as he swung 866 across her bows from the seaward side, and it had exploded with a shallow setting on its pistol just as the German's stern passed over it. A huge mound of white water swelling and then erupting, the ship's afterpart lifting with it, crashing down in a flood of sea swamping over and emerging then almost on her side, slowly righting as the huge disturbance settled. She'd have either no screws at all now, or ones that wouldn't turn on the twisted shafts. Her guns were silent and her upperworks were still bright with that internal fire.

Ben pushed the microphone into Stack's hand: 'The mike, you wanted.'

'Yeah. Ship's head, Cox'n?'

'South forty east, sir!'

'Steer that.' Towards 874, roughly. Barclay was

144

back on the bridge and was passing the order to cease fire, Stack reaching to the telegraphs and putting the three working engines to slow ahead. Ben's head singing from the comparative silence: it surprised him that he could hear any of these smaller sounds now. Even the click in the speaker as Stack switched on . . .

'Monkey—good on you, boy. Dog Three, how're you doing? Over.'

Silence: except for the fact you could barely hear yourself think. One thought however was clear: that the priority, urgency, was to clear out—quick.

Stack was trying again: 'Dog Three—Topdog. How's tricks, Ted? Over.'

'Topdog.' *Now*, he was answering. 'Dog Three. First lieutenant—Worbury. Skipper's died, sir. Had a head-wound . . . Sir, starboard outer's mended, and there are hopes for the starboard inner. Ten knots, meanwhile? Over.'

Bland dead. Oh, Jesus . . .

Stack was telling Baldy, 'Take station astern of me, Worbury. I'm damn sorry . . . Monkey, you're tail-ender. Course north, ten knots. Out.'

Furneaux would have heard that, would know the field was being cleared for him now.

CHAPTER EIGHT

He'd called the other two to within loud-hailer distance, one on each quarter, Chisholm's 562 to port and Heddingly's 564 starboard. All three still paddling northward—on an interception course to the convoy—on one engine apiece at revs for about

145

six knots, consequently tossing around a bit. He'd have carried on at this low speed, creeping in to close quarters as inconspicuously and quietly as possible, but radar had just reported new arrivals coming— apparently—to join the convoy, from the west, and it seemed inadvisable to hang back until the escort had been thus strengthened.

On his seat in the bridge's starboard forward corner, he switched on the fixed loudhailer system. He was listening-out on R/T but not using it himself at this stage; it could have amounted to telling the bastards you were coming. He'd heard Stack initiating the gunboats' withdrawal northwards, anyway ... Testing the hailer by tapping its microphone, then bawling into it 'D'you hear there?' and getting for answers a thump and then a booming, long-distance echo of his own voice across dark, jumpy sea ... He told them, 'Starter's orders, chaps— and we have to look slippy. Radar just picked up a middleweight and two widgers coming east from vicinity of AA—could be the T-class and R-boats we had a while ago. Joint's jumping, anyway—and radar shows the target now five thousand yards nor'- nor'-east—steering west, seventeen knots estimated. So—quarterline starboard, twenty knots for two miles, then slow to twelve. I'll steer to leave the nearer M to starboard, passing ahead of him to get in on the target's bow, and I'll disengage to port. You two go the other way—detour to starboard, cross astern of the M, approach from the quarter and disengage to starboard. OK? Anything unclear, speak *now*.'

Cocking an ear to the wind, for a few seconds ... But there was no interruption to the engines' drowned rumbling, wind and sea and battering hulls. Nothing to wait for, therefore. Loudhailer again:

'Right, chaps. Quarterline starboard—execute!'

Twenty knots wouldn't be exactly *sneaking* in. But with the target's escort about to be reinforced—the hell ... Time now—2342. Mile and a half to go, roughly: at twenty knots, four and a half minutes. And they were in quarterline now. Telegraphs to half-ahead, therefore, throttles easing open: no need for signals. He'd flapped his seat up out of the way, was on his feet behind all the controls, with his coxswain's burlier figure close on his left. Power building, 560 thrusting forward: stern-down and bow lifting, the start of the hammering impacts you felt all the way up your spinal column...

Hugh Lyon was returning from the after end of the bridge—the screened shelter behind it where the gunners waited—all but Vibart, gunlayer 3rd class, in the point-five turret, and Bellamy the Oerlikons' number two and loader, who for the time being was still up here as a lookout. So was Woods, on this starboard side; and Perrot, Leading Signalman, propped in the after corner between the flag-locker and the signal-lamps' stowage, keeping an eye open for signals from the other boats. Lyon paused there, between him and Woods, training his glasses too on the others—rather too highly visible, fast-moving explosions of brilliant white and widening, trailing wakes ... Lyon wondering—aware of a familiar pre-action tautness of his own nerves, and a slight shortness of breath—whether Mike Furneaux had any fears on this first appearance as a flotilla SO. He'd certainly shown none. Which was what made one wonder: total lack of fear, or vast self-confidence?

Achieving command itself would be the big one, Lyon supposed. After that, maybe, having a few

147

more boats tucked under one's wing wouldn't make so much difference?

Not to the Mike Furneaux's of this world, anyway.

A species apart. That was probably the answer. Horses for courses. By the same yardstick he, Lyon, was probably in his right niche as a *second*-in-command. Talking to Betty once he'd said something like 'When I get my command', and she'd goggled at him: '*Command?*' Then seen from his expression that he wasn't exactly overjoyed at this reaction, and covered up with some unconvincing waffle...

Ourselves as others see us, he'd thought. Moving up now to the forefront, port side. Maybe how Furneaux saw him too. Might well be—and he could be right, at that. You didn't *all* have to be bloody Errol Flynns.

John Flyte had gone down to the wheelhouse to try to prepare a radar plot, which would be made use of at later stages—from the time they slowed to twelve knots. Furneaux had told him to keep the picture up to the minute with everything that came from Davies but to pass on only what he, Furneaux, would want or need to know. Priority at the start would be the movements of the *Torpedoboot* and two *Raumboote* who'd been on their way back eastward—and might yet be there ahead of them.

2345. A minute and a half to go, roughly. Flyte would call up to the skipper when you'd run the distance, anyway.

'Perrot.' Furneaux, still with his glasses up, and not turning. 'Stand by with the blue lamp and "George twelve".'

'George twelve—aye aye, sir.'

Meaning 'speed twelve knots'. But—loudhailer, and now the blue lamp. Once the shooting started,

148

he'd be back on R/T, no doubt.

'Light showing green five-oh, could be a ship on fire, sir!'

'All right, Woods...'

Focusing on it, Lyon saw that that was exactly what it was. Some of the gunboats' handiwork, no doubt. An escort stopped and burning and left behind by the rest of the convoy as they steamed on westward. Furneaux had taken a quick look at it before resuming his sweeping across the bow.

'Bridge!'

Lyon ducked to the port-side branch of the voicepipe. 'Bridge.'

'Four and a half minutes coming up, sir.' Flyte paused for about two seconds. 'Time's up—*now.*'

'Pass "George twelve", signalman.' Furneaux eased the throttles back. The bumping-around was immediately worse again, as the revs came off and she slumped deeper in the waves, slamming through them.

'Bridge!'

Lyon answered again. Grabbing for stability at the correcting sphere on the port side of the binnacle: she'd dug her bow in and the sledgehammers were getting busy. Flyte told him, 'Only radar contact port side is on red two-zero, sir, Davies reckons the T-class, range about 024.'

'No R-boats?'

There should have been another 'T' as well. One on fire, one that had been standing by it.

'Not unless they're blanked-off behind that one. But there's another a degree or two to starboard— right ahead, almost—range 900 yards—'

'All right, Sub.' Furneaux, unruffled at hearing of an enemy right ahead at less than half a mile. It would

149

be the one he'd known was there, of course, the M-class sweeper on this inshore side. Engine-noise was down to a murmur, comparatively speaking—revs for only twelve knots, and Dumbflows engaged. Noisy, battering sea ... Furneaux called down to Flyte, 'Tell Davies watch that T-class and sweep for the R's and another T we seem to've lost track of.' He took a quick look out to starboard, saw the other two—that they'd cut their revs and were still in quarterline—and swung back, glasses up to look for this closer enemy, the M-class minesweeper.

'Port wheel, Cox'n. Steer north twenty-five west.'

'Port wheel. North twenty-five west, sir ...'

Closing throttles a bit more. Revs for about ten knots. Not having been spotted yet, despite a somewhat noisy arrival. Operative word, *yet*.

White water helped, of course. Searching ahead, from five or ten degrees on one bow to the other. The enemy units were all a great deal bigger than an MTB, you'd be ashamed of yourself—and as likely as not pay for it too—if you didn't see them before they came anywhere near seeing *you*. The burning ship was only a distant flickering, way out there to starboard, had no relevance to this picture. The night's second burning ship, in fact: the earlier one—unidentified, unexplained—had disappeared. Sunk, maybe. One's mind shrank from the thought of that one having been Mark Newbolt's 563. *Possibly*—with a lot of wishful thinking—it might have been something he'd run into ... The one now in sight, though, was just as well out of it—seeing that you had in any case to cope with two T-class—or three—as well as two 'M's and—somewhere, they couldn't have vanished into thin air—two *Raumboote* as well?

150

'There.' On the bow to starboard. 'Ship's head, Cox'n?'

'North twelve west, sir. Fifteen. Twenty...'

On green two-zero, one M-class sweeper. Furneaux pointed it out to Lyon. 'That's the M. Target's got to be somewhere the other side of her.'

'Course north twenty-five west, sir.'

Rolling hard. In the past half-hour the wind had come up quite a bit. Chisholm and Heddingly would be on their own now, acting independently; they'd have seen his own alteration to port in order to pass ahead of the 'M'.

'Bridge!'

Lyon leant to the voicepipe, reaching at the same time to hang up the gunnery telephone—having ordered Markwick, Wiltshire and Garfold to close up at their weapons...

'Bridge.'

'The T-class is about right ahead, sir, range two thousand yards. Still no R's.'

'Very good.' Straightening, he called towards Furneaux, 'That *Torpedoboot*, sir—'

'I heard.' With his glasses on the 'M' again. Bearing about forty on the bow, now. His problem being to pass ahead of it and then swing right-handed towards the target, at a distance from the 'M' that wouldn't be actually suicidal but still getting round under starboard wheel before actually rubbing noses with that bloody 'T'. He'd given the others the easier approach—at least, what should logically be the easier—passing astern of the sweeper with no other escort on this side to complicate matters for them. They could pass as far astern of the bastard as they liked.

Unless the 'M' astern of the target divined what

151

was happening and moved up to intervene.

But *that*, now, was the *Heilbronne*.

First sight of her. Star of the show, reason for being here at all—a darker mass separating itself to the left of the 'M'. Two funnels, and quite a lot of ship. 4,500 tons, allegedly. You'd have thought *all* of that, maybe more.

Anyway. Another ten degrees to port, maybe, to pass rather more safely ahead of this inshore 'M'. Not that 'safe' was really a good word for it ... But with a sixty-degree turn to starboard, say, immediately after crossing his bows, and you'd still be seven or eight hundred yards short of the 'T'. In on the target's bow—by that time probably—well, *surely*—being shot at—on a course obliquely towards the target, then hard a-port and fire maybe on the swing. At an ideal range—something like 400 yards.

Touch wood. Having still to watch which way any of these cats jumped. The other two MTBs might get in first; and whether the *Heilbronne* was hit or missed she'd surely be taking avoiding action.

'Steer ten degrees to port, Cox'n.'

'Ten degrees to port, sir.'

Starshell. Sixty on the bow and a mile to the north—mile and a half, maybe. Yellowish, *British*-type starshell for a change. Actually illuminating rockets, fired from a gunboat's forward six-pounder mounting. Not bad, actually, neither the timing nor the placing—giving the devil his due.

Poor old devil. But he was still a darned good man at sea. At home, he bored the pants off her, she'd said. He'd commented, smiling at her across a table in the Savoy Grill—three weeks ago—'One way of doing it, I suppose', and she'd murmured, 'On the whole, Mike, I prefer *your* way.' Shaking his head, shaking all that out of it. Thompson reporting the course as north thirty-five west ... The *Heilbronne* looked as big as a house, with the starshell-glow behind her. Course and speed—south seventy west, he estimated, and sixteen knots looked like a better bet than seventeen. He set the torpedo sight—optimistically—for a ninety on the bow shot. Glasses up again, then, seeing that the M-class sweeper was much clearer in outline too. One of the later, '37–'40 batch: the main differences being size and that she'd have two four-point-ones instead of only one. Training the glasses right: there was that other 'M'—to the right of the near one but a lot further away, probably astern of the *Heilbronne* by four or five hundred yards. From that position it could crack on speed to come up on either side, when its CO saw an attack developing. Chisholm's and Heddingly's worry, though—for the moment, anyway. He left it, swung his glasses left, passing over this nearer 'M' and the *Heilbronne* to check again on the *Torpedoboot.*

There. Identifiable by the two widely-spaced funnels and unusually low freeboard aft. While another rocket fizzed up and bloomed. Good for old Bob ... The 'T' was turning, though—away, to port. Furneaux swivelling back to the 'M'—having to watch all the cats at once, knowing he couldn't afford to take his eyes off any of them for more than a few seconds—muttering in his brain *Some bugger's got to spot us, damn it* ... And at that moment, too damn right, some bugger *had*—starshell, *green* starshell, burst almost slap overhead. 560 floodlit: men's faces greenish too.

He'd pushed the throttles shut. Telegraphs to stop.

To lie doggo, engines cut. Even under that green glow they didn't *have* to see you.

*   *   *

'Ready both tubes!'

Chisholm—562—had seen the green starshell out there to port, realized instantly what it meant—or roughly so—and cracked on speed. The time to attack being *now*—escorts distracted by Mike F. and lighting him up, poor bugger, while at the same time one had the benefit of Bob Stack's illuminants hanging in the sky, a palely yellow backdrop throwing the ex-banana boat and her consorts into ebony relief. Chisholm peering ahead through binoculars, shouting to PO Dan Martin, 'Five degrees to port, Cox'n!'

To aim initially at that M-class sweeper's stern, not to detour to starboard and then turn in astern of her as Mike had proposed, because (a) there'd be very little room for manoeuvre there inside her, (b) the 'M' was overhauling the target—obviously to fend off Mike's attack. If one had been there *now*—instead of in about fifty or sixty seconds, which was roughly the time it was going to take to get there—you'd have been as near as damnit ninety on the bow.

Might still be—touch wood. *Might.* Things could change within seconds, though—relative velocities being *entirely* relative...

'Tubes ready, sir.'

David Eden, sub-lieutenant. No relation to Anthony. Chisholm caught his arm. 'Tell the guns, no shooting without orders, not even returning fire.'

'Aye aye, sir. Close season, I'll tell 'em.'

Fine time for smart-arse jokes. He'd taken the

154

latches off the torpedo firing-levers. Left hand on PO Martin's shoulder, right arm pointing ahead. 'See him?'

Leaning forward over the wheel, peering...

'Yeah, blimey—'

'The target—with an escort overlapping her forepart on this side. Steer for the escort's bow—see?'

Five hundred yards, say, to that sweeper—which was plainer to see now as another of Stack's rockets broke open up there—and then maybe another four hundred to the target. If one fired just short of the 'M', therefore—which admittedly was begging a few questions, but *if* one did—torpedo running distance might be say five hundred. He let his glasses hang while he set the torpedo sight. Enemy speed— seventeen. And—eighty on the bow, say ... He swung the sight-bar over so that it clicked up against the stop at the seventeen-knot mark. A glance to starboard then at 564: abaft this boat's beam, distance about 150 yards. Heddingly sticking close: but *he* could take a wide swing at it, if he wanted.

When the moments came, though—one's own, then Heddingly's—you'd be playing it off the cuff. *Heilbronne* might be either stopped and sinking, or taking violent avoiding-action, or—whatever...

There were also one or two other escorts as yet unaccounted for, remember.

'Escort astern of the target's moving up, sir.'

Swinging his glasses right: just as the tracer came— blinding—from that other 'M', forging up from right to left—to come up between oneself and the target, probably ... Couldn't be certain—darkness, distance, and the blinding effect of that tracer to the left: guesswork had to be part of it, but—

'Oh, *damn!*'

155

Green floodlighting, from overhead. Lit up, and blinded, and tracer thickening, homing-in from more than one direction now...

'Hard a-starboard, Cox'n!'

To break off, get out of it, then try again.

* * *

Furneaux warned Lyon, 'Gunners hold their fire.' So as not to give the enemy an aiming-point before he had to: or before they spotted him anyway. He was closing in again: had been lying cut, feeling like something on a brightly-lit stage, but in fact they *hadn't* spotted him under their bloody starshell: there'd been a second one, and that had fizzled out now. The *Torpedoboot* which had fired the things hadn't in any case been turning towards—as he'd feared, for a tense half-minute or so; it was completing a full turn, reversing course to lead this pack back westward—having assumed the position of centre-forward, so to speak, and probably thinking in the course of the turn that he *might* have seen something, put up a couple of starshells on the off-chance, and drawn blank.

His taking up that station in the lead rather suggested that the R-boats whose presence one had been suspecting didn't have to be any part of this assembly, might only have happened to have been in company with the 'T' at that time—could by now be anywhere. But where in hell were the other *Torpedoboote*, for Pete's sake?

Tracer off to the right. A lot of it. 560 rolling more than pitching on this course and at low revs with wind and sea on the beam. Another rocket-starshell—only a mile or so to the north. Stack and his boys still at it.

156

Ears flapping for the sounds of torpedo-hits, no doubt...

Thinking—about the missing 'T's—that one should bear in mind their existence—as wild cards, so to speak—but not waste time worrying about them meanwhile. Them *or* the R-boats. Also, that it might be only a matter of time before the M-class which was preoccupied at the moment with either Chisholm or Heddingly, or both, woke up to this *other* alien presence: especially as in the next half-minute 560 would be crossing its bow. Not really a very healthy prospect. In fact one began to wonder—suddenly, a new angle on the situation—whether if the odds were weighed against one rather too heavily here—the closest threat being that *Torpedoboot*, but the 'M' as well—he might hold on, cross ahead of the *Heilbronne* and attack from seaward before either she or the escorts on that side knew he was there. *Might* be a good alternative. There wasn't going to be a hell of a lot of elbow-room whatever happened, and if the 'M' moved up, for instance, between him and the target, he'd be shut out—and stuck between these two, with no option then but to get out of it double-quick with nothing achieved. He'd dropped his glasses on their strap, had his hands on the telegraphs. Thinking about Chisholm and Heddingly: deciding that far from fouling things up for them, it might do them a good turn—taking enemy attention from that sector. They'd been told to disengage to starboard, nobody'd be getting in anyone else's way.

Telegraphs to full ahead. They'd see you *now*—any bloody second, anyway ... Throttles ...

Hadn't been a bad guess, that, either—a stream of tracer was coming lobbing from the 'T'—which was

157

on the port bow by this time, and travelling from right to left—and yet another green starshell had lit up, somewhere up behind his shoulder. *Everyone* wanting light ... 'Oerlikon return fire to port, point-fives starboard!' Lyon's shout of acknowledgement: 560 tucking her stern down and tilting her bow up, dark sea splitting and that sickly green tinting the spread of white. Explaining in a shout to Lyon as she gathered speed, 'Going through *there*.' An arm flung out, pointing. 'Shift the point-fives to this one when the time's right—if they're coming anywhere near us—OK?' Gunflash from the sweeper's foc's'l—a four-point-one, that would be, quite possibly not the first: an opening burst of tracer too, either 20-mm or 37-mm.

'Port wheel, Cox'n—' He'd grabbed his arm, to get his attention, shouting close to his ear—'then constant helm, weave twenty degrees each side.' Four-point-one shells were *definitely* to be avoided. Acknowledgement was inaudible but the tone would have been calm and level and all the way from Huddersfield. Gun-flashes at regular intervals now from the M's foc's'l—whoever it had been persecuting before must have high-tailed it, he guessed, leaving 560 as the sole object of its attentions now. Criss-crossing tracer was thickening from both directions: but it wouldn't be like this for long—forty knots wasn't a bad speed at which to run a gauntlet. And weaving as well ... Well up on the plane, a steady-enough platform for her own gunners—whose function was primarily to discourage the opposition, *en*courage *their* gunners to keep their heads down. Main purpose in life now being to get by and into a position to use torpedoes. Nothing else. The point-fives were shifting target, joining the Oerlikon firing

158

in bursts at the *Torpedoboot*'s stern—roughly abeam at this moment, range about 500 yards and—he saw this now, having half-expected it—under helm, turning to port: to bring its guns other than the stern ones into action. Had expected him to have gone to starboard: turning this way he was stern-to again, so that to gain the advantage he'd been after he'd have to continue right around—which would take him dangerously close to the bows of the sweeper and/or the *Heilbronne* as they ploughed on westward. Would also take him out of station in the convoy's van. Incomprehensible, but all and any such mis-judgements were entirely welcome. The end-on shape on the other beam now was the *Heilbronne*, and she was herself in action, tracer streaming out in all directions. The other two attacking, obviously: hadn't attacked yet, he hoped—there'd been no torpedo hits. Any moment now ... 560 had effectively outdistanced the sweeper—in any case it would have been impeded by having the 'T' in its line of fire in the last minute or so—and it was probably tied-up in that other *fracas* now, around the *Heilbronne*. Effectively, therefore—worst over, through the gauntlet? *Heilbronne* was abaft the beam to starboard—tracer and gunflashes in that sector still blinding when you looked back at it—the last starshell from the gunboats had faded and had not been replaced—and the *Torpedoboot*, still turning, was roughly beam-on. Still shooting, and 560 still weaving: there'd been a pause in the action but it had opened up again as the 'T' came on round in that tight turn. 37-mm with red tracer in it, four-point-one flashes too.

Hopes of having made it had been a little premature, in fact...

Hits *then*. He'd felt them, a rapid succession of what must have been 37-mm shells blasting up the port side from aft to for'ard as she'd swung that way: two seconds earlier he'd seen that stream of tracer arcing in closer, the gunner steadily correcting his aim before the turn just seconds ago.

The Oerlikon was out of it now. Only point-fives shooting back.

'Hard a-starboard!'

'Hard a-starboard, sir...'

To circle in—actually putting the wheel over sooner than he'd intended—and close in on the *Heilbronne*'s starboard bow. Well aware that she might be taking avoiding-action by the time one got there, but reckoning to get into torpedo-firing range anyway—and with any luck lose *this* bastard in the course of the turn. He yelled at Lyon to cease fire—to reduce the boat's obviously excessive visibility—but Lyon had gone down to check on and/or deal with the port-side damage, and it was Perrot, who'd told him this, who jumped to the forefront on the coxswain's left and jammed a thumb on the cease-fire button.

'Midships!'

Thompson acknowledging, taking the rudder off her: Furneaux easing the throttles back: again, to reduce one's conspicuousness. Spotting another *Torpedoboot* out there—out on the *Heilbronne*'s beam, roughly. *One* of the wild cards located ... She was no immediate threat, that far out. Might have been out there to ward off the gunboats, the starshell firers. Starshell incidentally having ceased now ... That one did seem to be returning towards the centre—he thought. Not easy to make out. In fact very difficult, confusing ... But—he swung his

160

glasses back to the nearer 'T', which had just opened fire again: and was turning inside 560's own wider turning-circle, putting himself right in there— precisely where one didn't want the bastard...

Tracer was again blinding. He'd thought to have been out of it by now.

The German was only chancing his arm, though. Browning, more or less. None of it was any cause for anxiety, at this stage.

'Port wheel, Cox'n.'

And still less throttle. An approach from the quarter would be a more practical proposition now. First step being to get in as close as possible unseen ... 'Ship's head?'

'South fifteen west, sir!'

'Steer due south.'

Explosion—back in the mêlée around the *Heilbronne*, a percussion you felt through the sea and the boat's hull. A flash—vertical streak of flame. Where the target *had* been, anyway—and a torpedo hit, for sure. There was a whole mass of tracer and gun-flashes in that area now. If the *Heilbronne* had been polished off—as she might have been, to sink a ship her size didn't necessarily take more than one hit—well, *Torpedoboote* were well worth torpedoing, when nothing larger offered. Or 'M's—there were two of those...

2355, the time of that hit.

Chisholm and Heddingly, if they hadn't disengaged already, surely would have by the time one got in there. So press on in—*now*.

'Steer for that tracer, Cox'n!'

Telegraphs to full ahead, throttles open. The thought in mind that Lyon was taking his time over it down there, that there had to be some problem. But

161

this was the moment, you couldn't pussyfoot around all bloody night–

Starshell—for God's sake . . .

One's own—yellowish, and right over the top. One had assumed the starshell exercise was over. If Stack had tried, he couldn't have done better—or worse . . . And the tracer was finding her now—multi-coloured, blinding in the start of its trajectory, thinning somewhat as it lifted seemingly slowly then cracked overhead in brilliant streaks. Not all of it so *far* overhead either—*definitely* finding her now, in this brilliance.

'Hard a-port—'

'Captain, sir—' Lyon fetching up hard between him and the coxswain—'Port tube support's smashed, Garfold's dead and—'

A shell-spout lifted close to starboard. And another hit, then. Right aft—a flash, and a heavy jar right through her. Revs decreasing sharply, engines stopping.

* * *

Chisholm was at 562's torpedo-sight, sighting over it with his binoculars.

'Come five degrees to port, Cox'n.'

On his way back in. He'd circled away at high speed, gaining enough bearing in the process; was moving in now at lowish revs—circumspectly enough to stand at least a chance of eluding that sweeper.

Heddingly was somewhere astern or on his quarter: having disengaged at roughly the same time—however many minutes ago that had been— and come back in more or less in company for *his* second shot at outwitting the defence . . . Bob Stack's

162

last starshell was dimming up there: had now flickered out. Until only a minute or two ago the gunboats had kept them overlapping—one fading, another replacing it before it died. Not this time, though. Not when you bloody needed it ... Action had all died away on the bow too—had apparently transferred itself to the convoy's other side. Mike F. looking for an easier way in, obviously.

Stooped at the torpedo-sight: having his work cut out to separate A from B and Y from Z: especially without the backing of Stack's starshell. 562 rolling hard, meanwhile.

'He's woke up again, sir!'

Shout from PO Martin—one hand up from the wheel, pointing towards tracer lifting, soaring this way—from the *Heilbronne*, then from the 'M' too—which one was passing astern of—*had* passed astern of, and closer than one should have risked, maybe—although in fact there'd been very little option, with the other one as well—the one still pushing up from the quarter. He'd had to steer to pass about halfway between them: *no* option, really ... Distance to the target now—six hundred, six-fifty? Explosive 37-mm shells thwacking over—the sounds of their passage as regular as heartbeats—while he opened the throttles to revs for about fifteen knots. The concentration of tracer was blinding but thank God the shooting wasn't all that accurate.

As yet, it wasn't.

Known as flying half-blind. Jolting, rolling, sea flying white and the tracer coming closer, now. Some closer than *that*, even—in that moment he'd felt at least one hit. Head down, grin and bear it. Grins, in fact, were optional ... He yelled at Eden, 'Stand by!'

'Stand by!'

Raikes on the port side—Henry Raikes, sub-lieutenant, spare officer—yelled the same thing down to the torpedoman on that side. Chisholm shouting urgently, his eyes squeezed half-shut against the continual, flashing brilliance of the tracer, 'Three degrees starboard, Cox'n!'

Almost on...

Knees bent, eyes on a level with the sight, hands on the firing-levers. Running-distance for the fish would be about five hundred yards. *Fucking* tracer... Blue flash for'ard, the scream of a ricochet; then, as the stream of red and yellow dazzle lifted, a section of the windscreen and deflectors on the port side virtually exploded—disintegrated, flew away.

Crouched at the sight, ignoring it...

'Fire both!'

Eden's shout repeated it, impulse cartridges fired—simultaneous muffled explosions on both sides: you heard the *whoosh* of the torpedoes' launching then: would have seen by the light of surrounding tracer—if you'd been so daft as to stick your head up high enough—the great fish plunging out ahead, streaks of silver and blue shellac in the constant flicker.

'Hard a-starboard!'

Jangling the telegraphs, and leaving them at full ahead: leaning on his throttles...

'Wheel's hard a-starboard, sir—'

'Steer north thirty east.'

Twenty seconds' running time, say. About eight seconds gone already. Glasses on 564, who was passing astern as 562 swung away to starboard—gathering speed, hammering her way up towards the plane. He'd changed his mind: 'North *ten* east, make it!' Martin acknowledging, easing the rudder off her.

164

Motive being to steer her closer in on the convoy's quarter so as to keep at least some of the enemy's attention, give John Heddingly a better chance ... Glasses up: on *Heilbronne* who was turning to port—an attempt at combing the tracks. Still watching her when the torpedo struck: deep hard knock of the explosion, upward shoot of flame—but not on *her*, on that sweeper—which had also turned, had been on her way round while still pouring out the flak.

Invisible in smoke, now. Hiding the *Heilbronne* too.

'Course north ten east, sir!'

Starshell. Gunboat starshell. First for some time ... And the smoke had blown away—like the whisking off of a magician's magic cloth under which the audience knew for sure there'd been some object although now there wasn't ... Telegraphs back to half-ahead, revs for twelve knots. Aware of one fish having missed, of *Heilbronne* untouched, steaming on. Aware of having cocked it up, in fact. All right, an M-class sweeper hit and sunk, but what the hell, you'd come here for the *Heilbronne*, not for—

Time—2355.

Glasses up, swinging round and seeing 564 at about thirty knots scooting across close astern, leaping across 562's wake.

'Port wheel, Cox'n.'

'Port wheel, sir ...'

An MTB that had fired its torpedoes might as well disengage and head for home, except that in some circumstances—such as *now*—it could assist by distracting attention from a boat that had *not* yet fired ... He put a hand on PO Martin's shoulder, and pointed: 'Steer for that bugger!'

'Aye, sir!'

Full ahead. Aiming at the M-class which until a few minutes ago had been astern of the *Heilbronne*, had since moved up, was more or less on her beam now.

'Ship's head?'

'North fifteen west, sir!'

Tracer starting up again—at *this* boat, not 564. Heddingly was detouring to port, they either hadn't noticed him or didn't yet regard him as a threat. Wouldn't know which was which anyway, which had fired or which hadn't. Tracer everywhere again now, and gun-flashes, most of it coming this way.

'Cox'n—weave between north fifteen west and north fifteen east. Constant helm.'

'Aye, sir!'

Conspicuous—as well as safer—weaving at high speed. Heddingly *was* getting a share of the flak now, but nothing like the amount he'd have had to cope with on his own. Another escort was engaging him, a *Torpedoboot* coming over across the *Heilbronne*'s bows. Had to be a 'T' because the 'M's were all accounted for—one destroyed by the gunboats, one just torpedoed by 562, and one surviving—*there*. Blinded again. He'd lost sight of 564 too.

*　　　*　　　*

'Stand by!'

John Heddingly—MTB 564 ... Down to about twenty knots, with *Heilbronne* massive-looking on the bow to starboard, range about five hundred yards and squirting tracer out on her port quarter for some reason—as well as this way—while seemingly holding a steady course, since turning back to about south

166

eighty west. Heddingly with eyes only for her, and his hands on the torpedo firing-levers. 'Two degrees to port, Cox'n!' Easing the throttles to bring her down to about fifteen knots. The escort broader on the bow had been giving him some unpleasantly close attention in the last half-minute, but hadn't been able to keep it up without hitting this other one—the *Torpedoboot*, to port—which unfortunately was showing less restraint.

'Steady as you go, Cox'n. Lovely—spot-on ... Stand by, Farrow!'

Hits on the port side, somewhere. 20-mm, probably. Port side aft. *Fuck 'em* ...

'Fire both!'

Echoes in other voices, port and starboard—and both fish gone. He'd heard it, felt it too, and 564 was suddenly three tons lighter. Needing speed now, you'd get it—she'd be almost airborne. Telegraphs at full ahead: throttles wide open: 'Hard a-starboard!'

'Hard a-starboard, sir ...'

Heilbronne was beginning a turn to port, damn her.

But—she'd left it a bit late—he thought. *Please God* ... And on the plus side, 564's own turn between her and the 'M' was silencing them both—for some brief but blessed interval while they couldn't shoot without potting each other.

Over his shoulder: 'Open fire!'

On the 'M'—at close range, a blast or two in passing. With only about fifteen seconds' running time left for the fish to get there, though. Surely by *now* ...

'Steer due east, Cox'n!'

Hit!

Solid underwater *thump*: column of muck soaring

167

twice the height of her own masts. Right for'ard—even right on her stem—as it looked from here. Another yard to the left—or if she'd started her turn a second earlier—that hit-by-a-whisker would have been a miss. With his glasses still up—tracer still lacing the sky, back there—looking back over the beam and then the quarter—564 getting up towards the plane, leaning hard into her disengaging turn-away—he knew he'd missed with the other fish, damn *near* missed with both. Because they'd (a) seen him coming (b) timed that turn almost to perfection. The one hit didn't seem to have done her all that much harm, either: the muck had cleared and he could see her—down by the bow, maybe, but not by much, and still under way, making at least a few knots through the water.

*   *   *

Mike Furneaux had heard that torpedo hit. Second one—making one each for Chisholm and Heddingly; a fair assumption therefore was that the *Heilbronne* would have been done for. Closer to home, though, had been the near-certainty that MTB 560 had come to the end of *her* road—so he'd thought half a minute ago.

A very long half-minute, at that. Long and by no means happy. But then—*now*—pushing the engineroom telephone back on to its hook, PO Motor Mechanic Coates having astonished him with the news that the centre engine could be used, it was like waking from nightmare.

Centre engine ahead. Easing the throttle open ...
'Steady as you go, Cox'n!'
'North fifty east, sir ...'

Keeping the wind astern, and keeping her close to the smoke. Not right in it where you couldn't breathe, but close enough not to *want* to breathe too deeply. Working up to about fifteen knots. That engine's fuel supply from the after tank compartment had been severed, Coates and his staff had connected it to the midships section of tanks within—well, within thirty seconds, for God's sake ... At the time of the hits which had stopped all three engines, though—hits which must have come from the *Torpedoboot* which had then been astern, having been in the deep field earlier—Furneaux had turned her to port, relying on the residual way she'd had on her to get her round—and sent young Flyte aft to start making smoke—which without the engine wouldn't have been any long-term solution, only an instant reaction—in preference to being blown to matchwood in those next few seconds.

Now, to sneak away. Then, establish communication with the rest of the unit and with Bob Stack. Get Lyon's report on damage and casualties first, though ...

CHAPTER NINE

'Pack up starshell!'

Barclay passed the order forward via the gunnery telephone: 'Starshell cease fire.' There'd been some disruption of the starshell firing anyway, a misfire with ensuing complications and they'd only got a couple of rounds away since then. The last one was still hanging up there, though low and fading, on the beam as 875 swung away to starboard, engine-noise building, increasing to revs for twenty knots, battering through a stiffly choppy sea, wind about force 3 from the west. A lot of white on the sea now and the wind still rising. All four engines were in commission again. The port outer had had its exhaust outlet punctured in several places and Bluett had had to stop it until repairs had been made; alternatives would have been to evacuate the engineroom or be gassed. A lot was happening at once though—not all of it entirely clear. There'd been torpedo hits down there to the south—two, widely spaced, a minute and a half between them, roughly—but no reports yet—and radar had chosen this time to come up with a double contact, Wheeler reporting two ships on a west-nor'-westerly bearing at a range of about five thousand yards. Hence the alteration of course and increase of speed. They could be R-boats—which had been in the vicinity not long ago—but whatever they were they'd be in a position, or might be, to intercept the MTBs as they withdrew. Had therefore to be intercepted themselves—dealt with, driven off, whatever.

Bob Stack's view, this was. Ben's was that they might be well enough clear—and perhaps on course for Cherbourg—could as well have been left to their own devices. Like any other red herrings. He wasn't being asked, though: there was no reason he should be, come to think of it.

'Course north sixty west, sir!'

Checking astern now: seeing 866 tucked in neatly there, Monkey not having needed any signal to follow round and adjust revs, maintaining his distance-astern. He'd worked with Bob Stack for so long that the connection was almost telepathic. There were only the two of them now; Baldy Worbury's hope of getting another engine going had not been realized—or realizable, his motor mechanic had told him—and he'd had other serious damage, as well as men killed and wounded. Stack had ordered him home to Newhaven, via the R/V position fifteen miles northeast of Pointe de Barfleur.

'Radar, bridge!'

'Bridge.' Ben would have got to it but Barclay was there ahead of him. Wheeler reporting, 'Right ahead, sir, range 048, moving right to left.'

'Make anything of 'em yet?'

'Not really, sir. Small, like—'

'R-boats?'

'Could be, sir.'

Stack had heard it, and had ordered port wheel. He had his glasses up, searching ahead. Ben too, on this port side where whenever anyone passed through the companionway with its black-out screening—as Barclay had just now for instance, checking on the condition of AB Merriman—who was comatose, apparently, heavily sedated—the wind howled up like owls screeching, through the damaged wheelhouse. He was thinking, with his left elbow hooked over the clamped twin Vickers 303, that things might not have been going all that well for the MTBs. Standard procedure was for them to fire both their torpedoes at once, and from those two widely-separated hits the inference was that (a) there'd been two attacks made and two misses, (b) one MTB had either not yet attacked or had missed with both its fish.

The second hit had been at 2356. It was a minute past midnight now. OK, so no reports yet— Furneaux might be waiting for his third boat to do its bit before he came on the air. That was a possibility.

There was another too, though.

875 making all of twenty knots. A couple of minutes, at most, should bring her into visibility range of the radar contacts.

'W/T office, bridge!'

He got to it, this time. Barclay was on the telephone to the guns, alerting them to the fact there were new enemies ahead, probably two R-boats.

He'd cracked the bridge of his nose on the voicepipe's rim. Stifling appropriate language in favour of the standard, toneless answer: 'Bridge...'

'Signals from the MTBs in the pipe, sir!'

Meaning the message-carrier, the little bucket you pulled up on its lanyard. He called to Stack, 'Going down to the plot, sir', and went below. Signals, plural, the telegraphist had said. Leaning over the chart-table, he pulled the cannister up, extracted a sheet of large-size signal pad and smoothed it out.

Two messages on the one sheet, in Telegraphist Ordway's blue-pencilled, copperplate hand...

MTB 560 from MTB 562. Attack completed, one hit on M-class sweeper which got in the way and has now sunk. Disengaging northeastward, no casualties or damage. Are you all right? Time of Origin 0002.

MTB 560 from MTB 564. Attack completed, one hit right forward on main target which however continuing westward at low speed. No casualties or damage, disengaging northeastward with 562 in sight. Do you require assistance? T.O.O. 0003.

Voicepipe again, from the W/T office: 'Plot, sir?'
'Yes, Willis?'

172

'More coming in, sir.'

'All right.'

In fact—thank God ... If there'd been continued silence from Mike Furneaux—as one's forebodings had suggested there might be—well, *two*, then. The boss *and* the new boy gone missing.

He'd forgotten to send the bloody bucket down. Dropping it in the pipe now, hearing it rattle through. Getting the reek of stale cigarette-smoke through the pipe and visualizing them in that cramped little office, the air blue with it, Ordway with a fag-end in his mouth no doubt while he scribbled away, the leading tel. Probably smoking too while he waited for it. Everyone smoked too much. Ben lit one of his own. Wondering about Furneaux—the fact that both Chisholm and Heddingly had had reason to suspect he might be in trouble. And so far only the two hits, two attacks that one knew of.

He got an updated position from the QH, and put it on the chart. Time—0010. Position Cap Levi 030 degrees 7800 yards. Wheeler, radar operator, was . talking to Stack about yet another contact. It was getting to be like Piccadilly bloody Circus around here, Ben thought.

'Plot!' Leading Tel. Willis again. 'In the pipe, sir!'

'Right.' Reeling it in ... Willis adding, 'There's more coming, sir.'

This was a short one:

Unit from MTB 560, repeated C-in-C
Portsmouth. Return independently to base. No
assistance required, thank you. T.O.O. 0008.

He was alive, anyway. Giving damn little away, but—extant. OK, taking less time on the air, for

173

Krauts to eavesdrop. Using W/T rather than R/T for that same reason, probably, also for range—the MTBs might be widely separated by this time—and to have the transmission picked up back in Newhaven as well as Portsmouth.

Waiting for the next instalment. Cigarette between his lips, eyes narrowed to keep the smoke out while using a rubber to clear old pencil-work from a plotting-diagram. If radar was suddenly going to find a whole profusion of bloody contacts ... A fleeting thought then as he marked a starting-position for this unit and tagged it 0011, eleven minutes past midnight: *This time* last *night* ...

'Plot!—' Willis again—'Signal in the bucket, sir!'

'OK.' He jerked it up. A thought in mind of men like himself and Furneaux coming to grief—as was always possible—and how many women might weep into their grog. He knew the answer in his own case: *one* ... Stack's voice booming suddenly from the R/T speaker: 'Dog two—Topdog. You receiving me? Over.'

Monkey was replying affirmatively. Stack ordering port wheel, meanwhile. Turning away from those radar contacts? Seen sense, maybe. Or had decided the new one should have priority. He'd have some reason, and it would be a good one. You could count on it. Correction to that recent thought, however: there'd be tears shed in Brisbane too. *And* by her old man. He shook the signal out of the carrier: hearing Stack again on the TCS telling Monkey, 'Altering to port. Those two are holding on—could be for Cherbourg—and we have a new one—tiddler—due south, 2,500 yards, could be more dangerous. Steering to leave him to starboard. Out.'

'Topdog—your tiddler—on its own, could be

174

Newbolt? At a pinch? Over.'

'Dog Two, I had the same wild surmise. But he'd be chipping-in on this now, surely. Out.'

Chipping-in on the R/T exchanges, he'd meant.

The new signal was from Furneaux addressed to Stack and repeated to the staff at Portsmouth.

MTB 560 to MGB 875 (R) C-in-C Portsmouth. One tube wrecked by gunfire and two engines knocked out. Stalking target westward, target speed reduced by torpedo hit from MTB 564. Intend attacking after overhauling in vicinity position AA. T.O.O. 0010.

Position AA meant close off Cap Levi.

He'd taken a beating, by the sound of it: the forebodings hadn't been entirely unjustified. With only one engine, in fact, he might well be heading for another. Even if the *Heilbronne*'s speed had been drastically reduced, allowing him to overhaul, there'd still be several escorts surrounding her, and speed was essential for manoeuvrability—especially after firing, when the time came to disengage.

Kamikaze stuff, otherwise.

And only one fish, for God's sake. But there you were: first time out as the MTBs' SO, he wouldn't want to leave his target afloat. In his shoes, who would?

Back at the pipe, Ben asked Willis whether there was anything else coming in; there wasn't, so he went back up to the bridge. Stack meanwhile had been on the R/T again, conferring with Monkey; his last words before switching off had been, 'I'll challenge first—depending on how it looks—otherwise engage starboard. Out.'

175

Ben relieved him of the microphone. 'Signals from the MTBs, sir—'

'Yeah—right, Ben—all that matters, in ten seconds flat.'

'Aye, sir.' Grabbing for support: wind and sea *were* getting up. 'Essentials are—Mike Furneaux's had one tube wrecked and he's on one engine, *Heilbronne*'s been hit and slowed but she's still afloat, continuing west. Mike's overhauling her, aims to get her with his one fish—near Cap Levi he reckons. He's sent Heddingly and Chisholm home.'

'Christ.' Digesting it ... Then: 'Glutton for punishment, old Mike. We'll have to stick around. After we've dealt with this bugger. *Could* be Newbolt, but—' A shake of the head ... 'Ben—get a signal out, tell 'em 874's on *her* way home, first lieutenant in command.'

'Aye aye, sir. Re this challenge—letters changed, at midnight?'

'Damn *right*—'

The signalman called, 'Challenge is F for Freddie, reply's Z for Zebra, sir.'

'Good on you, Miller...'

Down in the plot again—with the irreverent thought that punishment wasn't the only thing Mike Furneaux was a glutton for—he drafted a signal informing MTBs 562 and 564 that MGB 874 was on her way back to base via the R/V position which she'd be passing through at approximately 0040, with wounded on board, 1st Lt in command, and only one engine, making about ten knots. Motives behind this were (a) to reduce the danger of mistaken-identity encounters, (b) that the MTBs or one of them might elect to stay with Worbury in case his remaining engine packed up, and (c) the possibility of

176

transferring his wounded to one of them, getting them home and into hospital three times as fast.

If transference was a practical proposition—which wasn't by any means a certainty. A moderate sea like this one looked a lot bigger when you tried to hold two boats alongside each other for long enough to transfer even fit and agile personnel.

He put a time-of-origin of 0019 on the signal, sent it down the pipe and went back up to the bridge.

Barclay was using the telephone to the guns about holding their fire. 'There's a chance it could be MTB 563.'

'I think it *is*.' Stack—in a tone of surprise. Glasses up, looking out over the bow. Revs had been reduced: she was plunging along at something like twelve knots, plugging southward like a big fish on a line. Wind about force 3 rising 4, he guessed: having to wait for his night vision to re-establish itself before he'd be much use.

'Five degrees to port, Cox'n.'

Barclay shouting into a voicepipe: talking to Wheeler about picking up the *Heilbronne* and/or her escorts; 'Mad Priest' Wheeler reminding him, 'Not as good in the landward sector, sir. Lot of interference, like.'

'See what you can get. We need it.' Up from the pipe: glasses up too then. 'Sure it's him, sir?'

'No. Not *sure*, at all. Bloody miracle if it is … What d'you reckon, Ben?'

He was on it—at last. Whatever it was, it was about ten degrees on the starboard bow: broken water, the pale gleam of it, like sea sluicing around and over a half-tide rock and pluming up from time to time, the rock itself no more than a hollow centre to the disturbance. It *could* be. It had taken keen

177

eyesight to have spotted it in the first place, with the broken water all around. He answered Stack, 'Looks like an MTB. Although...'

Leaving it at that. No-one was listening to him, and in any case—well, to an extent you saw what you *wanted* to see. Although what the hell it could be if it *wasn't* an MTB...

'Miller.' Stack with the glasses still at his eyes ... *Everything* on the move—whatever it was out there soaring and dropping away again, the black white-patched slopes shifting and slanting this way and that, this gunboat hammering, pitching and rolling even harder—at low revs, and beam-on to it. In contrast, Stack and others as upright as cut-out figures mounted on gimbals ... Stack calling back to the signalman, 'Clear-glass Aldis, Miller, starboard side here ... Steer ten degrees to port, Cox'n.'

'Ten degrees to port, sir...'

Barclay into the 'phone to the guns, keeping the lads in touch with events: '—starboard bow, but I repeat, do not open fire before the order. We're about to challenge.'

'Standing by, sir...'

'Make the challenge!'

White beam lancing out, piercing the night—a lance with a spread of salt-spray around it. Two shorts, one long, one short. Pause: then the same again. Ben had his glasses on that patch of white—which looked decidedly like an MTB's humped and spreading wake; but if it *was* Mark Newbolt's there was no way of knowing what he'd been through or what state he might be in, whether for instance he'd have the updated recognition signals ready.

Except that—well, bloody fool if he didn't. He *was* heading south, must be regarding himself as fit for

178

action. Presumably. Even if he was—apparently—deaf to R/T.

A flash, over that swirl of wake: expanding into a beam like a searchlight probing this way. Long, long, short, short: Z for Zebra.

'Christ ... Miller—*blue* lamp now!' Joyous tone, and everyone feeling the same, probably all of them having at least privately given that crew up for lost ... 'Make to him, interrogative numerals five, six, three!'

'Aye, sir ...'

Blue-shaded lamp for its restricted visual range ... Barclay telling the gunners 'Correct reply, seems it *is* 563!'

Cheers on the wind. Stack shouting—to anyone in earshot—'Would've given you twenty to one against!' Miller's lamp finished passing that question, and the answer came immediately—'Affirmative'.

'Loudhailer—'

Miller gave Stack the microphone, and switched on. Barclay was answering a call from radar—Wheeler having to admit he'd been over-pessimistic, that his set had blips between red two-five and red three-oh at 2,500 and 3,000 yards. Stack had cut to outers, meanwhile, Miller's blue lamp winking astern to warn Monkey. 875 sliding up abeam of the MTB fifty yards clear to port—and Stack's magnified Aussie tones carrying clearly over the gap of heaving blackness: 'No R/T, Mark? How about W/T? What else don't you have—and *why* not?'

*   *   *

560 had two working engines now—centre and port. PO Coates had achieved this vast improvement despite his leading stoker, Willoughby, having been

179

thrown across the port engine, burnt and for a while knocked out, when a 20-mm shell had burst inside the engineroom, against the outer side of the starboard engine. The solid bulk of the engine itself had saved Coates, Willoughby and Stoker Hughes from far worse injury. Willoughby was conscious and back at work, helping to plug holes.

'I can have twenty-five knots, can I, when I need it?'

Lyon called, 'Red two-oh—escort of some kind!'

Coates was hedging: 'Sooner keep revs down, sir. Especially with the weight we got in aft.'

The aftermost compartment, containing steering-gear and the steering engine—as well as lub-oil tanks—was full of water that had flooded in through the shattered transom. The gear was still working perfectly, but the weight of the flooding was putting a stern-down angle on her; Coates' point was that the extra drag could only add to the strain on engines that were already in need of nursing.

'All right. And well done, Chief.'

He handed the 'phone to John Flyte, and put his glasses up. 'Red two-oh, Number One?'

'And less than a mile, I'd say.'

He was on it. A *Torpedoboot*: steering west—or west by south, say. He agreed: '*Much* less.' Under helm at this moment too, either zigzagging or changing its position in the screen. He was probing the immediate surroundings for a sight of the *Heilbronne*. He was here now, stalking again, as a direct result of Heddingly's report that the target was still afloat and *continuing westward at low speed*.

With only five or six miles to cover between here and Cherbourg. OK, so she wouldn't be getting out into the Atlantic now—not even round the corner to

180

Brest—but the brief had been to sink her, not just damage her.

'Flyte—revs for eighteen knots. Steer five degrees to starboard, Cox'n.'

'Five degrees starboard, sir...'

Revs increasing. 560 dragging her flooded stern like—Furneaux's own comment to Lyon a minute or two ago—like a duck with its arse full of shot. Another adverse factor was that as a result of the severing of the fuel-line to the centre engine her bilges aft were awash with 100-octane petrol. You wouldn't want *another* hit back there.

Lyon had answered a call from the W/T office. Furneaux, keeping his glasses up, cocked an ear.

'Signal to us from the SO, sir!'

'Let's hear it. Come another five degrees to starboard, Cox'n.'

To pass outside that escort, presumably. Furneaux informing Lyon and Flyte, 'The *Heilbronne*'s to the left of that *Torpedoboot*, and there's another T on her port quarter ... Go ahead, Number One.'

'Addressed to us from MGB 875, sir.' Lyon passed it on phrase by phrase from Turner, the telegraphist. 'MTB 563—' he'd gagged on it: '*Christ—563—*'

'Come on, what about her?'

'*—closing target from seaward steering due south towards Cap Levi. Has only one engine, Limited to eight knots, no W/T, R/T or radar. Newbolt is aware of your own intentions. My position AA 032 degrees three miles course south by west, will assist with starshell if you call for it.* Time of Origin—'

'Never mind that.'

181

Beyond this, he seemed not to be commenting. Binoculars back on the *Heilbronne*. Lost in thought, maybe ... Lyon put his own glasses up too: looking for the *Heilbronne* and then for the other escort which Furneaux had spotted.

'All right. Reduce to revs for twelve knots. Starboard wheel, Cox'n.'

'Starboard wheel, sir!'

Slowing, and turning away ...

Labouring round, as the revs decreased. Movements were sluggish anyway, with that weight of water holding her stern down, although this was the best way to make the turn as far as her engines were concerned.

'All the way round, Cox'n, and steer south. Number One—'

'Sir?'

'Here, a minute. You'd better understand this. Flyte, you too. You hearing this, Cox'n?'

He was. Holding the rudder on her, the boat rolling hard as she swung her stem through north, all the weather on her beam: John Flyte fetched-up in a slide beside them, cannoning into Lyon. Furneaux pointing southeastward—over the port quarter, as she was at this moment ... *'Heilbronne's* there—3,000 yards, roughly—with a *Torpedoboot* on her beam this side and another on her port quarter. *There*. Other escort or escorts ahead of her, obviously. I'd guess only one, the surviving M-class sweeper. Right? Well—Newbolt's supposed to be coming down on their beam, roughly—there, from the north. So if I'd gone on as I was, to attack from that beam—well, bugger's muddle to start with, and when this T spotted us we'd 've stirred it up for Newbolt too. You with me?'

182

'Yes—'

'So—round this way, passing astern of them—*well* astern, to get round that sod on the quarter there—then overhaul again, attack from inshore. *Diverting* attention from Newbolt. He'll have the best chance—with two fish. And we'll have room enough. *Heilbronne*'ll be a mile offshore, using the channel through the shallows there—whatever they're called—'

'Raz du Cap Levi.'

Flyte: earning himself a grunt ... 560 most of the way round, PO Thompson easing rudder off her. Furneaux had put his glasses up: briefing finished, Lyon realized. First ever, of its kind. Having so nearly *not* got away with it in that last scrimmage, hedging his bets on surviving the next?

*   *   *

563 rolling and pitching south-by-westward. Mark Newbolt upright on his seat, glasses up and sweeping across the bow. Foam sheeting over and flying away to port: too much of it, making her too visible by half even at this mere eight knots. Still having only the one wing engine, and half-power from it at most. PO Motor Mechanic Talbot's attempts to get another engine back into commission had come to nothing, and when Newbolt had tried to work up the revs on this starboard one—only minutes after getting under way after his close shave with the trawlers—she'd overheated, the supercharger seizing-up and the engine then jamming itself in neutral. They'd had to lie stopped—once again 'at the mercy of wind and wave', as Kingsmill had poetically described it—for another uncomfortable twenty minutes. There'd

183

been flare-ups of action in the southeast, tracer and other fireworks including starshell, and two or possibly three torpedo-hits. There'd also been doubts as to whether the MM was going to be able to get even this one engine going again: Newbolt had had visions of the action being finished down there between Barfleur and Levi and all concerned then legging it for home, leaving 563 stuck here until the *Luftwaffe* found her in the dawn.

Code-books and other secret publications had some while ago been put into the weighted sack ready for ditching, but this second time round he'd also considered the details of abandoning ship and how he'd set about sinking her.

Then Talbot's great news—again.

'We get back intact—' Kingsmill had suggested— 'ought to get Talbot knighted.'

Newbolt had thought, *And me shot* . . .

Not all that flippantly either. The boat and her crew were in this hole for the sole reason that he, Mark Newbolt, had cocked up. First, allowed himself to become separated from the unit; and second, rushed into action when it was the last thing he should have done.

And—incidentally—failed to send out an enemy report when he should have, before having his aerials shot away.

Cock-up followed by fuck-up. Vivid awareness of which had resulted in the decision to carry on southward in search of a target on which to use his fish. Knowing there'd been hits and that it was therefore odds-on that the *Heilbronne* had been sunk, but with a sharp distaste for the prospect of returning to Newhaven in this beat-up state and having achieved damn-all—beyond the destruction of a

184

Raumboot against which he shouldn't have been in action in the first place—and bringing back with him two perfectly good, unused torpedoes.

Being found by the gunboats had been a bloody miracle. Bob Stack in the guise of *deus ex machina*—yet another quote from Kingsmill, which Sworder had countered with 'Or fairy godmother, say.' Kingsmill's raucous laughter, then: 'Some fairy!'

Bucking and rolling southward. Stack and Moncrieff in their MGBs were following a mile or so astern.

'Ship red four-oh, sir!'

Sworder had sighted it. Newbolt swung his glasses to that bearing. To roughly where he'd been expecting it; in fact, searching for it: Stack having given him radar ranges and bearings—one large and one smaller blip . . .

'Warship green one-oh, sir!'

OD Holland, that had been, the lookout behind him on this starboard side. (*Singing* lookout—when he so far forgot himself and no-one had the heart to shut him up, or the noise was such that it didn't matter. Trivialities flashing in and out of mind while facing what might well prove cataclysmic.) He had the first of the two sightings in his glasses. A *Torpedoboot*. This side of the *Heilbronne*'s screen, obviously; on her beam, in fact: the escort that Holland had just picked up would be ahead of her or on her bow. He left Holland's to look after itself for the moment, concentrated on and around this one. Wanting a sight of the *Heilbronne*—logically, the larger of those radar contacts.

There. *There*. Large as life.

'Ready both, Tony.'

'Ready both, sir!'

185

The *Heilbronne* was down by the bow, for sure.
Quite a steep bow-down slant. There was a certain
amount of water-disturbance around her forepart,
but you wouldn't call it a bow-wave: she was making
about—three, four knots, he guessed. Five at the
most. And that escort—to the left of her, from this
point of view—was definitely a *Torpedoboot*. Range
about—fifteen hundred yards, say. He let his glasses
hang on their strap for a few moments while he closed
the throttle slightly—to more or less eliminate bow-
wave and wake—then set the torpedo-sight for a
ninety-on-the-bow shot and enemy speed four knots.
Or make it five. It would be no more than five, but
you could guess the German would be fairly
desperate to get into Cherbourg, nagging at his
engineers to squeeze the last half-knot out of her,
might be more easily satisfied with a round number
such as five. The for'ard bulkhead would be the
danger: there'd be a slowing effect from the damage
itself and from her angle in the water—her screws, for
instance, would be close to breaking surface—but the
risk of the bulkhead bursting would be worrying
them most.

'Tubes ready, sir. Close the guns up?'

'No. Not yet.'

And then the thought: *I'm off my bloody rocker* . . .

To expect to get away with this—pass ahead of
that sod unseen. Knowing that once seen you'd be
finished. Having only eight knots—but even without
that—any second *now*, expect the starshell!

He pushed the throttles shut.

Lie cut, let the sod pass, then cross astern of him at
a range where you'd have—well, at least a *hope* . . .

Kingsmill was beside him. Wanting to know what
was going on. Newbolt was aware also of the jut of
186

the Badger's beard this way. His shout came across only weather-noise now: 'Losing steerage way, sir!'

'Yeah. Going to cross astern of this one, not ahead.'

Then there'd be some catching up to do. But having eight knots, when the target had only four or five . . .

Let him get out to say twenty degrees on the bow, *then* go ahead. Estimating it roughly: half a mile to cover at four knots—seven and a half minutes. Going ahead then at eight knots with, say, a thousand yards to cover before you crossed his stern—add three and a half minutes.

'Tony—tell me when seven and a half minutes are up. Better get the torpedomen back up meanwhile.'

'Lost steerage way, sir . . .'

It was going to feel like a bloody hour. Other snags were (a) Mike F. might get his attack in first, and (b) if you failed, the target would be that much closer to Cherbourg.

This was *right*, though.

Not that you could count chickens, even this way. Giving oneself a better *chance*, that was all.

'Mid—'

'Sir?'

'Nip aft, let's have a puddle of smoke around us. Take one hand with you. Pickering, maybe. Leave him on it. A squirt now and then—OK?'

To thicken the darkness around her. It was only a matter of manipulating a couple of valves. The chemical from the cylinder expanded into 'smoke' when it came into contact with the damp sea air.

*　　*　　*

187

He'd told Kingsmill not to close the guns up yet, because he hadn't wanted itchy fingers too close to triggers at this stage. Not to run the slightest risk of it. Tubes being ready, incidentally, meant amongst other things that Torpedoman Lloyd, who still had some bullets in his thigh but who'd been treated and bandaged up by Kingsmill and was adamant that he was fit for duty, claimed to be feeling hardly any discomfort, was down there on the starboard tube, with AB Mottram to give him a hand if he should need one. And AB Burrows on the port side, as usual, each of them with a mallet handy.

They'd be back in shelter now, anyway, abaft the bridge.

'What's that, Tony?'

'Six minutes gone, sir.'

The *Torpedoboot* was about ten degrees on the bow to starboard. He'd reckoned on making it twenty, but—

No. Belay that. Wait for the seven and a half minutes. If he'd had to guess just then he'd have said four minutes gone, not six. Grit your teeth and count your blessings. Sitting again: making himself sit. When he'd ordered the tubes to the ready he'd flapped the seat up to give himself room behind the sight, and after making the hard decision he'd banged it down again. *Making* himself do it.

Patience not being one of his best-known virtues.

563 was tossing around like flotsam. Shrouded, some of the time, in the ectoplasmic smoke ... It wasn't easy to hold glasses steady—on the barely-visible smudge of the *Torpedoboot* inching slowly, slowly across the dark interlocking circles of the lenses: which were wet *again*, God damn it ...

'Skipper, sir—time's up!'

188

'Thank God.' He'd dried the front ends of the glasses, put them up again. Green two-oh, two-five even ... Glasses down: right hand on the starboard throttle, easing it open. 'Starboard wheel, Cox'n.' Thrum of power trembling through her. 'Steer due south.'

*　　　*　　　*

'Close up the torpedomen, Tony.'

Second time of asking. Sweating a bit now. He'd passed closer astern of the 'T' than he'd originally intended, and since then brought her round thirty degrees to starboard, to push up between it and the target. *Torpedoboot*—the nearest one, the only one which for the moment mattered most—thus broad on the bow to starboard, *Heilbronne* less so on the port bow and at a range now of about seven or eight hundred yards.

Call it seven-fifty. Might fire at six hundred. Less, for preference, but it was a matter of getting there— unspotted, getting as close in as you could while gaining enough bearing to be in a position for—well, it wouldn't be a beam shot.

Hundred on the bow, maybe.

Still some way to go, too, clawing in at a relative— overhauling—speed of only four knots—obliquely, aiming for the centre of the gap of sea between the target and that 'T'.

Thanking God meanwhile for the camouflage of broken water...

After firing, disengage to port, obviously. With the *Torpedoboot* where it was—as well as an 'M' farther up ahead there—and having only the starboard engine that would be the quick way round

189

in any case.

Well—hardly *quick*—at eight knots. And there was another 'T' back there, somewhere astern of the *Heilbronne*. Bugger 'd be putting *its* oar in, by that time.

'See the target, Cox'n?'

'Can just, sir.'

'Soon as the fish are away, hard a-port. Bring her to east-by-north, north-east say.' Over his shoulder then: 'Mid—after we've fired, start making smoke.'

'Aye aye, sir!'

Getting out, might risk pushing her up to ten or twelve—having fired, being then several tons lighter, that much less strain on the ailing engine?

God only knew where Mike F. would be coming from. Have to keep him in mind, as well as the other escorts. Range now—say six-fifty yards. The *Heilbronne* a slow-moving, bow-down two-funnelled hulk, dragging herself like some huge wounded animal painfully but doggedly southeastward. Wouldn't be able to get herself round all that quickly either, he guessed—thinking of her taking avoiding-action—with her bow that deep.

563 was rolling hard, suds piling over and streaming aft. He checked the settings on the torpedo-sight again—hundred on the bow, enemy speed four. OK ... Dispensing now with binoculars. Fingering the firing-levers, checking *them* for about the fourth time too—that he'd taken the safety-latches off.

Sufficient unto the night being the cock-ups thereof...

'Skipper, sir—'

'Yeah—*damn!*'

He'd heard it—what Sworder had seen—the 'T'

190

opening up—at last ... Twenty-millimetre—streams of it, mostly red—and doubtless the heavier stuff coming with it too by now. He'd had only a brief sight of the start of it as he'd more or less flinched that way a second ago, but he'd also heard the crack of a four-inch: instant assumption being *starshell coming*...

Concentrating on the target again now, and his relationship to it via the torpedo-sight. Having no way of doing anything about any of the rest of it—and not wanting to be blinded, either...

Range not much more than five hundred yards. Five-fifty, say.

The starshell burst open right overhead: green brilliance spreading and the tracer thickening—*Heilbronne* opened-up too now, gun-flashes and tracer from her afterpart—inescapable in its blinding effect, *this* lot.

'Stand by!'

Kingsmill bawled it too, for the men on the tubes to hear. Newbolt crouching, peering narrow-eyed along the sighting-bar, his fingers crooked around the twin firing-levers in the recess below it.

'I'll fire on the turn, Cox'n. Use five degrees of port wheel.'

'Aye, sir—'

'Port wheel *now*!'

Swinging the line of sight to meet the *Heilbronne*'s deep-ploughing stem—which seemed almost to hesitate, draw back for an instant before it crossed it. The two crossing each other *now*...

'Fire both!'

Muffled thumps from both sides, the jolt and double *whoosh* of the fish departing. The Badger was already winding-on more rudder. Newbolt with his glasses up: tracer coming in a storm—there'd been some hits back aft, he'd felt them. But he'd got her. As long as the fish ran straight. Please *God*, he had. Well, it was *certain*, it had been that kind of shot— when you felt it in your bones, *knew* you had.

The task now—the *really* tough one—was to get his boat and her crew away.

CHAPTER TEN

Furneaux's view of it was from the south: bringing 560 westward across the shallows to overhaul the *Heilbronne* on this inshore side, by that time needing to gain only about another five hundred yards before *he* could have turned in to attack. Would have too, wouldn't have waited for young Newbolt to make his move first; this wasn't a game of 'after you, Claude'. Especially with Cherbourg practically in spitting distance, minutes weren't for wasting. Anyway Newbolt had pulled it off, and 560's crew had been cheering—with the crash of the hit still echoing in their skulls after the leap of fire that had lit the sea between here and there ... Furneaux had barely had time to order starboard wheel and to open the port and centre throttles—to bring her up from twelve knots to about eighteen—before the big one—second hit, starting like the first but expanding laterally as well as vertically, covering most of the ship's length and with burning debris soaring out of it: the *Heilbronne* spilling her guts into the sky. She'd have had U-boat stores in her holds, of course, ammunition and torpedoes, maybe drums of shale—or whatever Kraut torpedoes ran on—

Furneaux realized: looking round at the others, the boat and surrounding sea lit up in spasms of new flare-ups: seeing John Flyte goggle-eyed and open-mouthed, Hugh Lyon too—astonishment in his darkly unshaven and, in Furneaux's view, slightly bovine countenance: a degree of shock, even momentary paralysis.

How many dead in those few seconds?

Some would be dying over *there*, too, though. Ones that *mattered*, over there.

Only the coxswain seemed totally unmoved. You might have thought that in Huddersfield this kind of thing was commonplace. Reminding Furneaux: 'Got starboard wheel on, sir.'

'Yes. Steer north, Cox'n.'

'Steer north, sir—'

R/T crackling: then Bob Stack's voice. As from some other world ... 'Dog Two—Topdog. George three-zero. Stand by to follow Master Gunner, engaging to starboard. Got to get past the bugger somehow, haven't we. Over.'

Atmospherics, then, louder than before. Volume turned up, somewhere ... Moncrieff's voice broke through it: 'Darned right, Topdog. Master gunner starboard it is. Out.'

PO Thompson intoning, 'Course north, sir ...'

Perrot, then—from the starboard side behind Furneaux: 'Green two-oh, sir—563, or *looks* like—'

'Wait ... Yes—yes, it *is*. Well done ...'

Mark Newbolt. The *Torpedoboote* were very *much* on him: it was their tracer that had, as it were, fingered him. He was on the bow to starboard—to the northeast—twelve or fifteen hundred yards away. *All* of fifteen hundred yards, probably ... The sea was on fire in that region—oil from the *Heilbronne*,

193

patches of wind-driven flames spreading over an area of several acres. Drifting east, of course. Newbolt—563—seemed to have port helm on. Alternatively—well, he'd had only one engine working, and if it was the starboard one his wheel might simply be untended. Please God that wasn't so, but one had to allow for the worst. Even the best wasn't all that promising: having turned away to port—as he must have, after firing—and—well, he might have steadied now. On—east-north-east, roughly ... On course as if to pass midway between those two—who weren't going to let him. The sea around him was jumping with shell-bursts and lashed by smaller stuff—which would include 37-mm, not all *that* small. There was a lot of tracer over and around him, and the *Torpedoboote* were closing in towards him from the east and north—dishing out the punishment generously, meanwhile—and a third, an 'M' that had been in the lead, was on its way back to lend a hand. Not in range yet, that one. The 'T' that was supposedly about to receive the gunboats' attentions had to be the one roughly due north from here—because up there was where Stack would be and the other, to the right, was the one that had been on the *Heilbronne*'s quarter before this lot started.

That would be the one to hit. But there was a choice here: whether the best thing would be to get to Newbolt—go straight for the ball, so to speak—and either distract enemy attention from him—giving him a fighting chance, if he was capable of using it—or to get in alongside him and take him and his crew off. In the process, putting *this* crew's heads on much the same block: especially having one's own uncertainties in the engineroom department. If you could get away with it, though—well, you'd have *done* it, all units could disengage. Whereas the alternative was to leave Newbolt on his own to survive—please God—for a few more minutes, and go for that 'T'. Snags in that choice being that with only one torpedo you'd have to get in good and close to make sure of it: and they'd see you coming, with all that burning sea behind you. As they'd be seeing Newbolt now. To start with you'd pass around this western end of it—its source, not only originally but where oil must still be floating up, he guessed, igniting when it joined the stuff already burning on the surface. But there was also the problem with the engines: potentially much the same as Newbolt's— lack of speed when it came to disengaging. Not easy, therefore ... But conclusive, if the gunboats were taking care of the other one.

You'd still have the 'M' to look out for, of course...

He had his glasses back on 563: wincing, at what might have been a four-inch hit on her forepart. Like a huge camera-flash, with bits flying in the split-second's brilliance. One of the bits had been fairly substantial, could have been his Oerlikon.

Lost him again—beyond the drifting fires. If that *had* been a four-inch hit—well, God help him ... Seeing an answer of sorts, though. Thinking about it while shifting his glasses to the 'T'—which was moving from left to right—the same way as the oil was spreading—spreading fast, with this still-rising wind driving it—the 'T' probably steering to head Newbolt off. If he was still there to be headed off ... Range from here about—1,200 yards. He lowered his glasses, let them hang on their strap, and reached to the throttles: eyes still straining to see beyond that patchwork of shifting light and darkness. The

195

burning oil made it harder to see, not easier. A constantly flickering effect, together with alternating light and dark as the flames were thrown up or sucked down in the troughs.

And that—plus the extent of the continuing eastward drift—was the answer. To make use of it.

He was easing the throttles open, for as near as he could get to twenty-five knots. In full awareness of Coates' warning about the flooded stern compartment.

Had to take *some* risks...

'Starboard wheel, Cox'n!'

Through the oil, not round it. Touch wood, semi-invisible damn near all the way ... 'Number One!'

'Sir—'

'Listen.' Letting the left hand know: which he was aware he hadn't done as much as he should have, in the recent past. A hand on Lyon's beefy shoulder: 'Listen—we're going to spoil the paintwork, somewhat...'

* * *

'Master Gunner open fire, sir?'

'No—hold on, Alan...'

Ben relaxed again—slightly. He'd pulled rank, more or less, in taking over the starboard twin Vickers .303s, for this 'Master Gunner' shoot. Had wanted to *be* the Master Gunner, but they hadn't let him, had granted that honour to 'Banjo' Bennet, gunlayer on the starboard point-fives. Well, fair enough ... The boat was up to her flat-out speed of thirty knots now, pounding southward with Moncrieff's 866 in close station astern and the *Torpedoboot* fine on the bow to port, steering about

196

east-south-east at seventeen or eighteen knots, easy to see—with glasses anyway, and by now probably with the naked eye—in silhouette against the widening drift of burning oil-fuel half a mile to the south.

Newbolt had to be somewhere in that lot. Poor bugger: getting it in the neck, and *then* some. At least half of it from this sod whom one was about to hit: but from this one and another of the same species, a mile or less away southeastward.

In very recent and vivid memory, had been the sights and sounds of young Newbolt's successful attack. The gunboats had been following him south at his own speed of eight knots—on silenced outers and a mile astern of him, having given him a head start. Radar, on the blink again, had lost him at less than *half* a mile, to Stack's extreme annoyance. He was on edge with concern for Newbolt and his crew anyway: shouting to himself at one stage, 'Eight knots, Christ's sake, what sort of bloody chance'd *that* give him?' Questioning, Ben realized, his own judgement in having let Newbolt go on with it, in his crippled state ... Anyway—there'd been the sight, sound and shock of the first torpedo hit—then the second—so you knew it couldn't have been Mike Furneaux's work, Furneaux having only one shot in his locker—and that holocaust ensuing—and the *Torpedoboot* a dark cut-out against it—as it had been a minute earlier, against German starshell—more or less in profile and also right in their way. The gunboats having to get down there in a hurry, and the German in any case much better knocked out of the game, if possible—for everyone's sake, but especially for Newbolt's. Stack had crash-started the inners, slamming them and the outers to full

197

ahead, 2,400 revs.

Pent-up anxiety translated into action—*that* far—
and then this further wait, sweating self-control...

Tracer, suddenly—coming *this* way. Bastards
woken up, or something...

'Go ahead, Alan!'

'Master Gunner, open fire!'

Barclay had yelled it into the telephone. Bennet as
Master Gunner had to start it. It was a procedure Ben
had seen used in gunnery exercises but never before in
action. The master gun—or rather guns, in a twin
mounting such as the point-five turret—were loaded
with 100 per cent green tracer, and picked the targets;
all other guns in all the accompanying boats followed
that lead, hitting where the green tracer hit. The
theory of it was that whatever got shot at got shot to
bits. In fact this would be a very limited use of the
technique, since there was to be only one target, with
no latitude—or time—for shifting between different
points of aim; the target was to be solely the
Torpedoboot's bridge. To hit him hard and leave him
reeling—with any luck the skipper and officers and
helmsman dead, controls and communications
shattered. It should be achievable here—touch
wood—touching in reality the cold steel of the twin
gas-operated Vickers—because you were catching
the bastard on the hop—through his having been
preoccupied with exacting revenge on poor
Newbolt—and hitting him at pretty well point-blank
range. The double stream of green tracer hitting him
now, Bennet not needing to use his open ring-sight
thereafter, only hosepiping the streams of it slightly
left to find the bridge and stay on it, pouring the stuff
in, Ben squeezing his own triggers and within a
second or two stone deaf, the vibration of the two
198

guns' extremely high rate of fire rattling his teeth while he guided his yellow tracer to merge with the green. Stack had ordered the wheel hard a-port, and 875 was leaning into the turn, in the course of it opening her after guns' arcs of fire to the enemy at a range of less than a hundred yards. Six-pounders, point-fives, Vickers and Oerlikons all hitting the same target with a mix of incendiary, high-explosive and armour-piercing, the six-pounders in particular delivering wholesale destruction in every burst: and the guns' racket, colossal on its own, combining with the roar of the four supercharged 1,250-horsepower Packards at full blast to create a volume of sound that was unbelievable. The German's bridge was already a mass of flame: Ben's bones and muscles juddering with his guns, firing on the beam now as into a furnace as the gunboat drew ahead, overhauling—firing abaft the beam, then on the quarter—with only one gun, though, the left one had jammed, damn it—

A bang on his shoulder—a fist—and Barclay's yell like a seagull's shriek to pierce the noise: 'Cease *fire*, Ben!'

He grumbled—inaudibly even to himself—'Spoilsport...' But he'd have needed to clear the left-hand gun, anyway, and change the pans on both. Wouldn't have had anything to shoot at now anyway: what was left of the engagement was visibly all astern—Monkey still at it, for the moment. It had only lasted seconds. Ben excusing himself to Barclay—although still not hearing his own voice—'Sorry, but you *know* I'm deaf...'

Stack, on R/T: 'Dog Two—d'you hear me? Over.' Waiting, then, he put his glasses up to look back astern at the bonfire-like *Torpedoboot*. It was sheering away to starboard: but there'd be no

199

steering from that bridge now, you could bet. *Nothing* from that bridge.

'Starboard wheel, Cox'n.'

'Starboard wheel, sir...'

R/T: a sudden roaring from the speaker—so loud Ben actually heard it: then it cut out and was replaced by Monkey's voice: 'Topdog, Dog Two. Heard you loud and clear. Over.'

'Dog Two. George two zero. Repeat, George two zero. And I'm altering thirty degrees to starboard. When we find Mark I'll go in close—alongside, if I can—while you give me a lee and/or see off any interference. God knows where Mike is. Out.'

'Roger, Topdog. Out.'

Telegraphs to half ahead, revs reducing to twenty knots. R/T again, then: 'Mike One—Topdog. What is your situation? Over.'

Atmospherics: nothing else.

Engines slowing, now; volume of sound lessening, and the gunboat's posture in the water levelling.

'Steer south forty-five east, Cox'n.'

'South forty-five east, sir...'

Stack had his glasses up again. Ben too: reflecting that this was the second time tonight that Furneaux had been lost—or seemed to be. The last time, it had sprung to mind—'unbidden', as such thoughts tended to be labelled—to wonder how matters involving Stack and Joan might be affected, if the bugger really *had* gone; and the answer had been that the only difference would be himself and Monkey relieved of any obligation to discuss the events of Saturday night. No other difference, because Furneaux himself was incidental. If she'd reverted to previous form—as she had, obviously—she'd very soon replace him. You could bet on it.

And *still* have a soft spot for her.

Extraordinary.

But—happy times. Exciting times. And she *had* got under one's skin, somewhat. Remembering it now one thought of *that* girl, not of this one ratting on old Bob.

Searching carefully with the binoculars. His ears felt as if they'd been stuffed with plasticine. There was still plenty of tracer down there: what Stack was steering for, no doubt. That other 'T': there was certainly nothing coming from the one they'd just hit. He was a blazing hulk, you could forget him: and the 'M' would as likely as not go to his assistance: no option really, it would have to. Two for the price of one, effectively.

Newbolt would be somewhere under that tracer. In what state, though—God only knew. It could be Furneaux they were shooting at now. *Could* be...

'No casualties, sir.' Barclay had pushed in beside Stack. 'And the only damage is superficial. CSA gear's gone for a burton, guardrail aft's carried away—oh, and the ventilator, and the steps at the back of the bridge here—all smashed. God knows how Michelson and Foster got away with it.'

'Devil looks after his own, they say.'

'Ah. *That's* a point...'

A bark of mirth from Charlie Sewell. Who'd been on that wheel for—what, close on seven hours. Time now being—0159. Barclay was saying, answering a question from Stack, 'A few holes for'ard, yes sir. Few *more*, that is. All above the waterline—as far as one can see.'

'Got off damn lightly.'

'Well—considering—'

The darkness split—a mile away. The tracer had

201

cut off; a streak of flame shot up, hung for a moment and then darkened, disappeared. The sound and shock arrived, then—that distinctive, underwater *thump*.

'My bloody oath.' Stack, with his glasses on it. 'My fucking bloody oath...'

'Steer for where it was, sir?'

'*Yes*, Cox'n. Ben, all engines full ahead—'

'Topdog.' Furneaux's voice, loud over the R/T ... 'Mike One. Kiss *that* one goodbye. Fish blew his stern off. Look—on my way to Mark, but I'd appreciate assistance. Got a few problems. Over...'

CHAPTER ELEVEN

Ben had never cut a man's arm off before, but he had a few minutes ago. Pausing in the wheelhouse now on his way back up to the bridge, for the more mundane task of checking the position again by QH. Young Carter, the Liverpudlian OD who had ambitions to become his navigational assistant, had fixed a mattress over the damage in the corner and port side, primarily for the sake of the blackout. It was a lot better than having to take the chart down to the wardroom, which was now also a sickbay and emergency operating theatre. The arm, belonging to Newbolt's spare officer, a midshipman by name of Sworder, had been connected to his shoulder only by sinews, which Ben had severed with a razor while Barclay had been struggling to cope with a spouting artery. After they'd embarked the dead and wounded Ben had gone down there to lend a hand, and become caught up in helping with some of the more urgent and basic tasks. They'd got them more or less settled now: Sworder unconscious in one of the wardroom bunks, full of morphine and with Barclay and AB Michelson binding-up the shoulder-stump—having tied the artery—and Mark Newbolt semi-conscious in another—with shell-fragments in his back and from ankle to shoulder in his left side—and in the forward mess, next door, a leading stoker by name of Chivers and a seaman torpedoman called Lloyd who according to Newbolt had been wounded in two separate actions. Merriman was in there too, of course. Barclay was being assisted by Charlie Sewell and this Michelson, the Oerlikon gunner who'd been brought up in a Barnardo's home.

ETA Newhaven—Ben had drafted the signal, one of several which would have gone out half an hour ago—was 0700. Wind was up to force 4 and by the feel of it still rising. She was making hard work of it, and a lot of men were being sick. Ben hadn't been yet but suspected it mightn't be long before he was. Alan Barclay, down there with the wounded, was about the same colour as the white-painted bulkheads, had looked as if he was either going to faint or cut his own throat with that razor; Ben had taken it from his hand, told him, 'Gimme—I'm a dab hand at this.'

He'd wrapped the arm up in a towel, and someone had taken it up and ditched it.

The ETA might hold good, he thought. If it had been less rough you might have reckoned on getting in by nearer 0630; but with revs on for twenty-three knots she was making-good less than twenty. An uncertainty from the navigational angle was whether wind was beating tide, or vice-versa. Wind from the west causing eastward drift, and the tidal stream setting westward at about two knots. You set the best course you could, knowing it would need adjusting from time to time: also that with the weather as it was, very accurate steering was a near-impossibility. Leading Seaman Harper was on the wheel now.

Furneaux, with Monkey in 866 keeping him company, wouldn't be in until nearer nine. There was a chance they'd be given some air-cover after first light—Stack had asked for it, as insurance against opportunism by the *Luftwaffe*. But Furneaux's best speed was eighteen knots, which in these conditions would bring him down to nearer twelve: MTBs, being flat-bottomed, tended to get blown around like leaves. Stack had left Monkey to escort him home in case of more total breakdown. Most of 560's engine and hull-damage had been sustained earlier in the night, but in that final stage of the action Furneaux had had a direct hit in his wheelhouse, blast and fragments from it killing his spare officer—John Flyte, a sub-lieutenant—and wounding Mike himself, his coxswain, signalman and an AB named Bellamy, who was a celebrity in the flotilla by virtue of being captain of its football team. Furneaux had told Stack over R/T that he'd been hit in his legs, left arm and shoulder, that the coxswain and signalman had also been hit in the legs, and Bellamy in his back. You could imagine how it must have been, the blast back into the forefront of the bridge. Johnny Flyte had been in the wheelhouse when the shell had exploded in there, apparently: he wouldn't have known much, if anything, about it. There'd been no question of embarking any of them: for one thing it had been a hell of a job getting Newbolt's dead and wounded out—near-impossible, in fact, but necessary—and for another Furneaux had passed the R/T microphone to his first lieutenant, Hugh Lyon,

204

who'd added another major item to the report of damage—that the steering-gear compartment was holed and flooded, virtually open to the sea—but had assured Stack that he had it all in hand and, while glad of MGB 866's company, was confident of getting the boat home.

*   *   *

Ben went up into the bridge. 'Tiny' Harper looming huge at the wheel, Stack on his seat in the starboard fore corner—as always, with binoculars at his eyes.

Fresh air was a great improvement on the vomit-scented fug below.

'ETA 0700 looks reasonable so far, sir.'

'Good.' Glasses down ... 'Get the signals out, did they?'

'Oh, strewth—*yes*. Sorry, skipper, should've told you. You saw Monkey's—'

'Negative. Didn't expect much else—uh?'

Moncrieff had signalled that he'd found no survivors from the *Torpedoboot*. Stack had told him to make a search of the area where it had gone down, but not to hang around, not to search at all if the M-class sweeper had been anywhere near by that time. Furneaux was to have started for home right away, Monkey to make his search and then catch up with him.

'You did darned well, Ben, getting Mark and his boys out.'

'Bit hectic, wasn't it?'

'Thought we'd seen the last of you, one time.'

'That was this clumsy bugger Harper's fault.'

'Beg pardon, sir?'

'I'm not picking any fights with *you*, Harper.'

205

'No. Well—glad o' that, sir.'

'Specially as you made a first-class job of it yourself. Not only in general terms either, I *might* have gone in if you'd been less quick on the ball.'

'Thank you, sir.'

It hadn't been easy to find 563, in the first place. The fact she'd been on fire hadn't helped—she'd looked like just another of the smaller patches of burning oil, with which the entire seascape had been covered by that time. But Furneaux had been on his way over to Mark, to stand by him, and Stack had called him on R/T again, asked him to switch on 560's fighting lights, and this had led them to him. 563 had been low in the water, immobile and with a fire in her afterpart; proximity of fire to high-octane petrol storage naturally turning thoughts towards the possibility of explosions, and presenting the alternatives either of keeping well clear—which was hardly realistic—or getting on board immediately to evacuate the survivors double-quick and *then* clear off. There *were* survivors: both gunboats were using Aldis lamps as searchlights while Stack was bringing 875 cautiously in towards the wreck—Harper hurriedly rigging a scrambling-net over the port side, meanwhile, and Monkey manoeuvring 866 up close to windward, beam-on, to provide a lee—and at least two men were seen waving from Newbolt's bridge. Stack had reduced to outers at low revs, was nosing up on the windward side, and as he closed in the relative rise and fall of the two boats—indicative of the difficulties to be faced in boarding, let alone transferring wounded—became more plainly daunting with every yard's diminution of the gap. The MTB's movements were comparatively sluggish, since she was waterlogged, but the gunboat was

206

pitching and rolling like something idiots might pay for in a funfair. Barclay meanwhile, mustering volunteers to go over, had been including himself in the boarding party, and Stack had vetoed this, on the grounds that it was the first lieutenant's job to organize the reception of the wounded, get them below and fix them up, to whatever extent was possible. Ben had therefore taken his place and gone on down, found Harper and a few others preparing to leap over as soon as they were up close enough. He'd excluded Harper, who'd be a lot more useful on the gunboat's deck—using his size and strength to haul men on board—and picked only two to go over with him: Harrison, layer of the for'ard six-pounder, and Lynch, leading motor mechanic.

'It's going to be a bastard, fewer the better. I go first—then you, Harrison...'

He jumped at what looked as good a moment as any—the MTB well up, the gunboat in a roll to port. Landing in a sprawl and a stink of smouldering wood, paintwork and metal, and men in the shattered bridge dragging themselves back to make way for him. There were dead as well as live ones. Newbolt had been sitting, propped against the binnacle: he had multiple wounds, it seemed from neck to knees, and was conscious but weak, presumably from loss of blood. There was a lot of it around. His first lieutenant, Kingsmill, was dead beside him, CPO 'Badger' Gilchrist was dead too but in a sitting position, jammed between Kingsmill and the wheel. Ben grabbed the others and pulled them inboard as they came over. The rise and fall between the two boats was frightening: Stack was doing his best to hold the gunboat clear, but they were crashing together all the time, the gunboat tending to override

207

the MTB, and the gap between them when there was one was a potential death-trap.

They'd cleared the bridge first. The dead as well as the living. Partly out of a horror of leaving anyone who might *not* be dead, partly so they'd have proper funerals in due course. They had to be just slung over, from the top of the MTB's rise, caught then in the arms of Harper, Michelson, Barclay and 'Banjo' Bennet. Two of Newbolt's men who had no serious injuries themselves helped with the transfer of their mates before following them over. Ben had elicited from Newbolt that the SPs—code-books and suchlike—had already been ditched. He and Lynch made a final search below—the water in her forepart was waist-deep and surging to and fro as the sea flung her around, and the internal lights weren't working—while Newbolt's PO Motor Mechanic, Talbot—who had a head-wound and blood flowing down that side of him—stood by to break the fuel pipes that led from the tanks to the engines. Ben sent Lynch back into the gunboat—Harrison had already gone over—and yelled at Talbot, 'OK, do it!' The MM ducked out of sight, back into the confines of the boat, which was not only on fire but rising and falling ten or twelve feet several times a minute, rolling savagely and smashing itself against the gunboat alongside. She might have slipped under at any time, with all that water in her, and weakened bulkheads. You had to make sure of her destruction, that was all, not leave her with even a remote chance of salvage by the enemy. The fire was another hazard, adding considerably to the danger of the job the MM was doing. Having done it, he came up—staggering, needing help now despite having insisted that the head-wound was only a scratch—leaving the petrol gushing through down there and the fire still burning only feet away from it. Ben hoisted him up and over, into the arms of Bennet and Michelson, and then followed—misjudging his grab for the scrambling-net and avoiding having at least one leg crushed, probably only by Harper seeing it happen and heaving him up to safety.

His own idea had been to use a Very pistol from a range of a few yards, but Talbot had panted that it would be best to shove off and then do the job with tracer. When this was done—a burst of tracer from the port-side Vickers—the explosion was accompanied by a sheet of flame that would have incinerated anything within fifty feet of it.

*　　*　　*

'*Was* a bit hectic...'

In the bridge still, with Stack. Harper at the wheel.

The reason for pushing on ahead of Monkey and Furneaux was to get the wounded back as soon as possible. In some cases an hour or two might make the difference between life and death. In Newhaven there'd be ambulances and doctors on the quayside: by the time Furneaux's 560 was alongside, this lot would be in hospital and the ambulances back again waiting for his.

Stack said—something he'd said before, only in different words—'*Hell* of a price to pay, Ben.'

'I know. Fucking awful...'

He was going to have to start talking about the other thing soon: if he was going to at all. He thought he'd have to. There might never be a better chance: alone with him, and Stack seemingly in a confiding mood. Saying now—in further reference to the dead

and wounded, the high price of the battle won—
'Could be asked—you or I might ask it, even—was
finishing-off the *Heilbronne* worth the candle? She
wasn't getting out into the Atlantic, was she, once
John Heddingly'd scored. Not without major
repairs—dry-docking, for a start?'

'There'd be a dry dock in Cherbourg, surely.'

'Yeah, but—'

'Orders were to sink her, anyway.'

'That's true ... Ours not to reason why, uh?'

'She *could* have been mended quick enough. If
those bastards decide this or that's a rush job, bloody
do it—they don't mess about, crack their bloody
whips and it happens. And from Cherbourg, then—'

'You're right, of course.'

From Cherbourg, repaired possibly within days,
she could have slipped out at any time they chose,
with nothing anywhere near enough to stop her.
Then the U-boat war would have been given a leg-
up—maybe in some area even a major boost: could
have provided the straw to break the donkey's back.
The price *did* have to be accepted.

But he was a thoughtful man, old Bob. Concerned,
utterly decent. Didn't look like it—to people who
didn't know him he looked like a bruiser—but he *felt*
things. In this other business, in fact, he was the only
truly decent character in the whole line-up and,
incidentally, the one who was going to be hurt, no
matter what.

So tell him. Get it over with.

Part of the dilemma was your own cowardice. So
commit yourself.

'Bob—'

'Hang on. Something I want to put to you, while
we're on our own.' Ben had been going to say, 'When

there's a chance of a really private word'—and Stack was now looking round at the dark bulk of Harper behind the wheel: raising his voice to add '—to all intents and purposes, that is, on our own.'

'I'm not hearing nothing, sir.' Shifting his feet, swaying against the direction of each heavy roll. The wind *was* still rising. 'Cloth ears is what I got, sir.'

'I'll take your word for it, Harper.' Back to nearer-to-normal tone: only high and loud enough to beat the engines' noise, sea and weather noise ... 'Ben—so happens, cloth ears come into this, in a way. I want to tell you that as a navigator here, you're wasted. A kid sub-lieutenant straight out of King Alfred, given a few weeks' sea-time—'

'My own thoughts exactly. In the 15th Flotilla it was different. Never realized *how* different.'

'Point is, I don't consider your bloody ear's all that important. Seriously, Ben. You had plenty of experience as a Number One—in fact you wouldn't 've been far off getting your own boat *then*—OK, in a short boat, but what the hell, you've done quite a time in these, now ... D'you get on all right with the quack at *Aggressive*, by the way?'

The doctor, at the Newhaven base. Name of Morrison. Dan Morrison. Ben glimpsed a certain ray of light but instantly decided not to believe in it. Cowardice again: fear of jumping too soon, hoping for too much ... Lowering his glasses though—about half-way—and staring at the hunched, goon-suited shape with its own proboscis-like binocular extension slowly sweeping the wilderness of sea ahead.

'Yeah. I'd say so. Nice fellow.'

'He'll pass you A1 if I ask him nicely and you swear your hearing doesn't cause you any problems. We'll

211

need clearance at higher levels too, but—I pull *some* weight—and it's my flotilla, damn it . . .'

'You wouldn't believe how fine-tuned my ear is at this moment.'

'Fact is, Ben—it's bullshit. What's wrong with a skipper making use of *other* men's sharp ears? Use lookouts' *eyes*, don't we?'

'A skipper . . . If I could *believe* this—'

'You can believe I'll try. OK, so it's a long shot . . . Maybe a refresher spell as a first lieutenant 'd be a good first move. If we could get *that* far. But you have the experience, and I'd say the talent.'

'Jesus Christ . . .'

'No guarantees, Ben. Let's have *that* clear.'

'Of course—'

'Well, I'll work on it.'

*　　*　　*

It wouldn't have been easy to have followed that with *Oh, by the way, d'you know your wife's a tart?*

He'd offered to take over the watch, give Stack an hour or two below, but he hadn't wanted it.

'I don't sleep all that much. Specially at sea.'

He went down, lit a cigarette, checked the position, called up suggesting an adjustment of two degrees to port, then went below and for'ard to see whether Barclay needed help or a breath of air.

Carter was in the galley, braced against the boat's gyrations while slicing bread for sandwiches.

'Spam again, sir. Tea or kye for you?'

'Kye'd be fine. You fit now, Carter?'

'Reckon I'll live, sir.'

Earlier, he'd had his head in a bucket.

Command, for Pete's sake!

212

So darned improbable it would be better not to think of it as much more than a daydream—born of Stack's good heart as well as his natural Aussie disinclination to be bound by unnecessary rules and regulations. Odds-on, it wouldn't come to anything...

And what the hell—you were at sea, not stuck ashore behind some desk, as you might have been. Count your blessings.

Barclay, asleep at the wardroom table, was woken by Ben's entry. He looked better too. Not exactly blooming, but less like one of his own patients. Buckets were still in evidence, but had at least been emptied. The wounded—Newbolt and the snotty, and PO Motor Mechanic Talbot—the rest were next door—were either sleeping or unconscious. Heavily doped, of course. Barclay lurched out into the galley flat with him, and thence into the forward messdeck, where Charlie Sewell was dozing with his head on his folded arms. He didn't wake, but Michelson the Oerlikon gunner did, and came out into the flat. He'd stayed to help after taking part in the embarkation and helping to carry some of the wounded down here. A square-built man, red-headed, middle twenties. The patients were all quiet, he said. The one in most discomfort was Newbolt's radar operator, an AB named Pickering, who had facial damage and might have lost his eyes. Barclay had padded and bandaged not only his face but also both his hands, wrapping them almost to the size of footballs so that he wouldn't easily be able to pull the coverings off his eyes—which in pain, fright and darkness might have been a natural thing, especially when emerging into semi-consciousness.

Nightmare. Remembering Stack's sadness:
213

thinking, *here's* the price.

Barclay muttered, 'Just all blood. You can't tell.' He added, 'Thank God for morphine.'

'And roll on Newhaven.'

'Yeah, crikey...'

'Reckon the snotty 'll make it?'

'Christ knows. Tell you one thing, *I'd* never make a doctor... Grateful for your help though, by the way.'

Two and a half hours to go, yet; possibly even three. It was about four-thirty. Ben offered Michelson a cigarette.

'Thanks, sir. Finished all mine.'

'Sandwiches and kye coming up, mind you. Carter's doing it now. Think the cox'n 'd like a shake?'

'I'd let 'im be, sir. Bear with a sore 'ead, otherwise.' He suggested to Barclay, 'If you want a break, sir— it's all quiet, an' I *could* shake him if I had to.'

'I'll take you up on that.' Barclay nodded. 'Any problems, shake him and come and find me. Wheelhouse or bridge—OK?'

They got sandwiches from Carter, and went up into the plot. Carter went on through, into the bridge with Stack's, Harper's and others' rations. Ben commented, 'Good bloke, that Michelson', and Barclay glanced at him almost angrily: 'They're *all* good blokes. They're the best, the cream, every bloody one of 'em.' It was about the longest and certainly the most fervent statement Ben had ever heard him make.

The kye was excellent, and the sandwiches weren't bad. Nowadays it seemed always to be either spam or corned beef, whereas in the Dartmouth flotilla it had been mostly ham. More pigs in the West Country, perhaps.

214

'Not getting *your* head down, Ben?'

'Not yet, anyway.'

'Lucky you had your crash in the afternoon.'

'Less luck than bloody exhaustion.' Sipping the red-hot kye. '*And* foresight.'

'Good party, was it?'

'Terrific.'

Tell Rosie, he thought. Imagining it: this evening, say about seven o'clock—or later, if she was working late—tell her—well, first, *I love you*, and then *Listen, I've been told there's a chance I'll be getting a command. Well—it's only a very, very small chance . . . But darling, listen to* this *now—*

'You were dropping off.'

'I was?'

Barclay nodded, drained his mug then pushed the rest of a sandwich into his mouth. 'I'll leave you to it. *Ought* to get your head down, Ben. I had a long kip down there. Might spell the skipper for an hour or so now.'

'He doesn't want it. I offered.'

'May have changed his mind. I'll ask him, anyway.'

'OK.'

Thinking about Rosie again. The cigarette-stub was burning his fingers. He pressed it out, and lit a new one.

Rosie, listen—that's not all. The conveyance I knock around in is due for an overhaul. So I may get a few days off—in which case—well, mid-week wouldn't be so good, would it, I mean your flat-mate being around, but—

Buckinghamshire, maybe. Meet her family. If *she*

215

could steal a few days.

'Snoozing, Ben?'

Stack: down from the bridge. Ben began to move, to surrender the folding seat to him, but he didn't want it.

'Been sitting all night.' He leant against the bulkhead—for stability. His blue-black beard looked more like five days' growth than a single night's. 'I'll take a smoke from you, though—save me a trip below.'

'Of course. Everyone smokes mine. Here...'

'Want to talk to you, Ben. Couldn't up there, with our friend cloth-ears, bless his heart—'

'But we did talk. Tell you, it's left me groggy. Can't begin to say how grateful—'

'Not that. Something else. Very—personal.' His stormlighter flared, went out: he swore, tried again. It needed shielding, in the draft from the mattress-covered shell-damage in that corner. Letting the smoke trickle out now, from the first inhalation: eyes shut for a moment, revelling in it ... Then: 'When we spoke last evening, Ben—after the first briefing? Yeah, well. I didn't tell you the truth. There'd hardly have been time, anyway, but—other reasons too. Such as—for instance—well, who *does* like admitting failure?'

'Failure?' Ben frowned. 'What kind of—'

'If you want it in one word—marital. Joan and I are finished. When we talked then I at least *implied* to you that—well, I couldn't face telling you, that's all.'

'Christ Almighty...'

'I'm a dull bastard to live with—that's the long and short of it. I suppose when we married it didn't show—you know, the excitement, eye of the beholder, all that—and I still am nuts about her,

216

in a way—'

'Well, for God's sake—'

'Excuse me, sir—more kye, or—'

'No thank you, Carter.'

Ben glanced at him, shook his head. Thinking—about Stack and Joan, this revelation—*No need to tell him. He's telling* me...

Carter had gone on down.

'Bob, I'm *damn* sorry. Don't know what else to say, I—'

'What it comes down to is I'm—a son of the soil, you might say. No ladies' man. Not good at polite conversation, all that. Lousy dancer, too—that's a major failing ... And—well, *this* is what I think about.' A gesture of one hand, indicating the ship, these surroundings ... 'Dare say talk about too. Not the sort of conversation a girl enjoys. I can understand that. But you *have* to live it—don't you? It's not a part-time job, I mean...'

Expelling smoke: and inhaling another lungful immediately. Shaking his head ... 'That's about it. *Can't* invite you to bring your sheila down—nowhere to bring her, we're giving up the house. That's to say, I am—it belongs to one of her relations. And now you know ... You're really stuck on this one, Ben—that right?'

'Hard and fast.'

'Mutual?'

'Seems to be.'

'You had a big thing going with Joan, didn't you?'

'With—Joan...' Looking at that blaze of blue eyes, narrowed through drifting smoke: wondering what the *hell* ... He nodded. 'In those days—yeah. Had a lot of fun. Before *you* hove in sight, of course.'

'Of course ... Look—it's OK, Ben, water under

the bridge.' Another shake of the head ... 'Hangs on in a man's mind, though—which is partly why I didn't bring myself to be straight with you last evening. Truth is—going back a bit—when you wrote from Dartmouth—see, it was all beginning to fall apart *then*, I was trying to keep it together and I thought having you join us here might be about the last thing I needed.'

'You're telling me you had some notion I'd—I and Joan—'

'It's all *right*, Ben. How I *felt*, this was. Simply for the record—clearing the air—'

'I'll make *this* clear here and now. There'd be no circumstances, ever, under which I'd bloody *dream* of—'

'OK. OK. I accept that. I'm telling you the whole thing, that's all. You and I hadn't been in touch for—what, two years, and—'

'How come you still did it for me—got me up here, I mean?'

'Because—Ben, in my philosophy, if there's a challenge you're safer meeting it head-on. Otherwise you could spend your whole life running and ducking—couldn't you?'

'But you truly thought *I*'d—'

'Or she might. Old flames rekindled?'

'I can't *believe*—'

'Let's be frank about it. I don't hold it against you that you and she used to—run around together. Before my time—none of my business. And Joan's line was always that you were just good friends. Want to know how I caught on to the truth of it?'

'Which truth?'

'Ben, that is *not* being frank.'

'All right. How?'

218

'With hindsight, mind you. Not at the time, only retrospectively. It was the way she—distanced herself from you. She visited you once in hospital for the sole reason I nagged her into it. Right after you got clobbered, that was, you still weren't clear was it Christmas or fucking Easter. She used that as an excuse to stay away ... And then they moved you down to Haslar, and we were busy—me at sea and then getting to be an SO, plus the fuss of getting married, her family walking all over me, Joan resigning from that upper-crust outfit to join MTC—so as to get paid, that was—but she didn't even send you postcards, or enquire whether you were alive, dead, crippled ... Wasn't natural, her writing you out of her life like that. If the two of you had been just friends, you'd 've gone on being friends. Wouldn't you?'

'*I* would.'

'There you are, then.'

'Some sort of case proved, you reckon?'

'To *my* mind. Not that it concerns us in the least, now. I wanted you to know I know—that's all. So you and I don't have to—sort of tiptoe around each other, henceforth. OK?'

There was a pause. Ben said—needing *something* to say—'Amongst my souvenirs of those times—hospital, etcetera—I still have a front-page news-splash about your wedding. Some East Anglian paper, Monkey sent it to me at Haslar. Your photo and Joan's—gladrags, medals—remember the headline?'

'Sort of.' Stack looked embarrassed. 'There were a lot of 'em, though.'

'Aussie Gunboat Hero Weds Sister of Belted Earl?'

'Yeah. Christ.' Stubbing out his cigarette. Other

hand on the deckhead, steadying himself against the roll. 'Should've known better, shouldn't he? My *God* he should.' A shrug. 'Maybe she should've too ... Ben—change of subject now. Tell me about *your* girl.'

* * *

He'd told him all about her: including the fact he thought she *would* go back into what she called 'the field', meaning German-occupied France—and that the prospect scared him witless. That he thought—from some things she'd said or nearly said, and questions she'd evaded—that she'd been through some particularly harrowing experience in the course of her last deployment, got away somehow but still had nightmares about it. As she had—night before this last one. He hadn't mentioned that to Stack, of course; only that she seemed to have some compulsion to go back and he wished to God he knew how to dissuade her.

'You can't. If that's her job, and she's set on doing it. No more than she could stop you going to sea.'

He'd shrugged. 'It's a point, but the comparison's not all that close.'

'You say it scares *you* witless. That's the beef, eh?' There'd been a sneer in his tone. 'How about her? How about bloody thousands of 'em—wives of bomber crews for instance, think *they're* not bloody terrified?'

* * *

Ring her tonight.

(And see Monkey as soon as he gets in, warn him

220

off. If it came out later that they'd all been there—
well, Bob could be induced to understand, he wasn't
stupid.)

A long way from it.

Ben had been remembering snatches of Rosie's
pillow-talk the other night, murmured exchanges in
the dusty-smelling dark, that old four-poster. Two
things she'd tried to explain, in a drowsy, shorthand
kind of way. The first was that in her job now she was
helping with the briefing—'preparation' was the
word she'd used—of agents who were on the point of
going in: while clearly—as things stood at this
moment—*not* going back in herself. She'd asked
simply, *Why* aren't I? How can I look them in the
face, wish them good luck and bloody well stay put?

The other was an image in her memory of a girl-
agent on a beach in Brittany who'd been on her way
in when Rosie had been coming out. This other
girl—she was tall, Rosie had said—gaunt-looking,
was the impression she'd had—on the beach in the
dark of a moonless night and keeping herself to
herself, *needing* to be alone to fight her own fears—
even panic. Which was something Rosie had
understood completely. She'd told him, with her
arms tight round his neck in that infinitely kinder,
softer darkness: '*I*'m that girl, Ben. She's *me*.'

(He'd been there too, on that beach, but she'd
forgotten this and in any case it was hardly relevant.)

Stack had been right—in his own blunt fashion:
Rosie most likely would go back into France. And if
she did, you'd just have to live with it. In hope and
prayer—and a lot of the time, for sure, in bloody
anguish. But you didn't have to give up on it *yet*.
Once she makes her mind up—if she does—OK,
accept it, grin and bloody bear it, help her. Knowing

how it scares *her*. 'Terrifies' would be a better word. In the night, that nightmare. And Rosie all alone: about as much alone, in her line of work, as it's possible to be. So go on trying, don't give up before you have to. *Try*...

Stirring: stretching. Glancing at the deckwatch. Waking up to the fact it was time to check the position and course again, perhaps amend the ETA. Then maybe take a look up top. Barclay was up there; Stack had gone down to visit the wounded. He stubbed out a cigarette, swung round to focus on the figures in the windows of the QH box. Time now, 0508. And it was all right. ETA 0730, no change. He went up into the dawn light: less 'light' than a polish on grey, tumbling sea. A cold, hard beginning to the day. Barclay was in the skipper's starboard forward corner, Harper still at the wheel. Ben put his glasses up and found the land—the Downs—in black silhouette between streaky, paling sky and lower obscurity where Newhaven had to be. Seeing the port in his mind's eye, and the ambulances waiting on the quayside; as likely as not the same ones that would have been there yesterday morning to meet Roddy King's unit. Training on across the bow: he was looking for Beachy Head now. Thinking of the ambulances, and wondering how a bookmaker might set the odds for or against any individual's long-term survival, in this racket. Reminding himself then—just as he found the high right-hand edge he'd been searching for—that in his own case it wouldn't be such a big deal either way unless Rosie came through too.

The LARGE PRINT HOME LIBRARY

If you have enjoyed this Large Print book and would like to build up your own collection of Large Print books and have them delivered direct to your door, please contact The Large Print Home Library.

The Large Print Home Library offers you a full service:

☆ **Created to support your local library**

☆ **Delivery direct to your door**

☆ **Easy-to-read type & attractively bound**

☆ **The very best authors**

☆ **Special low prices**

For further details either call Customer Services on 01225 443400 or write to us at:

**The Large Print Home Library
FREEPOST (BA 1686/1)
Bath BA2 3SZ**